Be
My
Valentine

To _____

From _____

A Red Hot Valentine's Day

Lacy Danes, Megan Hart,
Jackie Kessler, and Jess Michaels

red

AVON

An Imprint of HarperCollins*Publishers*

A RED HOT VALENTINE'S DAY. Copyright © 2009 by HarperCollins Publishers.
"Torn Desires" Copyright © 2009 by Lacy Danes
"Get There" Copyright © 2009 by Megan Hart
"Hell Is Where the Heart Is" Copyright © 2009 by Jacqueline H. Kessler
"By Valentine's Day" Copyright © 2009 by Jesse Petersen

HarperCollins books may be purchased for educational, business, or sales promotional use. For information please write: Special Markets Department, HarperCollins
Publishers, 10 East 53rd Street, New York, NY 10022.

FIRST AVON PAPERBACK EDITION PUBLISHED 2009.

Designed by Diahann Sturge

Library of Congress Cataloging-in-Publication Data
    A red hot Valentine's Day / Lacy Danes . . . [et al.]. — 1st ed.
        p. cm.
ISBN 978-0-06-168939-0
1. Valentine's Day—Fiction   2. Erotic stories, American.   3. American fiction—
Women authors. I. Danes, Lacy.
PS648.E7R439   2009
813'. 08508—dc22   2008029142

09 10 11 12   OV/RRD   10 9 8 7 6 5 4 3 2 1

Contents

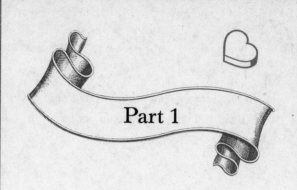

Part 1

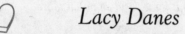

Torn Desires

by

Lacy Danes

To the two men who inspired this story;
Without you, this story would not be . . .
Lacy

To Eric,
Thank you for your unwavering support . . .
and editing skills! Grin.
We have been through so much, and this is proof we can
and do work well together.
Hugs and kisses and so much more,
Lacy

To my wonderful Mom and Dad.
I love you always.
Hugs and kisses,
Lacy

To my friends and fellow authors: Eden Bradley, Lillian Feisty,
Eva Gale, Crystal Jordan, and Shelli Stevens.
You are the best friends a girl could ask for.
Thank you for making me laugh, cry, smile, and boogie down.
Kisses,
Lacy

12th Day of September
In the year of our Lord, 1822

Miss Anne Cathcort,

I have come to the point in my life that I am now in need of a second wife. My first wife passed over two years hence and left me with my son and heir.

Some particulars on the woman I seek:

I am looking for a well-bred woman. Title and estate are not necessary.

A woman who already has a child of her own. One child preferred over more, though women with additional children, if all other qualities are present, will be considered.

A woman who knows how to be a loving good mother.

She must have a cheerful disposition and have expertise in the marital act. She shall not shy away from anything I may ask in this realm. I am quite vigorous and I am in search of a woman who enjoys the same.

These qualities in one woman I have had a hard time finding in my own search. I wish to employ you and your greater search techniques.

The Earl of Quinton.

Chapter 1

"Do you have to go?"

Sophia rolled over on her side and stared as Quinton pushed from her and sat up. "Yes I do, Sophia. We talked about this. I need to go. My son is expecting me to help him with his toy boat."

His son was his excuse this time. . . .

Stop Sophia! His son is important. You know that. She pushed up onto her hands. The covers slid down to pool about her stomach as her dark brown hair spilled in a mass of unruly curls. She hated her hair, but at this moment it provided a much needed veil against Quinton's eyes. She stared as Quinton pulled up his breeches and slid the button through the holes at the waist. He was beautifully built; stocky with a broad chest and large powerful thighs. He certainly did not spend his days idly. Her brow pinched tight. What did he do all day?

"Don't give me that look, Sophia! You know how much I hate that look."

She tore her gaze away from him but she couldn't keep it away.

Her gaze snapped back as he pulled his cotton shirt over his head, hiding his hairy chest from view. She so loved to play with the tiny curls as her head lay on his shoulder and she listened to him breathe. She loved those moments . . . skin to skin.

He tucked his shirttail into his waistband.

He did need to go. She simply hated that they never did anything besides this.

"Pardon my behavior, Quinton. I simply wish you didn't always rush off right after bedding me. It makes me feel . . . well like futter is all you came here for." Tears welled up in her eyes and her heart pinched.

"Not true, Sophia. I enjoy your company. You are my lady. I simply need to head home; Gretchen will only entertain Jake for so long before she needs to head home to her family. You know that."

A deep sigh pushed passed Sophia's lips. *Dash it all, Sophia, stop being so childish.* She settled back on the mattress and watched as he buttoned up the top buttons of his shirt. *He has family obligations and I do not. He needs to go and you know that.*

"I will see you tomorrow, my lady. You know one day you will be precisely that."

Her lips curved into a smile. Indeed, yes, she wanted to be his lady. The lady of Elm Place. It had been almost a year since he started pursuing her and almost two since his wife's death. Surely he wished for a mother for Jake sooner rather than later.

Unease flipped her stomach. Things between them always seemed a bit off . . . not quite true between them.

He walked toward her and bowed his head, "Until tomorrow, my lady. Shall we picnic on Crest Hill?"

"Oh yes! That would be delightful." Maybe she was wrong.

They did spend time doing things out of the bed. They simply seemed so far removed.

Quinton pulled on his tall black boots and buttoned his waist-coat. He grabbed his deep gray greatcoat off her chair by the door and draped the garment over his forearm, smiling down at her. "You are beautiful Sophia. I am still in awe that you have cast your favors on me."

He leaned in and kissed her hard on the lips. She relaxed into the harsh pressure and little waves of light flashed to her eyes. Her toes curled and she grabbed hold of the loose fabric on his arms.

"*Mmmm.*"

His lips pulled away and his hands grasped hers on either side. He pulled her fingers from the cloth of his shirt. "Enough, Sophia. I shall never leave if you do not let go."

He stared down at her and attempted to frown, but his lips kept twitching up.

"Ha! Would not leaving be so horrid, Quinton?"

He turned away from her and walked toward the door "We have discussed this before, Sophia. I will see you tomorrow." His boots sounded on the wood floor of her small cottage. The door opened and then he was gone.

She lay and stared at the cracks in the plaster ceiling. A small part of her didn't really believe Quinton was interested in her for his lady. Why would he be?

She had made the mistake of allowing him to bed her. She grinned. A wonderful mistake.

Her hands trailed down her stomach to the swollen lips of her cunny. His cock fit in her so wonderfully. Her fingers wandered farther down her slit to the bed linens and the large wet spot she lay in. That spot was one of the best sensations she ever experienced. A mistake all the same.

George had taken her innocence on their wedding night, but they never reached the kind of bliss she had with Quinton. She barely knew George before he went off to fight for king and country.

She squeezed her eyes shut. What did he look like? His short blond hair, sparkling blue eyes, and his tall lean figure came to mind.

She sighed. She wished she could remember him better. She was thankful she had this home because of him. She had no dowry and could not have survived longer living with so many siblings underfoot. He had rescued her and gave her this life.

She rolled onto her side and sat up. Well she certainly could not spend the rest of the day in bed. There were things to do in this life she had, and the sun and dirt were calling to her.

Alistair sat across from Anne in her overdone plush carriage. He shook his head and stared out the window. How in damnation had she talked him into coming with her to the country, to the estate of a gentleman whom he didn't know?

He inhaled long and deep through his nose, hoping to settle the unease in his stomach.

"Stop scowling, Alistair. This is supposed to be relaxing for you. Remember?"

Oh, so that was the reason. He needed to relax. How this was going to relax him he certainly had not a clue. He found fencing and playing cards relaxing. Not inhaling the smell of cows and talking wife business of Anne's.

"Indeed my memory is sharp, Anne. I simply do not have a

clue how you got me into this carriage on the way to a place I have
no desire to be."

"Well, dear. If you don't remember, then I shall have to
remind you." She reached across the seat and placed her hand on
his cock. "Besides you said you would protect me and my girls, as
Lord Quinton has a reputation."

Protection? Indeed. He would protect any one of the girls he
bedded, and Anne certainly knew how to use her hands. . . . His
cock flooded, stretching the skin taunt. "*Mmmm.* I suppose I
should stop thinking with my pego because this trip I have the
feeling will drive me daft in the attic. Did you smell the cows
as we passed that last farm?" Bile rose in his throat just at the
thought of it.

Anne's fingers undid the buttons to his breeches and her knowing hand slid inside, freeing his hard erection.

He shifted his hips and pressed his need toward her. Futter in
the carriage would make things only marginally better, but better
was the only way to go.

Her hand wrapped about his shaft and she gripped. His shoulders relaxed and he closed his eyes letting her do what she was so
good at.

"Only have a few moments before we arrive, Alistair. So I will
not be able to give you a proper release. Do you still wish me to
continue?"

"Right you will and you will give me release if I have to keep
you in the carriage with the footmen rushing about."

"You rogue." She hissed as her lips came down on his cock and
sucked him all the way back deep into her throat.

He fisted his hands on the seat, then slid them up into her hair.
He grasped her head and thrust up, controlling the stroke and the
depth of her oral delights.

Her tongue swirled and saliva drizzled down his length. "*Uh, Uh.*" Each press into her mouth sent pleasure pulsing through his soul. This is what he lived for. This is what relaxed him and was the only thing Anne provided him with. Well that and friendship . . . and for him that was all he knew.

"*Uh, Uh.*" Her tongue fluttered into the eye of his head. His buttocks clenched and his legs jerked. He wanted to be buried deep in her cunt, making her scream so the footmen heard. But he knew better than to ask that of her on this trip. Besides, she certainly didn't have a sponge in on a carriage ride to a visit a client.

"Take me deep, Anne." She slid forward and he pressed her head down all the way until the soft flesh on the back of her throat touched the tip of his cock head.

She gagged.

"*Uh. . .yes.*" He wanted to thrust deep into her. "Sit back and lay on the seat so I can thrust into your mouth, Anne."

She slid back, her black hair amazingly still pinned up in perfection. He never understood how she did that. He kneeled down on the floor of the cab and put one of his feet up on the bench she lay on.

She licked her lips and opened her mouth. His cock, still glistening from her saliva, twitched, and he placed the tip to her plush lips. She angled her head and he slid into her.

Each press, his thrusts grew harder and faster. Her lips glided over his hardness like oiled flesh. The light futtering taps of her tongue flicking all about his peg made his seed rise quickly. Anne knew exactly how to please him. He braced his hands on the wall of the cab.

His buttocks clenched. Anne groaned. The vibrating sensation pushed him over the edge. His head grew light and his sack tingled. A quick jolt pulled the carriage to an abrupt halt, tossing him back from Anne's sweet depths and onto the carriage seat he had resided on. His cock glistened with Anne's saliva and his muscles clenched on the verge of release.

"Damn it. What is going on?" His cock twitched and he clenched his teeth in outrage at the denial of his spend.

Anne laughed and sat up on the carriage seat. "I am uncertain, Alistair."

His blood raged and all thought concentrated on his twitching peg.

"Bo! Come here, Bo! Get out of the carriage's way!" A woman's voice came from outside the carriage.

A dog barked and barked.

"Bo! Come here, Bo!"

"Damnation. A stupid dog denied me my pleasure." Alistair hastily buttoned up his breeches and sprung to the door. He pushed it open and hopped down. Mud spattered up his boots and his pantaloons. He rolled his eyes and blew out a tense breath. Where was that blasted mutt? His hands fisted in want to strangle that dog.

His feet hit the ground and he strode forward.

"Ma'am, please remove yourself from the road. We need to pass." The driver's shrill voice pierced Alistair's ears.

"No worries, Jenks. I shall remove her and the mutt myself." His teeth ground together as all the pleasurable sensations he had raging through his body turned to anger.

He rounded the last of the four horses. There running about the road was a woman with dark brown hair pinned up. She ran chasing after a small black-and-rust-colored puppy.

The scene, if he had not just been denied his pleasure, would have made him laugh. She chased after the mutt. The mutt ran from her. Her face, a delicious shade of scarlet, either from embarrassment or from exertion, shot heat through his gut.

"I am so sorry, sir. If I could catch him, I would remove him myself."

"Stop chasing him. He thinks it is a game," Alistair growled.

She continued as if she had not heard him, which was a distinct possibility. Women often paid him no mind. He strode forward and wrapped his arms about her firm waist.

She jumped and pulled away from him as he hoisted her up into the air. "Wh—what are you about?" Her legs and arms struggled and thrashed thudding against his frame.

An utterly feminine floral scent filled his senses and all of his muscles locked. Her thighs brushed along his front and her calf firmly rubbed his pego.

His cock wept in his trousers and his balls contracted. Insufferable! Damnation! He was too close to spending. A slight strain developed in his sack. He shifted uncomfortably.

He didn't even truly know what this chit looked like and he wanted to spread her legs to the side of him and burry his peg deep in her pussy. He held in a cringe. *See what happens, Alistair, when you do not spend you become uncivilized.*

The puppy growled and nipped at his ankles. He gritted his teeth. Having raised five pups from his bitch Grete, he knew full well this mutt would not cease. He was sorely tempted to kick the whelp.

He spun about and strode from the road. At the side, he ever so slowly lowered her back to earth. Her body slid down his rock hard erection. There was no way she had not noticed the press of his sex along her body.

She staggered back and placed her hands on the top of the rock wall lining the road. The puppy placed himself firmly between them. She stared at his breeches.

"Ma'am." His voice came out deep, aroused, annoyed. "Please do keep your mutt out of the road or a carriage shall run him up."

She continued to stare at his breeches, then slowly looked up at him.

Beautiful. Wild curls sprang in rings about her round doll face. Eyes, deep as the fresh grass she stood upon. Tingles raced up his neck in anticipation of—

"Pardon, sir." Her face grew incredibility red as she stared him straight in the eyes. "Your *um* . . ." Her plush red lips parted and her tongue darted out. "Your *umm* . . . button's undone."

Alistair glanced down to see the tip of his stiff peg poking through the side of his flap.

He scowled, and with the side of his hand pushed his peg back into his pants. What did it matter really?

She smiled and cocked her head to the side. "I was in my garden here, sir, and we heard the carriages and Bo simply bolted though the gate. I shall do better from now on." Her hand rose and rubbed her cheek smearing dirt across the porcelain white surface.

He swallowed hard. She even made dirt look appetizing. Indeed he would have her on her hands and knees in her garden, as she pulled weeds or whatever women did there. *Ummm* . . . He would flip up her skirts and slide so slowly into her wet cunny from behind. A moan burst from him and he coughed to cover the sudden sound.

The smell of long, sweet, sweaty sex, mixed with the floral tones on her skin assaulted him. She had recently futtered.

He held back the urge to reach down between her legs to see how swollen her pouting ruffles were. Would she mind if he simply lifted her skirts right here and diddled her against the wall?

"Alistair." Anne's laughing tone came from the carriage. "Thank you for taking care of our . . . obstacle. Now shall I move on without you and let the little miss take care of your needs? Or shall you be joining me?"

A laugh burst from his chest. Only Anne would say such a thing as if it were normal and proper. "Pardon her ma'am. She is quite of the fallen variety." He glanced over his shoulder at the carriage. "Where is this damned Elm Place anyhow, Anne?"

"Oh!" The woman in front of him raised her hand and pointed to the dense line of shrubs abutting the stone wall. "There is Elm Place, sir."

"Well then, Anne. I shall walk, seeing I have to make myself presentable for arrival."

"Indeed, Alistair. Drive on, Jenks." The carriage door shut and then rolled past them, followed by two more, which held two women for Lord Quinton to choose from as brides.

He turned back to the miss before him. "I am Alistair Taylor the third son of the marquis of Lanktor. And who may this little pup be?"

Chapter 2

Should she answer such a man? He didn't even flinch at the mention of being undone. Simply pushed his peg inside and buttoned up as though his prick sticking out happened all the time.

To consider not answering was silliness of course. She needed to answer. Besides, he only asked about Bo. He stood there with those beautiful brown eyes and stared at her. Her knees weakened. Now answer him, Sophia. "Indeed. He is Bo, sir."

"Be a good pup now, Bo. No more chasing carriages." The tall brown-haired man bent and scratched Bo behind the ears.

Bo squirmed and wiggled at the caress. Sophia shifted her stance. In her mind his fingers wiggled and tickled her skin as she squirmed against him. *My God, Sophia! Why are you thinking such thoughts? Quinton only left here a few hours ago.*

Alistair smiled and dimples puckered the flesh of his cheeks. A stunning man; all posh elegance and calm. He appeared to not have a care in the world. A capital man of rank.

Who was she to judge him; a low member of blood, that is what she was. She had never had a coming out in town. Her oldest sister was the only one of her family her pa could give a dowry to.

If it had not been for George, she would in all likelihood be living on the side building of her father's estate with her next oldest sister. Sigh. In all respects she was very lucky to have this home; George's brother had not wished her to move and had simply signed the property over to her father, stating her residence or her offspring on the property was a stipulation in the sale.

"So, ma'am, Elm Place is on the other side of the hedge?" He motioned with his hand in the direction of the house.

"Oh, indeed, sir." Her gaze went unseeing to the opening in the hedge that led to Elm Place.

Why was this man here? Why had Quinton not said anything to her about his visitors? The image of the woman in fancy dress peering out of the carriage flooded her thoughts. Who was the beautiful woman headed to Quinton's door?

Sophia's heart raced in her breast and the hair on the back of her neck stood. Something was amiss. Whoever that woman was, Sophia didn't want her to meet Quinton.

She swallowed hard and her stomach flipped. Her gaze still fixed on the opening in the hedge.

Quinton had omitted the information that this woman and his other guests arrived today. Nothing good ever came from finding out such information. He was hiding something from her and her soul screamed the information was not in her favor.

"I am not much for fresh country air . . . walks and such. Is there a shortcut to the house, ma'am?"

She turned her gaze back to him. His brown eyes searched her face as if he looked for some deep meaning to her hesitation. Were her emotions, her thoughts, clear to him simply by his gaze?

Shake yourself out of this pondery, Sophia. He asked you a question. Walks . . . Country air . . . Shortcut . . .

"Oh. . ." She could show him how to get to Elm Place and maybe get a better idea what was afoot with Quinton while they strolled. "Indeed, sir. Let me fetch my warmer cloak, and I will show you."

She ran into her cottage and grabbed her deep green wool cloak from the hook by the entrance. She glanced in the mirror that hung by the door. She frowned as she beheld her unruly hair. Strands stuck out at all angles in a mass of curls she never could tame. Her hand rose as if to straighten them, and she stopped half way to her hair.

Quinton would be furious to see her in such a state. He hated when she appeared as she worked as a peasant.

A devious grin turned her lips and her eyes brightened back at her. She wouldn't remove a thing . . . not even the mud on her cheek. He should have told her company was arriving. The logical reason for him excluding that knowledge eluded her.

She walked back out the door with her chin held a little higher. Shutting Bo into the gate, she strode toward the tall, handsome man. His sable eyes sparked with mirth as his gaze slid over her body in a lick of desire, then settled on her hands clutching her shawl closed.

Goosepins raced her skin and her eyes widened. Handsome, devilishly so. She certainly could use a good flirtation to brighten her spirits. *Goodness, Sophia. You are a taken woman. This man should not turn your head. Your fearful feelings about Quinton are simply that. Fears.*

She strolled up beside Alistair. "Follow me, sir. I shall take you to Elm Place."

"Very well." His lips twitched up as if he had gotten exactly what he had wanted; her to escort him to Quinton. Well he would have a shock to find out she was taken by the very man they went to see.

They walked along in silence. A small break in the large laurel hedge emerged, and they turned into a grassy field. "We will cut across the field here and then into the covered lane, which leads to the house."

"Very well, ma'am."

He walked so close to her. Too close. Silliness, Sophia; he is a proper distance from you. His hands are clasped behind his back. He is not trying to touch you in any form.

Simply his nearness caressed her. Calmed her. Made her feel as if she wished to bury her head on his shoulder and tell him all her struggles, her worries, her fears about being who she was.

The sensation was very different from the one that Quinton inspired. Quinton was all futter and pleasure. She never really walked with Quinton as such.

Even if Alistair bluntly told her he never walked in the country, somehow this felt natural. The wind blew across the field as they walked, and the crisp fall air reddened her skin and made her ears hurt.

She stared at Alistair, then back at the grass before them. The green grass would soon fade to brown and the crisp sunny days turn to rain. A blast of chill air blew and a chill raced down her spine.

She glanced at his face; he gazed about him, not really fidgeting but not calm. Well she should start asking questions if she wanted any kind of information from him about his stay.

"What brings you to Elm Place, sir?"

He laughed a deep joyful sound. Her lips curled up and her belly tightened with suppressed laughter. His laugh alone lightened her.

"Anne, the woman in the carriage is one of my *um* . . ." He glanced at her from the corner of his eye, then back to the ground before him.

"Your paramour?"

"Indeed. In a sense she is. Though we have no romantic involvement . . . simply pleasure . . . friendship."

Anne was *one* of his paramours. . . . How many did one man need? Sophia's brow pinched and she scowled as she glanced at him. A handsome devil, indeed. One who was worse than a dog sniffing for scraps.

"Anne said I needed a few days in the country. I was thinking with my peg at the moment and said yes before I realized what exactly she suggested."

They turned the corner onto the long vine-covered lane that led to the side of the house, and Sophia shivered. The sun no longer warmed her skin, and her wool shawl was inadequate in the damp of the covered lane.

"What was she suggesting, sir?"

He stopped, and she stopped and turned toward him. "Everything well, sir?"

She stared unable to move as his fingers trailed up the edges of her wrap to her fists clutching her cloak together at her breast. "No not well at all actually."

Her heart lodged in her throat and her eyes widened. What was he about? She should knock his hands away, she should—

He grasped her hands and repositioned them higher up on the cloth by her neck, then pulled her wrap tight by fisting her hands. "If you keep it held closely to your neck, less heat can escape. All shall be better now." His hands brushed against her breast as they retreated.

A purposeful brush or on accident she did not know. Her entire body trembled as his musky scent filled her nostrils. How strange a man who does not like the country or a walk in the woods wears a scent that smells like them?

She glanced down at her hands clutched in the wool of her cloak. He watched out for her welfare. The sincerity in the kind gesture knocked her back a step in thought, and her body trembled. "Pardon, sir?" spilled from her mouth before she realized she'd spoken aloud.

A kind smile curved his lips and he winked at her. "You should stop your quivering with your cloak tightly closed like that."

Would she? No. Her legs shook of an entirely different accord: him.

"Anne is here on business. She thought I could protect her while she was here and I could take deep breaths of refreshing air while she did business. Problem is . . . the smell of livestock is enough to make me cast my accounts."

A laugh burst past her lips before she could recover it. "You jest, sir."

"Oh, I kid you not." He turned back toward the house and stepped forward causing her to step with him to continue the conversation.

"I shall have to tell you all of the paths to avoid on your tortuous walks through the countryside."

"You shall show me yourself." His shoulder and arm brushed into hers as they continued to walk.

"Well I—"she bit her lower lip, then looked down at her feet. What was wrong with her? Stop reacting to this man this way. She certainly could not see him again after this. She needed to be honest with him about where her sights were cast. "I would like that, but I fear I have given my favors to another man. He would object, sir."

"Come now. You were home alone. What man would leave you on a lovely day like today? Though I certainly respect your telling me. As you are aware of my avoidance of 'fowl' scents, I still would enjoy your escort around the area."

She swallowed hard and they reached the end of the covered walk and stepped back out into the glorious sun.

"Bloody." His hand rose and he shielded his eye from the sun. "Should have grabbed my hat from the carriage."

"No worries, sir. The sun will be in your eye but a moment."

They strode three steps and the sun dipped beyond the eave of the house. "This is Elm Place, sir. And Lord Quinton and the rest of your party shall be in the parlor, I imagine. The front door is just around corner."

"Very well, ma'am. I shall call on you tomorrow at noontime, and we can take a stroll before feasting in one of Lord Quinton's covered gardens. The air is too chill to risk your taking a chill by dining in the damp air." He leaned toward her as if to kiss her. Her heart jumped into her throat. No, don't let him! Her eyes widened and her tongue slid out and wet her lips. He hovered a breath's whisper from her face. Their eyes locked.

"I wish you a fine evening, ma'am. Be ready at noontime tomorrow." He pulled back and stepped away from her.

She swallowed hard and stared at him as he walked past her and around the corner of the house. *Sigh*. Tomorrow. Noontime.

She turned and stepped back into the damp of the covered walk. She had only come here once or twice since Quinton and she began. Quinton was more comfortable with her at her place, or in the wilderness, because of his son.

Oh no! Quinton had asked her to picnic tomorrow. She bit her lip. Then again he would most likely cancel, as he had guests. Something always seemed to come up. . . .

Quinton stared out the window of the parlor and watched as Sophia walked up the covered path with a tall broad-shouldered man. His heart sped in his chest and his throat tightened. Was he the man Miss Cathcort had mentioned to him? Her gentleman friend?

The man stopped, and Sophia turned toward him. He wrapped his fingers about her fingers clutching her cloak.

How dare he touch her? Quinton's teeth clenched.

Sophia leaned toward him, and her neck arched seductively.

Damn her. What was she doing?

The man unwrapped her fingers and moved them up higher on her cloak.

"You might want to set the glass down if you are going to clench your fingers so tightly, Lord Quinton. Any tighter and you shall surely cut your hand," came a feminine voice.

Quinton glanced down at the glass of scotch he held in his hand; his knuckles paper thin, white. He closed his eyes.

Miss Cathcort stepped up beside him. She glanced over his shoulder and watched as Sophia and her friend stopped at the edge of the house.

"She is a handsome woman, Lord Quinton. Are you involved with her? Your mistress, perhaps?"

He turned toward Miss Cathcort. He needed to tell her the truth. He worked his jaw, to relax the muscles he had held taut, then blew out a tense breath.

Sophia turned and headed back toward the covered walk. The sunlight caught her hair and glistened in the soft curls she pinned behind her ears. She was not his mistress. She was so much more to him. Yet he had difficulty letting her meet Jake. A woman who had children of her own is what he wanted for his son. Siblings his son's own age and a woman who knew how to be a mother.

"No, Miss Cathcort. She is not my paramour. Rather someone I had considered to be my lady."

"Oh well, well. So my ladies have blood competition."

Quinton swallowed hard. "No, Miss Cathcort. She does not fit quite what I desire for Lady of Elm Place. Though she has touched my mind and spirit."

"Very powerful emotions, Lord Quinton. Something I am sure you are considering, even if she does not meet your social needs."

Sophia turned out of sight, and Quinton closed his eyes and savored the memory for one simple tick of the clock. He would give these women a fair chance. Sophia would always be next door waiting for him if things didn't work.

♡ *Chapter 3*

The next day ... hell and passion collide

"Bo! Bo! Stop whining." Sophia grasped her gloves and pulled them on. "Silly dog."

Bo jumped up and lightly bit her kid-gloved hand. He shook his head and pulled her toward the door.

She reached down and grabbed the door handle. Bo let go of her hand and raced out the back of the cottage toward the sun-patch field.

She hoped Quinton would be out on his morning walk. She needed to ask him why he had not told her about his . . . company. Her stomach flipped and her insides wobbled. She had not been able to eat since they arrived. Her entire world wobbled on what he would say to her, and her soul was positive things were not good.

They walked up the hill and toward the estate trails.

A woman's giggle floated on the slight crisp breeze. Sophia stopped still. The bathhouse resided only a short way over the hill.

Sickening curiosity crawled up her spine. She wanted to know what the woman Anne's features possessed. Did she have large breasts and a slim waist? Were her legs fat and the skin dimpled beneath her petticoats? No. What she saw of Anne was beautiful. Logic would say the rest of her body would be so as well.

Sigh.

Sophia lifted her foot and went to step in the direction of the bathhouse. Her knees twitched, but her will stayed firm. *Pass on by, Sophia, pass on by.*

Bo continued off in the direction of their normal routine. *Indeed, follow Bo.* The path to the bathhouse only leads to contorted thoughts and an aching soul. Don't do it, Sophia.

Her feet moved and she continued down the slightly worn path toward the pond and the ducks. Bo so loved to torment those ducks.

A woman's laugh, followed by a deep chuckle, came from the direction of the bathhouse.

That chuckle was Alastair's. The sound warmed her to her toes and she smiled. No, Sophia! Quinton is your suitor; but Quinton also lied. What would it hurt to see what his friends possessed and maybe to hear more about why they are at Elm Place?

She swallowed and turned in the direction of the bathhouse. Her feet moved light and swift, and she glanced all about, making sure no one saw her approach. She walked into the woods.

What are you doing, Sophia? Quinton would slap you for this. You would slap yourself. The image of her hand slapping her cheek came to mind, and she held in a giggle and rolled her eyes at herself.

Bo bounded after her, dashing in and out of trees while sniffing the ground. She came up to the bathhouse, which sat next to the pond. Bo bounded to the water in search of his ducks.

More giggles came from the bathhouse. "Shush, Anne. I am trying to enjoy this long soak. If you want to play, go find Lord Quinton and have a quick futter."

"Alistair, stop being such a limp weed."

Sophia held back a giggle. Limp weed? Somehow, she could not fathom Alistair being *limp*. The word did not fit him.

"I shall do as I wish, Anne. I want to find that pretty little thing and bed her soundly."

Sophia's hand covered the gasp that threatened to press from her mouth. Oh my! He wanted to futter with her. Goosepins of excitement raced her skin and heat bloomed low in her belly. What would doing the act with Alistair, a man who had no embarrassment about his peg being exposed, be like?

Though he had simply said pretty little thing. She supposed she was a bit presumptuous to think he referred to her.

Push the thought from your mind, Sophia. Alistair is not the kind of man who loved. Who offered security. He was the kind of man who had multiple dalliances!

"Very well, Alistair. If the country miss is what you crave, then have her. You know I don't need futter simply to futter. I am sure Lord Quinton's affairs will more than fulfill my needs."

"Quinton?" His name pressed past Sophia's lips and her heart sank. Anne was here to . . . to do what with Quinton?

Sophia had no idea.

Think Sophia. Surely she missed something he said to her. Her mind and her stomach flipped and tumbled. Footsteps fell on the earth behind her. Sophia's gaze turned to see two additional women at the foot of the trail to the lake and bathhouse.

Oh no! If she didn't move, they would see her spying.

She quickly dashed to the bathhouse wall and tucked herself around the side of the marble structure. Her back to the smooth surface, she held herself so very still. Her heart beat through her and controlled her breath. She closed her eyes. Please don't let them see her.

The women's footfalls approached, and Sophia held her breath, not wanting to make a single sound.

"Lord Quinton certainly is handsome."

"Indeed. I hope Miss Cathcort can arrange something for one of us with him. This estate is beautiful and his son is so delightful. My daughter will simply adore him."

They had met Jake. Sophia's heart pinched. She had longed to meet him for the past year. Quinton always had some excuse for her not to.

The door to the bathhouse opened. "Mary. Olivia." Anne's cheery voice floated through the air. "Alistair is inside. Behave if either of you have any interest in Lord Quinton. Do not give into Alistair's persuasions."

"Anne. Why would I go for one of your girls when I could have had one or both of them already . . . and for all you know, I have." Alistair's tone held a note of humor. He truly was a confident and scandalous dog.

Anne scoffed and the other women giggled.

"Anne, did Lord Quinton express interest in either one of us?"

"He said you were both stunning and your bloodlines and stations were exactly what he searched for in his wife."

"His . . . his wife?" Sophia's face froze and a chill raced down her spine.

The door to the bathhouse closed. Footsteps fell on the trail and faded off into the distance.

Quinton had not told her about his visitors because he . . . He . . .

Tears welled in her eyes and her heart pinched. She worked her throat but couldn't even say the words again.

Maybe they all jested. Or maybe Sophia was simply Quinton's dove. She shivered straight down to her soul. How could she have been so naive?

Sophia strained to hear what went on inside, hoping more information would come to her. She closed her eyes and leaned up against the cool wall.

Concentrating on the sounds inside of the structure, she bit her lip. Please let this all be a jest. Low murmurs was all she could discern within the stone structure.

"My, aren't you the curious thing?" Warm coffee-filled breath fanned her face.

Sophia's eyes popped open as Alistair's arms braced the wall on either side of her.

She swallowed hard. His heat seeped through her clothing and warmed her skin. She shivered as the chill from the shock dissipated.

She stared into soft brown eyes, as damp hair curled in dark brown waves about his face. My God, he was handsome. She swallowed hard once again. *Duck beneath his arm, Sophia . . . walk away.*

His lip quirked up. "What exactly are you curious about, dear miss?"

"Sir." She pulled her face from the intense desire in his eyes and stared at the dirt and fallen leaves on the ground around them.

"Very well, then. Shall we walk or would you prefer this?" His hand rose and traced the line of her cheekbone down to her lips.

Her mouth fell open to protest. Not a sound came out. Her head fell back against the stone wall and she closed her eyes.

His smooth finger traced the top contour of her mouth. Her lips trembled, and the heat of his touch on her skin captivated her. Tingles raced down her spine and her stomach flipped. She could not move; all she could do was feel him.

Quinton's touch, let alone kiss, never immobilized her. She swallowed hard, and bursts of light flashed behind her eyelids.

His fingertip glided along her bottom pout and pulled the lip down. Her eyelids fluttered open. His face was less than a finger's width away. He was about to kiss her!

His lips came down soft and gentle . . . nothing like Quinton's. They fluttered and nibbled. No harsh intensity . . . no pulling back for air. Time ceased to matter.

Alistair's kiss lingered. Slowly his lips pressed and grabbed her upper one.

She moaned, and the essence of coffee and soap filled her taste-buds. Her nipples peaked. His tongue traced the plump surface he had captured.

Sophia's heart raced. This was wrong; Quinton was everything she had ever craved and wanted. Or was he?

His companionship had never quite felt genuine and then this . . . He had women here for . . . God, she still couldn't say the blast word! Her relationship with Quinton was not well. His respect of her was amiss.

Alistair's tongue fluttered into her mouth and circled hers, then retreated. Heat flooded her belly and trickled lower, wetting her cunt lips.

She could not deny she wanted to experience this act; Alastair's kisses.

He was a tempting rogue. His confidence was nonesuch, and that alone was an enticement to her.

His tongue teased her lower lip. She wanted him to go deeper.

To kiss her harder, to pull her to him and crush her mouth with his until she couldn't breathe and she gasped for air. Would he?

Please, please let his desire possess her and wipe away all of this brumblebroth of emotions she swam in.

His tongue continued a slow light flutter along her lips. She moaned in frustration, wanting more. Pressing up against him, her breast touched his chest. Her lips pressed firmly to his. She kissed him back with a longing she had not realized she had deep in her gut.

Alastair called to a deep dark desire lingering in her. She wanted to experience him. He was different.

She was lost, head-deep, swimming in unforeseen and unknown territory. The right and the wrong of kissing him tore her in two.

She wanted to find out exactly what Alistair could offer her. What made him so different? What made Alistair, Alistair?

Alistair pulled back a breath, as she tried to deepen the kiss once more. His body pressed to hers. One knee slid between her legs and his foot tapped her feet farther apart.

Her body shook and she opened her hips, her long skirts caught between his probing leg and the wall behind her.

His lips slid, kissing her cheek in feather line to her ear. Breath as warm as the steam from the bath warmed her to her soul. She was safe here in this moment with this man. He would never let anything happen to her. She mentally shook herself. How did she know such a thing simply from a kiss?

Molten heat spread up her belly and she relaxed into him. Her body trembled. The sensation overwhelmed her. Wet tongue traced the curve of her ear and dipped into the cup. A moan pressed from her lungs.

"Dear sweet miss. Your inexperience is as sticky as honey. I am a bear that simply cannot resist." His words raised the fine hairs on her neck. His tongue traveled down the soft flesh of her throat to the curve, and he bit.

Warm, wet pressure tingled through her sex bud as if his mouth and teeth pressed to her cunny and not the exposed skin above her cloak. How did that happen? Oh, she wanted to know more.

Her hips arched into his thigh, and she reached for the ache in her womb to be soothed. The core of her womb burned hotter and hotter. Desire pulsed through her veins, and she was ready to erupt.

Beneath the fabric of his breeches, the hard ridge of his peg teased her inner thigh. She pressed her mound insistently against his prick and moaned. His cock swelled further as the desire to join pulsed through them. She wanted to gaze upon his phallus and touch the smooth skin.

The shape beneath his breeches was narrower than Quinton's but equal in length. She couldn't remember what George's peg felt like, and she so wanted to know how men were different. Specifically, how Alistair liked to futter.

His fingers dove beneath the folds of her pelisses and gripped her breast. She wanted his hand on her bare skin, not all the layers of clothing that lay between them. She wiggled and tried to get his fingers to move farther up to touch the bare skin of her chest. His fingers moved lower.

Oh God! Indeed, lower.

Fingers trailed to her waist . . . then dipped to her thigh. He inched up the fabric of her garments, adjusting the cloth so that her skirts disentangled from their legs.

The cool air seeped through the thin cotton of her stockings and washed her skin in ice. Her heart sped. She wanted to cuddle into him, to feel his naked heat as his peg parted the folds of her sex and entered her.

His fingers glided up the small bit of bare skin at the top of her thighs. Her pussy quivered, and delicious tendrils of want crawled through her.

He was about to touch her cunny. To finger-futter her in the open of the woods . . . where anyone could see.

She swallowed hard as exhilaration rushed through her veins. She squirmed wantonly against him.

His icy-cold fingers parted the folds of her and his hand pressed fully against her humid flesh. She jumped at the unexpected contrast. His lips and tongue trailed back to her mouth. Soft and gentle, his tongue fluttered.

She wanted more, more of his kiss, more of him. She closed her lips firmly on his and sucked his tongue into her mouth.

He moaned, and one large finger glided effortlessly down her slit. She rocked her hips against his intrusion. My God, she had not realized how wet her cunny grew. She moaned in her throat.

The tip of his finger dipped into her opening, and she bucked and spread her thighs wide. She wanted him to ease her ache no matter how wrong it was. His fingers . . . oh. . . .

He slid his middle finger deep within her pussy and pulled from her kiss.

"My aren't we an eager little miss?" his tongue traced her lower lip, and he gently bit as he slid his finger back out then in more harshly. The palm of his hand pressed to her mound and he rubbed her hairs side to side.

Exquisite warmth flooded her sex and her cunt gaped open.

"Indeed. You do desire me." He released her lip. His tongue traveled down over her chin and to her neck. He leaned in and his shoulder pressed to hers holding her still.

Yes, indeed, she wanted him.

He angled himself against her and slid his fingers in and out of her flesh with quick and fast motions. Each press of his fingers mixed pleasure and insanity. A deep needing pressure blossomed into a blissful pain.

She opened her hips and pressed down against his fingers next withdrawal. His hand continued to move quickly in and out, in and out of her. Her cunt opened wide and her flesh tingled. The urge to push down against his invasion over took her. Her lower abdomen clenched, and the pressure released in a gush of warm trickles of fluid from her body.

"Oh, you are a wanton wench. Spending in my hand like that." The words hissed against her ear.

Fire raced down her spine and straight to her wet cunny.

"Reach down and unbutton my flap."

Her hand trembled . . . and she hesitated. She wanted to feel him, to see what his peg was like. Quinton had lied to her and searched for a wife other than her. She was a fool to have believed in him. This act was real and now and promised nothing more.

Her hand rose and went to the buttons of his flap with quick jerky motions. Her fingers undid the top button and then the next lower on the left side, then undid the top button and the next lower on the right.

The tips of her fingers glided along the smooth skin of his lower abdomen and through the springy curls of his sex. His cock lay along his right thigh. She wrapped his peg with her hand and pulled his length from the confines of his breeches.

"Ummm . . ." He grasped her skirts and pulled them up higher.

Her legs trembled in the cool morning breeze. His tongue swooped into the cup of her ear and his hands grasped her bottom. He lifted her.

Should she do this? Panic tightened her chest and she grasped his shoulders. Her legs gripped the outside of his hips, opening her cunt to him. He pressed his body to hers and the head of his cock parted her weeping flesh and thrust into her as if a knife cutting through butter.

She cried out at the quickness of the joining of their bodies.

He leaned in and bit her earlobe. "Noisy little miss, are you not? The fun I could have teaching you to let go of your restraint and scream louder. . ." He rubbed his pelvis against her open mound. "And louder." He pulled his length out of her and then slid back in.

"Oh! Ah!"

"Indeed you are a noisy wench. Shall we see if we can get the girls inside to hear you?"

Sophia bit her lip and squirmed as she tried to hold in another deep moan. He bit her neck and pulled out to the ridge on the tip of his hard head. The flange of his cock caught the weeping flesh of her pussy opening. Tingles of heat tightened her muscles. He rocked his hips with small motions in the opening of her.

A deep pressure pooled in her sex. He slid back in all the way. Her mouth fell open and she tilted her head back against the wall. An animallike growl pressed from the depths of her soul.

No matter how confused she was, this moment she flew on pleasure, on exhilaration of doing this act here with his man. The pressure in her womb released, and wetness drizzled from her sex and down the crack of her bum. He pushed in again. Her entire body shook against him.

"You are so wet." He stared down at her with heavy-lidded eyes.

"Don't most women get wet between their thighs?" Heat raced through her and she tightened her cunny muscles about his cock.

He laughed outright. "Indeed. Each one is different, and each one to a different degree."

He pushed into her again, stilled, and held himself buried within her.

Alistair glanced up as the door to the bathhouse slammed shut. The low murmur of voices floated out on the breeze. Someone joined the ladies within. He held Sophia's legs tight to him and glanced down into her beautiful green eyes.

"What is it?"

What was it, indeed? She was a gorgeous woman, who thought she belonged to Lord Quinton. Lord Quinton was a rogue and a disrespectable man and she'd just learned of his faults.

Lord Quinton was about to futter two widows to see if they met his carnal act requirements. Sophia couldn't hear that test or by twisted fate become witness to the act. He needed to remove them from this location and quickly.

"I have the urge to take you in a bed. Though I believe you are on your daily ritual. So instead, may I join you?" He lowered her legs back to the earth. His pleasure be damned . . . no woman deserved to have her undoing flaunted right before her nose. Lord Quinton's behavior simply was not proper. Alistair cringed to himself. *Proper?* When had that word ever gained consideration in his thoughts? His lip quirked up. He normally would wish to join the scoundrel Lord Quinton. Where had this spark of morals come from?

She leaned back against the wall behind her. "You stop in the middle of futter because you want to walk with me?"

It was ridiculous . . . beyond. "Indeed. I am not always rational. Or practical . . . but my pleasure is important, and I feel we should stroll along the path with Bo."

Her eyes grew wide "Oh, Bo!" She glanced around the woods. "Where is Bo?" She straightened her skirts, covering the curve of her ivory thighs, and glanced seductively up at him through her lashes.

That look alone made him want to scoop her up in his arms and protect her from the world. He shook himself. He did not even know her, yet was compelled to protect her like one of his girls. She was *not* one of his girls. The mutt . . . concentrate on the mutt, not the wench with the tight, watering pussy.

"Please, no vapors over a wandering mutt. I will find your pup." He offered her his arm, and she wrapped her fingers about his coat sleeve. They turned in the direction of the pond.

"He loves to chase the ducks."

"As any self-respecting mutt does." He winked at her. He had gone daft in the attic. She was much more than futter to him, but how he got here to this strange unfamiliar place in less than one meaningful conversation he had not one blasted clue. He scowled. This trip to the fresh air certainly was filled with one foul-smelling hazard after another.

Chapter 4

Show and tell

Anne had instructed Quinton that Olivia and Mary would be waiting for him in the bathhouse. They waited, eager to show him their physical sides and demonstrate to him their expertise in the art of passion.

He hesitated by the door to the bathhouse. Never in his life had he thought of searching for a wife this way. Eleanor he had simply fallen for as he saw her across the dance floor. She required so very little searching; and then there was Sophia.

Naive, innocent, Sophia. He closed his eyes and sighed.

Sophia grasped his soul with the ever-changing passion in her eyes. Her very existence seemed to change everything about him. They had met when out on a walk. He saw her twirling on top of Crest Hill. The sun glinted off her unruly mane and her smile. . . . Her smile and spirit lifted him from the dreariness of mourning and added joy to his everyday existence.

She had enlivened him and made him realize he wanted a

second wife, but her lack of children and her lack of proper behavior where society was concerned were the very things he knew would not serve him in his position. She would never be presentable. The image of Sophia with mud under her nails as she sat at one of the marquis of Lanktor's balls made his stomach sink. She was the perfect mistress for him.

His close friends and peers would frown upon him for choosing such a woman, even if she was of blood, and so he had turned to Miss Cathcort.

He hoped Miss Cathcort's renowned skills for finding suitable second and third wives for those who did not have the time to search lived up to the claims. He would soon find out. This was the one aspect beyond children he would not compromise on. Sophia had fulfilled his every desire in this realm. Whoever became the Lady of Elm Place needed to do the same with equal vigor.

Quinton turned the handle and stepped into the bathhouse. Steam washed over him. He coughed at the contrast from the cold outside air.

"Lord Quinton. How are you this morning?" Olivia pushed her coopery gold hair back behind her ears and smiled.

"Very well, Olivia, and may I ask after your health?" He stepped farther into the room. Both women remained in their chemise. The steam dampened their skin, causing the fabric to stick to the peaks. Their nipples shone delightfully through the thin cotton fabric.

"I am quite fine, sir." She giggled, and her robust figure jiggled slightly from the exuberance.

"And, Mary, how do you fare this fine morning?" Indeed the day was improving with every tick of the clock.

"I too am quite fine today and most days, sir." Her dark eyes swallowed his discomfort at being here as if he somehow read her thoughts before she'd even spoken them.

They both possessed stunning beauty. Though Mary had one advantage over Olivia in that she stood only to his shoulder, which for him was a reward in itself. He fell short of most men in height, and she was one of very few who did not match him.

Sophia was another.

He closed the door to the bathhouse and steam flowed all around him. Stepping forward, he unbuttoned his greatcoat and placed the garment on the hook by the door. He turned to find Olivia and Mary standing and facing him.

"What do you wish us to do for you, sir?"

Good question. He had no idea. Anne had called this his physical inspection to see if either of the girls met his needs. He had never done anything like this. His heart beat rapidly in his chest and his hand rose and touched his chin. What to do was a good question.

Both women portrayed a vision of loveliness, and by the smells of their cunny oil, they were more than ready for his inspection of the passions in the act.

He strode toward them and grasped one of each of the girl's hands. Olivia's plush hand fit securely in his whereas his other hand dwarfed Mary's petite fingers. His gaze darted back and forth between them. What to do? A physical inspection would be a start.

"I wish for you both to undress for me."

Olivia giggled and looked up at him from beneath her lashes. "Oh, indeed, sir. Shall you undress for us, too?"

His lips quirked up and up again at her playful, coy attitude. "That I shall. That I shall."

"Oh, good." Mary's small hand squeezed his. His gaze went

to her, and she beamed up at him. The excitement of the moment shown so clearly in her eye. Her eyes expressed so much. Just like Sophia's. He shook his head.

Stop thinking of her, Quinton. You will only end up raining on the moment. You need to give these girls a chance. Sophia will be there when this is over.

He released the girls' hands and turned and sat on the large marble ledge of the bathhouse.

Do this, Quinton. Finding a new wife is for your own good.

"I will greatly enjoy savoring both of your charms. Mary, I wish you to disrobe first."

Mary stared him straight in the eyes and smiled. Her hands rose to the cotton ribbon that held the neckline of her shift tight. Dainty fingers wrapped the string and she pulled. The bow untied, and the crisp cotton shift slipped slightly down her shoulder revealing rich creamy peach skin, which reddened upon his stare.

A blush. How delightful.

"Slip it down your shoulders, Mary."

How far did her modesty reach? Would she do all he asked but simply blush a deeper red? He intended to find out.

Her fingertips slid beneath the loose collar and along her collarbone. Reaching the shoulder, she hesitated and her gaze snapped back to his. He smiled at her, reassuring her with a smile that this was indeed what he wished. He was pleased with her and this moment no doubt would exceed his expectations.

"Once you have disrobed, Mary, I would like you to disrobe Olivia. You both will get more acquainted this day."

Her eyes widened but a glint of thrill flashed in their depths. Her fingers pushed the fabric over her shoulder and the garment fell to her elbow. Her breasts stood in small rounded mounds with coral-tipped nipples. Succulent fruit ready to be plucked and devoured. His mouth watered. He would indeed taste them.

She unbent her elbow and the garment fell the rest of the way down her body to pool at her feet on the gray marble floor. Stunning! Small and waiflike her personality radiated from her as if her body was too small for all she could do.

"Very nice, Mary. You are a vision of loveliness so acute, you will undo any fine gentleman's restraint. Now for Olivia." He continued to stare at Mary. Her loveliness mesmerized him.

Quinton swallowed the large lump in his throat. Never had he even imagined doing such a thing. Well that was a bit of a jest; of course, he had imagined seeing two women together doing as he willed. He simply had never comprehended he could get two women of breeding to do this in front of him.

Mary turned to Olivia and undid the tie to her shift. Then walking around behind her loosened the shoulders and slid her sift down her arms. The fabric caught on her hard nipples.

Olivia giggled and shimmied her shoulders, shaking her large breasts. She was the livelier of the two women. He certainly made note of her enthusiasm for the final evaluation.

He held in a chuckle to himself. Her laugh would either be a source of constant smiles or scowls. The shift slid down her body to reveal a woman with shapely curves. Her breasts were large and round, her hips swelled in a wave down to her plush thighs. She was a woman like one would see in a painting, but a half stone too much.

Nevertheless two very beautiful women stood before him. Beautiful and very different. He closed his eyes and Sophia's green eyes, her medium-sized breasts and generous hips flashed to mind. *Sigh.*

How could he stop her image from coming to mind when he did what he needed to. He couldn't.

"Stand back-to-back please."

Olivia and Mary complied. Mary's head came to the middle of Olivia's shoulder blades.

Quinton stood and walked to the two women. He stood facing Olivia. Her breasts were her most handsome physical feature and her light heart was her advantage in personality. He reached out and circled the tip of her nipple. Her body trembled, and a deep throaty purr erupted from her.

A noise as such, he could get used to hearing upon his touch. He trailed his fingers down her stomach to her hips. She shifted and separated her legs slightly for him. His fingers dipped down between her legs and into the warm oil of her cunny lips.

Her hips rotated to ease the entry of his fingers into her pussy and to maximize the friction of his vigorous digits.

"*Mmmm,* you are delightfully wet, Olivia." He slid his fingers deeper back until he found her pussy hole. One fingertip, he slid into her opening. She spread her hips and bent her knees slightly to allow him easier access to her. Her legs shook and her hand wrapped his forearm for stability. Indeed, she wanted him.

He pushed all the way into her, his palm rubbing on her bliss button. The warm velvet walls of her cunt grasped his finger as if holding onto something she held dear. "Your cunny is wonderfully tight. Do you wish for more of my attentions, Olivia? Would you like me to finger-frig you until you spend?"

"Oh, indeed, sir. Indeed. You may do whatever you wish to me, sir." Her chest labored in and out.

How quickly would she spend for him? He rubbed his palm against her plush mound and wiggled his finger in out of her. The slick spongy walls of her cunt grasped his hand. Her legs shook and her breath came in labored puffs. She leaned against him and her fingers dug into the fine tweed of his jacket.

"Oh, sir. Oh yes, more of that, please."

"You do like that, don't you?"

He wiggled his palm from side to side as the bud of her sex throbbed beneath his touch. His other hand trailed up to her breast, and he pinched her bud. Such a succulent peach, her juices quickly coated his adventuresome digits buried deep in her cunt.

She screamed. *"Ahhhhhhh!"*

Her body shook and the walls of her pussy grasped hard to his finger.

A nice spend, indeed, but nothing like Sophia's. When Sophia spent her entire body came alive. She gushed her spend from her like an erupting volcano or waterfall washing his hand or his prick in delicious molten warmth. He inhaled deep. *If you keep comparing them to her, you will never be satisfied with one of them. Appreciate them for who they are, Quinton.*

"Delightful, Olivia. You are so filled with salacious pleasure."

She straightened herself and released his arm. "Indeed you have wonderful fingers, sir."

"Thank you, Olivia. I enjoyed frigging you."

Quinton stepped to the left and around to Mary. Her long black hair hung in a thick black sheen down to her bottom. Her waiflike form covered almost entirely in hair. He smiled down at her. Raising his hand he ran his fingers through the long silk-soft tresses. "Your hair is stunning, Mary."

"Thank you." The words barely a whisper passed though parted plush lips. He licked his. He would indeed like to kiss her.

He let his hands glide down her waist to her hips. There he grasped her and pulled her slightly toward him. Her hands fluttered up and braced his chest, holding herself slightly from his body.

A tremor ran thought him. Indeed, he wanted her. He walked his fingers around to her bottom and dipped into the crack of her bum. Dew met his fingers. *Ah*, she was aroused. He slid the tip of his finger down the soft skin at the base of the crevice. His hand wrapped the swell of her bottom and his fingers slipped into the folds of her cunny.

A whimper bubbled in her chest, and her fingers gasped the lapels of his tweed coat.

He couldn't quite reach the opening to her cunny. Reaching down with his opposite hand, he scooped her up.

"Wrap your legs about me, Mary."

Mary complied. Her small figure light and airy wrapped his body. Her pussy opened to his fingers as she held herself to him. Three fingers slid into her slit. Creamy thick custard met his touch, and he pushed farther in. Her body jerked as her hands pulled at his shoulders. She lifted her body and sank back down onto his fingers, frigging herself on his hand, as he held still. She moaned and worked her body against him. Her cunt opened and opened to him. Her muscles loosened with each deep press onto his hand.

He tucked his thumb and pinky together against the tips of his other fingers to make a wider cone for her to ride on. He imagined his thick cock in his fingers' place. She would easily accommodate him.

She slid back down onto him, and the new width of his fingers elicited a shudder and a deeper moan from her. He pushed up and she pushed down; her skin stretched about his probe.

She continued to push down. *"Oh, oh, oh, oh."* His fingers slid in up to his knuckles. His eyes widened: with just a little pressure from him, his entire hand would slide into her pussy.

She rose back up and slid back down his fingers. With his hand covered in her thick white cream, his knuckles slipped in and he wiggled his fingers inside her.

She screamed. The slick creamy walls of her clutched and then released his fingers' assault. Her body shook and trembled as she steadied herself on his hand. She stilled herself and moaned.

His heart pounded in his chest. "Everything well, Mary?" She was so light. If she had been heavier, like Olivia or Sophia, this position would have been impossible.

"Indeed, sir. Oh how I adore this. I feel so full, so stretched."

He pushed a little more, and a fraction more of his hand slid into her. Her body convulsed and her muscles grabbed his hand in a grip that made him tremble to the core. What would her cunny's grip feel like about his cock? His peg twitched in his breeches he wanted to find out. He slowly pulled his hand out of her.

Every miniscule retraction his hand made, her body quaked in his arms. His fingers left her gaping.

She slid down his body and he held her steady for a moment as her feet hit the ground.

"Amazing." Olivia's voice came from just behind Mary.

"Indeed. I think so as well." Quinton said, and swallowed.

"Do we get to inspect you as well, sir?" Mary's hands slid down his torso and lightly grazed his cock. My God he wanted such, but he knew where that would lead. Both of them being his possible wife, he simply could not allow himself to do such a thing before they were wed. Thoughts of their tongues entwined about his peg, before sampling their sweet cunts, was more than any decent man could resist. He needed to; one of them, after all, would be his wife.

"No, sweet girls. You are both stunning and have your very own true talents and advantages." He reached up and wiped their cunt scents on each of their cheeks. He needed release and he needed to think which of these women would fit him.

"Finish your morning bath, ladies, and we will meet back at the house." Quinton's heart hammered in his chest. He had never ever desired finger-frigging a woman that hard, but now that he had, he wanted to do it again, and this time to Sophia. God, he could just imagine the gush of fluid that would run down his hand and arm. She would scream so loud that all the neighbors would know she was fully claimed by him and him alone. He closed his eyes as Mary and Olivia and the sweet feel of each one's pussy came to mind.

Which one cunny varied most from Sophia's? He should keep his activities as varied as possible to experience the most from life. Though Sophia was of high blood, she had accepted him into her bed with very little persuasion, and he had no doubt she would continue doing so. He grinned. That he certainly could count on from her.

Quinton pulled open the door to the bathhouse and stepped out onto the path back to the house. He could go see her now. His heart wanted to and his cock wanted release after the temptation of the two women he pleasured. He sighed. What would she think of him if she knew he had just finger-frigged two women? What would she say when he told her he would wed one of these ladies?

His stomach twisted. She would leave him. That he knew for certain. Until he made a decision on which woman he would wed there truly was no reason to tangle things up. He would keep the pretense up for a bit longer.

Chapter 5

Sophia and Alistair walked along looking for Bo. They checked by the pond where he loved to chase the ducks but he was not there. Her heart beat in her chest as panic sliced through her. How could she be so careless to simply leave him be for her own curiosity? Her heart sank to the bottom of her heels.

"Don't worry, ma'am. He knows this area."

"Yes he does."

"Then don't fret. As any good mutt knows where food and warmth reside; when he gets hungry he will be home."

That did make sense. She simply worried he would get lost and not know where home was.

"You are worried he will not know how to come home. Dogs have an amazing sense of smell, so you don't have to worry about him finding his way. He will come back to you."

She nodded her head and hoped he was correct.

"I have raised several pups and know what I am speaking of, ma'am. You have no worries; perhaps he is already at your home.

Shall we venture to your bed so I may take my pleasure with you?"
He grinned at her.

His pleasure . . . indeed. He was not different than Quinton
in that regard. She stared at him and the sensations of his cock
sliding so effortlessly into the opening of her pussy danced in her
head. She wanted to forget about Quinton and his broken promise and do for another man.

She glanced up at Alistair from beneath her lashes. Trying to
assess simply how serious he was about taking his pleasure, nothing more.

"Alistair, will you take me, nothing more? I have simply received a bit of information that should have caused a fit of vapors
today and I don't wish any complications. Simply enjoyment.
Nothing more than simple pleasure to help me feel better."

He stopped still and turned to her. "Dear sweet miss. You
are something of an oddity for a blooded educated woman."
He laughed. "Pleasure with no complications is all my history
speaks."

Her lips quirked up. "Indeed, sir. Silly question. I suppose I
simply needed to know."

"You have nothing to fret with me. I am very well at perusing
my own pleasure, ma'am. I shall help you to forget your love with
a time you will not soon forget."

"Well then, sir. We shall see if Bo has wandered home."

Alistair cringed at the pain that was so very evident in Sophia's
voice. He wanted to protect her from the uncertainties that were
Lord Quinton. Lord Quinton undoubtedly felt for Sophia. That
was certain. He simply would not commit to her. Alistair had no
inkling of why.

He would discover that reason. Even if it required him to sit by the fire with Sophia and listen to her woes.

"Indeed, ma'am. Let's see if Bo is at home. On the way please tell me what it is you so wished with Lord Quinton." *Stop this, Alistair. Never have you wished the knowledge of a person's woe other than a bad port or blunt blown on a horse slower than a pig at the pole. Fresh air certainly had ill effect on his mind.*

Her face flushed a brilliant shade of crimson. His chest tightened. How far did the sweet miss blush? Was the mound of her sex a rosy hue as they walked?

"*Ah,* well. I see we shall have a very interesting conversation on the way back. Shall I start with a question or do you simply wish to confess all your scandalous thoughts?"

Her eyes widened and she glared at him.

"Come now, Miss Sophia. I know your thoughts are so very less than innocent." It wasn't like he hadn't heard it all before. Sophia was a well-bred second or third or even lower sister. She married and happened to simply have her husband die at Waterloo. The boredom from arranged marriages caused most women to simply want to feel. So what were Miss Sophia's thoughts? Were they wicked or were they simply of settling down and marrying again?

"Very well, Alistair. When I met Lord Quinton, he was a pure gentleman toward me. He courted me like any other woman with higher blood. He took me driving in his pantheon, picnics on the estate in the gardens. He then kissed me . . ." Her voice trailed off and the look in her eyes grew dreamy. "I had never been kissed the likes before. It was as if every bit of me burst into flames. I simply didn't know what to do. He continued to kiss me and one thing led to another, and we futtered right there in his gardens. Shame overcame me afterward, and I refused to see him for some time. But that one time had been so delightful after several days of him pursuing me, I decided the next time he came by we simply would futter again."

Alistair laughed outright. "So you gave yourself to him. Denied him, then gave yourself to him again?"

Her lips quirked up. "I suppose that does sound absurd doesn't it? Well from there on we futtered whenever he came by, but we simply stopped doing much else. I would always ask to do other activities. He would say yes we will picnic on the hill or drive to the lake. When the time came he always seemed to need to spend his attentions elsewhere. He even told me I would be his lady of Elm Place and mother to his son someday. I feel that was a false."

The rogue! Alistair's teeth clenched tight. How could any self-respecting gentleman raise the hopes of such a fine woman. He inwardly cringed. *You, yourself Alistair, have often shrugged off gentlemanly behaviors in search of your own pleasure. Who are you to judge?* "I am truly sorry, Sophia. He is not a man of integrity. He is worse than a wolf at the henhouse." He grasped Sophia's hand to try to brace her for the information he had to bestow. "I am here with Anne. She is a matchmaker of sorts for men looking for specific needs in a second wife. Lord Quinton contacted her with specific requirements." He stopped just beside the gate to her home and turned to her.

Tears silently ran down her cheek. The scoundrel! My God if he ever saw the bastard again he would uncork him.

"Sophia. I will help take your mind off that fop of a man." He leaned down and kissed her salty tear-stained cheeks, then pressed his lips firmly to her mouth.

Her lips stayed firmly closed. He traced the slit of her mouth with his tongue and she yielded. Her body leaned against his. Her fingers rose and fisted in his coat, pulling and gripping him.

Leaning down he wrapped one of his arms beneath her leg and the other about her torso and lifted her.

She moaned softly into his mouth then pulled from his embrace. "Alistair, show me how to forget him."

He pushed through the door to her cottage and shut it with the heel of his boot. Forgetting was something he could not help her do, but to help her see there was more she could yearn for. She had nothing to be insecure about a future filled with passion and . . . love. Such a striking woman should never fear such a fate as loneliness. Alistair shook himself. Such dribble coming from his mind. Is this what fresh air and a long soak in the tub did to him? Anne was right: he had become a limp weed. He gritted his teeth.

"Where is your room?"

She pointed down a long hall. "At the end."

He held her tightly to his chest. The floral tones of her skin captivated his senses. His stomach fell. *What in damnation caused his stomach to ripple such?*

Reaching the room he set her feet on the floor. "Sophia, please take off your cloak and boots." His tongue glided out and wet his lips. Grasp yourself, Alistair; you want to have your pleasure with her so stop with all these mad thoughts.

He turned and closed the door to her room, then walked to a small chair she had set in the corner. His heart beat a steady hard pulse in his chest. Blast and damn Anne. He would never forgive her for this trip.

He unbuttoned his coat and slid it down and off his shoulders. Reaching up, he unwound his cravat and pulled it from his neck. He laid both items on the back of the chair and inhaled deep. Turning, he sat facing Sophia.

She stood by the side of the bed. Cloak off, boots removed with her hands clasped behind her back. Her gaze wouldn't meet his.

"Sophia, do you wish to change your mind?"

"No!"

"What is on your mind, then?"

"I simply wish to join with you, Alistair, and hear you take your pleasure."

"You do not wish for your own? To be brought to the edge of bliss and pushed over?"

"I—I." She glanced up at him and then bit her lip. "I simply wish to know what futter with you is like. If it brings me to spend, that is nice. If it does not . . ." Her face grew intensely red. "I have a false phallus. My husband got it for me before he left for the war."

"A false phallus?" He grinned. "You are a naughty wench, indeed. You wish me to do as I wish with you, then?"

"Indeed, sir."

Alistair's heart pounded in his chest. She offered him her body to do with what he wished. The problem was her body alone was so much less than what he wanted. His throat closed and he swallowed only to cough on his spit.

He had the desire to get inside her mind and know what kind of tea she liked to drink. If she wished the horrid stinking water sweet and with milk. He wanted to know what if anything made her thrilled. What in damnation had this wench done to him? The urge to protect her was one thing, to bring her tea and cookies appalled him! *Futter her, Alistair. Make sure her pup returns, then leave.*

"Sophia, take off all of your clothing. Do so one piece at a time."

Sophia's hands rose and her fingers traced the neckline of her dress. "You will need to unbutton me."

He stared at her from across the room, his cock hard as a stone false prick, and his heart beating like the first time he saw a wet nurse's breasts. "Step forward and come to me."

Sophia stepped forward and stood directly before him.

"Turn about."

She turned and her skirts brushed the insides of his thighs. Tingles, as if someone ran a feather taunting his nerves flowed up his legs to his cock. He twitched in the confines of his trousers. He had not found his release since yesterday's interruption in the carriage . . . followed by him stopping his spend as he futtered Sophia against the wall of the bathhouse.

His sack grew tender and the pressure of release promised him a blissful eruption. He reached up, and his fingertips brushed along the short row of buttons. He pinched each one through the hole as quickly as he could.

"I am done, Sophia. Now step back so I can watch you undress."

Sophia stepped forward two steps and turned. Her dress catching on her heel and sliding from her shoulders to the floor. She giggled and turned to face him. "I suppose I won't be *slowly* taking my dress off." She smiled so vividly, joy sparked her eyes.

The wench! His gaze slid over her pale skin and deep brown hair. Her green eyes showed her emotions as if a painting for all to see.

Her figure, concealed in her white shift and half corset, was plush with curves. She would make any man pant like a cat in heat.

His cock twitched in his breeches. What indeed would he do with her? "Do you need assistance with your corset as well, Sophia?"

She tilted her head to the side. "Do you wish me to remove my corset, Alistair?"

"Indeed I wish to see your naked form."

"Then I shall remove it for you." She grasped the top of the garment and pushed it slightly together. One fastener at a time she undid the garment. The corset fell to the floor and left her standing in her chemise and stockings.

"The shift, Sophia."

She grasped the hem of the cotton shift and lifted it up and over her head in a movement that was quick and entirely unseductive.

The wench! She did that on purpose.

She stood before him naked, except for her wool stockings, and his cock dribbled in his pants. His attraction to her was not simply physical. *Stop that, Alistair . . . Any further thought was simply ridiculous.* He never wanted more than friendship from his girls. This strife pulsing though him had to be that idiot Quinton. His poor behavior made him want Sophia to remain safe. Unease and unfamiliar panic sliced through him.

"Lay back on the bed, Sophia." She turned toward the bed and crawled upon it. Her bottom displayed to him in complete round temptation. "Stay like so!" He couldn't allow himself to see her obtain her release. He simply needed to take his in her and leave. He hated the thought of treating her in such a manner, but whatever caused these strange urges and sensations in him simply would not do! "Do you have an herb cloth or lemon or something of the sort, Sophia?"

"Indeed, sir. I have them on the stand by the window."

He glanced to the bed stand by the window and saw long strips of cotton and a bottle of oil infused with herbs. He grasped one of the strips and placed it in a bowl, then poured the oil over it, soaking the cloth thoroughly. He grasped the bowl and walked back to Sophia.

"May I?" He placed his hand on the round swell of her bottom.

"Yes."

He set the bowl on the sheets between her legs. His hand slid down the crack of her bottom to her pussy. He parted her swollen folds and slid his fingers into her. Warm slick wet cunt oil greeted him. She moaned and shifted her bottom invitingly. As he pressed his finger all the way in, she arched her back and pushed her bottom up to him.

"You are so ready for a thorough ravaging, Sophia."

"*Mmmmm.*" Her body quivered.

His fingers slid in and out of her with ease. He added a second and on exit he spread her opening wide.

"*Oh! Mmmm. Oh!*" She stilled.

His opposite hand reached down between her legs and grasped the piece of cotton soaked in the oil. He picked it up and allowed some of the excess oil to drizzle into the bowl. He placed the cloth at her opening and pushed the wad up inside as far as his fingers could reach. He removed his fingers and rubbed her ivory bottom gently with his hands.

"Are you ready for me, Sophia?"

"Yes, oh, yes. Please take your pleasure in me."

He unfastened the buttons to his flap and pulled his cock out. "Lean down on your shoulders Sophia and place your hands on the small of your back."

She hesitated and glanced back over her shoulder at him.

"Sophia?" He slipped his fingers into her cunt and back out. The warmth of her and increased slickness from the sponge tightened his sack, and his cock wavered in the air seeking out the warmth of her. He wanted to be buried deep in her spongy soft flesh. "Sweet, ma'am, you are so ready for me . . . Your hands on your back. Now."

She leaned down and placed her shoulders on the bed covers. Her head turned to the side, and her hands reached back.

"Grasp your wrists."

Her fingers wrapped about the opposite wrists and her bottom arched up into the perfect position for deep thrusts.

He grasped her hip and knelt up on the bed behind her. His prick head glided between the upturned cheeks of her bottom. The hot oil of her cunny touched the tip of his prick and he slid forward. The velvet softness of her inside encased him in slick molten warmth.

He grasped each one of her wrists in his and pulled her into him. Using her arms as if ropes he moved her back and forth. His prick slid in and out of her with force. Their skin slapped together.

The sight of cock disappearing into her was a sight he relished. My God, he needed to spend this time and this time he would fill Sophia with his seed and erase that rogue from her mind.

She moaned and shook. Her inner muscles rippled. He increased the ferocity of his buck. Her bum hit his legs and thighs and a sensuous wave of pleasure tightened all his muscles. His sack hit her pussy. The sound alone kept him teetering on the edge of spending. Her sweet dewed flesh clasped him. *"Oh! Oh! Oh!"*

"Sophia I want you to not make a sound, do you understand me, even if you are going to spend I don't want to hear a whisper from you. Only your breath."

Her entire body trembled at those words. He knew she would

enjoy being told what to do. Her body quaked. A spend close for her.

As he pushed into her wet flesh, all the muscles of his stomach flamed, and warmth spread through his being.

She shook and her muscles clenched tight. Her breath came out in a tumble and her cunny watered.

My God! The hot molten liquid undid him. His head spun and the first of the mind-numbing squirts sprayed from him as if he emptied his soul into her. Fever spread through him and he screamed. "Sweet woman!"

He released her hands and they flopped to either side of her. His hand steadied himself on her bottom. "Sophia, I am going to stand back and button my flap. I want you to roll onto your back and grab your false phallus and start to frig yourself. I will leave now and go search for Bo. I want you to make yourself spend one more time after I leave. Now not a sound as I stand back."

He pushed himself back from her, his softening cock sliding from her body as his seed dripped to the bedclothes below. She turned over as he buttoned his flap. Their eyes met and held. A content smile crossed her face, and she lowered her gaze from him.

His skin tingled everywhere simply from her expression. What in damnation was he thinking? He sat in the chair and pulled on his boots. He needed to fence, or to play cards. He needed a very stiff drink and miles between him and the fresh stink of county air and twisting thoughts.

She reached to the side of her bed and pulled out a green stone phallus. He stood and pulled on his coat. He walked to her and leaned down. His lips pressed to the salty sex scented skin of her cheek. "I want you to make all the noise you want as you spend without me this time."

He pushed away from her and walked to the door. Pulling the door open, he walked down the hallway. Now, where to find a wandering pup?

He smiled to himself. It was growing clear: Sophia meant more than simple pleasure to him. . . . He was searching for her pup and so well on the way to making a blunder out of his existence. He inhaled deep and sighed. Find the pup, uncork Quinton, and leave. That was the plan indeed. Why had he gotten out of Anne's stinking carriage?

♡ *Chapter 6*

Quinton pushed open the door to Sophia's cottage. Bo did not greet him at the door as usual, nor was there a sound anywhere. His brow drew tight. Where was Bo? Was Sophia home? He walked forward, his boots echoing on the hardwood floor. He had always liked this house, though her husband had never kept it quite as nice as he would.

He strode forward and down the hall toward her bedroom. The door stood closed. He walked to it and inhaled deep. What exactly would he say to her? *"Sophia. I know I lied to you, but can you please forgive me and let me futter you now? I so need to feel your body shaking beneath mine."* He rolled his eyes. Never would she accept that.

He grasped the handle on the door. A low moan came from behind it. His brow drew together and he froze his hand, gripping the door handle a fraction tighter.

He placed his ear to the crack in the doorframe and listened. The familiar sound of the bed creaking echoed behind the door. She made very little sound. Something was amiss.

"Sweet woman!" Alistair's smooth polished groan rose every fine hair on Quinn's neck, and his teeth clenched tight.

Alistair just buttered Sophia. *His* Sophia.

How dare she do such a thing to him? How dare she . . .

Get ahold of yourself, Quinn. You are looking for a different bride, when you told her she was your lady. She may be yours now . . . but searching elsewhere for fulfillment of your marital needs is not something she would take lightly. The shock when you tell her will devastate her.

Maybe she already knew. That really was the only reason he could think of for her futtering another man when he fulfilled her so thoroughly in the act.

Alistair's mumbles grew closer to the door. Quinton strode back down the hall and ducked into the next bedroom.

He shut the door slightly and peered out the crack in the back of the door. Alistair opened the door to Sophia's room and walked down the hall to the main room. The door to the outside opened and closed and then there was silence. Quinton opened the door and stepped back out into the hallway. He turned toward Sophia's room and his heart lodged in his throat.

Sophia lay on her bed. Her thighs open and her stone prick out in her hand.

Alistair had not fulfilled her.

Relief flooded Quinton and his chest loosened. She placed the stone between her legs and slowly moved the cock back and forth. She closed her eyes and her hips arched with each slip of the false phallus. Quinn's cock flooded with blood filling him to that same rigidity as the fake phallus in her hand.

The need to be inside her, claiming her, after Alistair had so recklessly left her aching for more swallowed him whole.

He undid the buttons to his trousers and then carefully watching her movements slid first one boot off then the other. He slid his trousers down. And stepped out of them, leaving them in there exact location on the floor in the hall. She continued to futter herself, her hips arching and flexing to each stroke.

He strode into her room. She made no movement to indicate awareness of his presence. He walked up to her and stood gazing down on the beauty that was she. Her ivory skin and doll round face. Her amazing green eyes, which now were hidden by her lids. The expression on her face was one of close rapture.

She slid the phallus down into her opening. Her pussy lips pouted open and the white cream of Alistair's seed coated the outside of her nether lips. Possession flooded Quinton. He would be damned if he couldn't prove to her that she was his no matter whom she tried to replace him with. "You appear in need of a good release, Sophia. I would be more than happy to oblige."

Sophia jumped and opened her eyes. Quinton stood over her. His trousers and boot removed and his beautiful thick cock standing straight from his body. Her heart lodged in her throat. Had Alistair and he passed on the path back to Elm Place, or had he been here in this house listening to them futter?

My God! What had she done? Quinton would be livid if he knew. Yet, she wanted to have Quinton give her release. She wanted for him to slide his thick cock inside her and make her gush like he always did. She wanted that delicious wet spot on the sheets and the scent of their futter lingering in the house for days. No, Sophia, that is wrong. The desire to futter another man when she just had futtered another was scandalous and wicked.

Her heart sped, and a thrilling chill raced her skin.

Stop, Sophia. You need to tell Quinton what happened even if he already knows. She was indeed a wanton. A wanton, who wanted to have her release with this man one last time before sending him away for good. An intense gushing release unlike the one Alistair provided her with. One Quinton knew how to do well.

Alistair thrilled her in an entirely different way, but the futter between them was not as practiced, there was a strain to the act, all caused by Quinton and his lies. Futter with Quinton had always surpassed her expectations. She wanted to feel that rush one more time no matter how scandalous this act would be.

She slid the cold hard stone prick to the side. Quinton's fingers wrapped about the object and he pulled it from her hands.

"Spread your legs wide, Sophia." The cold stone phallus pressed to her bottom hole and she squirmed. Slowly bit by bit the tip pressed into her bottom. The tight muscled pucker stretched about the inanimate object sending delicious arousing pain pulsing though her. Heat washed thought her sex and bottom. Her nipples bloomed into hard heavy mounds.

Quinton kneeled up between her legs and continued to press the stone cock into her. He reached his hand around her thigh and grasped the base. Leaning down, the tip of his hot cock spread the lips of her pussy wide. She trembled. Her entire body coming alive with delight and knowledge of this primal act they shared. Release and bliss would soon be hers if only for a simple moment.

He pressed slowly into her wet and slick pussy. She had never been so scandalous in all of her life. The stone cock in her behind and his thick warm prick filled her beyond full. She cried out, on the verge of unconsciousness.

"Quinton, oh Quinton, futter me!"

"Yes, Sophia. I will bring you the release you so crave." He pulled both the stone prick out and his cock, then pushed back the driving forces that split her in two. The pressure in her womb too much to bear, she cried out and pushed against the intense tension. A gush of fluid trickled down her bottom.

"Indeed, Sophia. Indeed. He did not take care of you. Only I can make you feel like this."

Oh, he did make her feel so good . . . Oh God.

Quinton knew. Her body contracted, and another gush of her spend washed them both in hot wet warmth.

Her heart sped and her eyelids fluttered open.

His cock slid in and out, in and out. The slick walls of her cunt gaped open to him, and grasping his hard cock. She screamed. Her fingers found his thighs and clenched as a wave of bliss washed up and over her once more. Every muscle in her body contracted.

How Quinton did this to her she never would understand. Their bodies simply fit together. She had wondered if their futter was more than most. She had only one other partner, her husband, and futter between them had been nothing like this.

Alistair had proved to her though he had experience and knowledge like none she had ever met, his body did not fit with hers like Quinton's did.

Simply the feel of Quinton's cock in the opening of her pussy and she came to life. The stretching pressure when the head pushed against the so-sensitive spot inside her made her gush.

Quinton groaned and his stroke increased. He would spend in her and rightly quick. She spread her legs as wide as she could and wrapped her hands about her thighs. He pressed into her and her pussy tingled and throbbed. The pressure built so great.

He pressed forward and stopped. "Oh!" His prick twitched within her swollen walls. "You are a naughty girl, Sophia. Yet we fit together like nonesuch. I cannot stay away from you. You are mine, Sophia. Do you understand me?"

She trembled. In this act indeed she would never find another man who could satisfy her as Quinton, but in other ways . . . Alistair was more of a companion than Quinton ever had been and Alistair would show her new and exciting ways to futter. No doubt. With experience he may be able to satisfy her greatly. She trembled.

Quinton pulled out and pushed in again the head of his cock rubbed on the special place within her. She shattered. Deep in her gut she pushed down against him, a flood of liquid spending from her body, washed her pussy and his cock in raining heat.

"Oh, yes dear. That is it; spend on me. Make me proud."

She spread her legs wider to give him easier access and moaned. He pulled out until the head of his thick prick teased the opening of her cunt, then pressed back in and continued. His face a slate washed in passion; eyes closed, mouth in a slight smile, his breath came in short moans. He cock speared her flesh with all his effort.

"Oh, Sophia." He pushed in again. His cock twitched within her and the warm gush of seed flooded her depths. Each pulse he pushed forward, and as he pulled back the seed ran from her down the crack of her bottom and onto the bedclothes below. She soaked in his seed, in hers, and in Alistair's. Never had she experienced such an amount of fluid.

He panted, leaned up, and slowly pulled the hard phallus from her bottom. The false cock exited her tight pucker. She shook with a force that pushed Quinton's softening cock from her cunny.

She stared up at Quinton. The man she had pinned her hopes and dreams on, the man who deceived her. Her heart pinched and tears welled in her eyes. She closed them.

He does not deserve your tears, Sophia. You have always wished for more from him and he always had excuses. Today you learned why.

He does not desire you for more than this act. He is a rogue. He is a man with his own priorities, of which you are not one.

Anger spread through her belly as she stared up at him, tears running down her face in a silent torrent that she simply could not stop.

"Sophia. Why did you futter Alistair?" Quinton's words came out harsh and scolding.

"I-I am not sure you have a right to ask me that, Quinton. I heard the other girls saying you were going to wed one of them. I was jealous, angry, and hurt." She inhaled deeply and closed her eyes. A chill raced her skin. "Yesterday before your guests arrived, you said I was to be your lady. You deceived me, Quinton." She opened her eyes.

Quinton stared at her, then closed his eyes. "I-I am sorry, Sophia. There is such a large part of me that wants just what I told you. That you could be my lady."

"You lie! Your actions prove otherwise. You had your last futter. Now go leave me to my bad decisions and my dog."

"Sophia. I still don't understand. I want you. I don't care if you fucked Alistair so long as you promise never to do so again."

"Alistair was there and confident and made no claims that he was anything but bent on finding his own release. I found comfort in that kind of integrity after hearing about your lies. How silly it was of me to believe you cared about anything other than futter with me. Leave me now!"

Quinton pushed up from the bed and sat back on his heels. He stared down at her. She could not stand to see the disappointment in his eyes. Sharing the act with Alistair had been wrong. So very, very wrong. Even if Quinton didn't care, she had no idea what she had done until this exact moment.

No one would ever respect her if this became gossip. She would be labeled the town jezebel or worse. If her husband's brother found out, he could very well remove her from this house. Her life would fall apart around her.

She turned her head to the side as tears continued to roll down her cheek. Her gut twisted and her heart ached. What had she done?

Quinton stood from the bed. "Please consider what I have said, Sophia. I want you. I want to continue to pleasure you just as I did now."

His footfalls indicated he left the room and she wrapped her arms about herself and cried. Her body rocked back and forth on the mattress as soul-deep sobs pressed from her breath. *Please, let no one find out what I have done.*

Chapter 7

Alistair jostled a very wet and shivering pup in his hands as he turned the corner in the hedge leading from Elm Place to Sophia's little cottage. Bo's tongue slid out and licked his chin.

He smiled. "What a sweet, stupid mutt you are. Now stop using that devilish tongue of yours to get on my good side. You have caused my life to scramble." He cringed as the wetness of Bo's fur soaked through his waistcoat and shirt. "Stupid mutt."

The door to Sophia's cottage opened, and Quinton strode out shaking his head. "Stupid. Idiotic fool."

Alistair stopped at the gate as Lord Quinton strode toward him. Alistair's fingers fisted in Bo's fur. The scoundrel would regret having come to Sophia's. His heart beat rapidly in his chest.

He reached across the wall with Bo in hand and set the mutt on the other side. His hands fisted. If Lord Quinton said one thing to him, he would uncork him right here and now. The gumption he possessed coming to see her after his deceptions!

His heart pounded in this throat. Maybe it didn't matter if

he said something or not. Lord Quinton deserved a good pummeling.

Bo bounded over to Lord Quinton. "There you are little pup. Your mama certainly could use a little kiss from you."

Alistair cleared his throat. "I imagine after seeing you she can use all the comfort she can get."

Lord Quinton's head jerked back. Their gazes locked.

What indeed would Lord Quinton do? The lying fop. He didn't have the sack to uncork him. Where as Alistair had marbles in spades.

"You have more spine than I thought to come here. What I don't understand is why you deceived her when you employed Anne. Anne will find you what you are seeking. She never fails."

"Anne is a dove of a different sort, Alistair. As you are well aware. She sells her services to anyone who employs her talents. She is not more than an overpriced wench."

"You . . . you . . . unclean son of damnation." Alistair dove over the wall and straight into him. They landed in a hard lump on the cold earth. Limbs tangled and hands slapped.

Alistair never lost his position on top of Lord Quinton. He sat with his legs astride him and pushed himself up. He stared down at Lord Quinton, pinned beneath him on the ground. "You never deserved such a woman. Or the services of such a talent as Anne. She is the best at what she does and she does not sell herself out. Not even to me. For what you have done to Sophia, you deserve your sack to be cut. If I only had the sheeas I would do the deed right now myself."

"Really. Anne certainly has you tied about her tiny nip."

"She does have me. I am her confidant and protector. And I

have what you crave. I desire Sophia for more than a mistress. . . .
She needs me."

"You are worse than a dog, Alistair, and she very well knows it.
She would never have had you in her bed if I had not lied."

"But you did, and I have had her. I will not let go."

"No one has me." The calm voice of Sophia turned both their
heads in the direction of the cottage door. "I don't want either of
you." She stood like an avenging angel with all the fury of hell
in her eyes, her long cloak wrapped about her as she shook with
anger. "I made a very big mistake in what I did. The circumstances were nothing like I have ever experienced, but it does not
make up for my poor behavior. I won't be speaking to either one
of you again." She turned calmly and closed the door to the cottage.

Crack. Lord Quinton's fist hit Alistair squarely in the nose.
Blood sprayed across Lord Quinton's face. Alistair wavered on
top of him and his life went black.

On the 15th Day of January
In the year of our Lord, 1823

Lord Quinton,

*I am afraid after seeing your behavior on our visit to Elm
Place in the month of November, I regret to inform you that
I will not be providing one of my girls to you. I also refrain
from any further contact and will be sending your monies back
minus the cost for my expenses thus far.*

Miss Anne Cathcort.

Alistair stared at Anne. Why was she doing this?

"What do you think, Alistair? Is this letter sufficient?" Anne sat at her desk and rolled her pen between her fingers. "Or do I need to mention your scuffle with him over the dove no one achieved?"

The hairs on the back of Alistair's neck rose. Sophia was no one's dove. She had all the class of a lady. Alistair stared at Anne as she tilted her head to the side and considered her missive.

He was well aware of Anne's game. "If you feel you need to send something, it will suffice, Anne. It has been several months since that hellish trip to the country. He no doubt is not expecting any word from you or your girls."

"Do you suppose he is back with the lovely? Or do you think she truly kept her word?"

Alistair had sent several letters to Sophia after returning to London that very same night, and the only word he got back from her was that she was no longer living in her cottage and now resided in London with her aunt. He stared unseeing at his fingers as he absently cleaned invisible dirt from beneath his polished nails.

"You have genuine feelings for her, don't you?"

Alistair's gaze snapped to Anne. Her eyes were filled with compassion. She knew Alistair better than anyone.

"Quite so. I have since I jumped out the carriage and first saw her . . . her and that stupid mutt of hers."

"Stupid mutt or not, Alistair, I have never seen you quite so over a woman." She tilted her head to the side considering him. "I think this is something that you should not shy away from. If you love her—or whatever you wish to call how you are feeling—you should tell her."

Never in all of his life had a woman entered his heart. Not even his mother. "You believe I love her? Is this what love does to a person, Anne? Makes them sad and fidgety and daft? I do believe the country air simply made me ill." He rubbed his temple. "I believe I should see a doctor because certainly I am touched in the head!"

"Love is a madness of sorts, Alistair. I know we never really talk much about my past. But love no matter if it is requited is powerful. It affects us in so many unforeseen ways. The emotion ruined me and forced me to wish to help others find their way. For me watching you . . . the biggest indicator is your lack of interest in other women since we returned."

Love! His heart did jump in his chest when he thought of Sophia. Yet at the same time it pinched in pain.

"Saint Valentine's Day will be upon us in a fortnight. You should do something for her . . . something to show her how you really feel. If you like, I shall help you. I am doing so for another of my clients."

Show her how I feel.

He shook his head. He didn't truly know what was happening to him. Anne was correct. He had not futtered a soul since that day with Sophia.

Anne had used her mouth on him once and he had asked her to stop. He cringed. Stop! That was not the only part of him going soft. If word got round the club, he would be looking for another table to drink port and play hazard at.

Something indeed needed to happen, or else he was going to go mad. He needed to futter just like he needed wine.

"Well, Alistair?"

Alistair stared at Anne. She had never given him bad advice yet. "I will follow your advice, but I shall do this on my own."

* * *

Sophia sat with yet another unopened letter from Quinton folded in her hand. She stared at folded yellow parchment with the red seal. She should open the missive. This was the fourth she'd received since arriving at her aunt's for the New Year, and each she had tossed into the fire without reading.

She had not told him where she had gone, yet he had somehow found her. There was a part of her that wished to open the letter . . . a part that longed for the passion they had shared to have been more than simply futter partners. Her mind knew better. If the letters said anything at all, it would be simply to restate what he had previously expressed: *"I want you. I want to continue to pleasure you this way."*

She sighed.

Then there was Alistair. . . One week after he'd left Elm Place she received a letter from a Mr. Alistair Taylor. She opened it, only to read two sentences.

"You deserve more than what he or I can offer you, Sophia. Your decision was sound."

In a weak moment she had sent a short missive to him in reply, explaining her soon-to-be change of residence. A small part of her had hoped she would run into him here in the capital. She realized sending such a note when Alistair was who he was only gave her false hope.

"Ma'am, there is a gentleman here to see Miss Sophia." The butler held out the silver platter with the calling card perched on top.

Sophia held her breath, not wanting it to be her past coming to haunt her here once again. "Who is it Aunt?"

"It is Mr. Taylor." Her aunt glanced over at her. "He is the third son to the marquis of Lanktor. Do you know him, dear?"

All the hairs on her arm rose, and her brow drew tight. She had not expected this . . . "Possibly."

"Show him in then, Burton."

Sophia sat perched on the edge of her seat. All the memories came flooding back of his determination to bed her, him pushing her up against the bathhouse wall, him telling her what to do in bed as he found his release had haunted her dreams since that day.

She had not futtered since. She had simply wished to forget she craved such shameful things. To forget the scandalous, wanton behavior she had exhibited.

The door opened and Burton stepped into the room. "Mr. Alistair Taylor."

Alistair walked in, his fair hair slicked back from his face, excitement dancing in his eyes. Her breath caught. He certainly was handsome. . . . He bowed to her aunt, and the muscles of his cheek twitched. He turned to her and bowed. "Good morning. I hope you are well."

"We certainly are, Mr. Taylor. To what do we owe this kind intrusion on our staid day?"

Sophia laughed. "Aunt, am I that boring?"

Her aunt winked at her. "No, dear, but I am."

Alistair coughed to hide his laugh. "I have come in the spirit of Saint Valentine's, ma'am."

"Saint Valentine? What do you mean, Mr. Taylor?" Her aunt's eyes lit, and she glanced from Sophia to Alistair and back again.

"Please do call me, Alistair, ma'am."

"Very well."

"Surely you know of Saint Valentine's Day?"

"Only its reference by Chaucer as being a day for lovers, Alistair."

"Indeed." Alistair winked at her aunt, then strode over to Sophia. The musky scent of the woods made the flesh of her cunny tingle. Damn him. What was he up to?

"Will you allow me?" he held out a folded parchment to Sophia. Sophia stared at the missive. "Alistair, what is this about?"

"Please take it, Miss Sophia, and you shall see."

Sophia's fingers gripped the thick paper. She placed the parchment in her lap over the letter from Quinton. Oh, two letters . . . one from a man who lied to her and the other from a man who stood an arm's reach away. She would only open one.

"Open it, Sophia."

She cracked the crimson wax seal with the marquis of Lanktor crest. Her fingers shook as she unfolded the paper. Within the folded sheet resided a finely cut paper heart. She picked it up, and on one side of the heart she read . . .

Miss Sophia,

You have been in my thoughts since the day I pulled you from the road. You and your stupid mutt. You have never left my thoughts. . . . Your strife endeared you to me. And your soul's expression slid you deep into my heart. You are the only woman who has ever resided there. I wish you to be mine, Sophia. Mine in heart, body, and soul. I wish us to share all things . . . will you be my lover, my dear friend, and wife?

Alistair

Sophia stared at the heart and tears trickled down her face. She had in no way expected this from Alistair. He was a man who made no excuses for who he was. But could she trust him? He had said he had his girls.

"What about your girls, Alistair?"

"My girls have all been very disappointed since I returned from my trip to the country . . . for I have not been able to concentrate on one of them. I will always be honest with you, Sophia. I will be yours and yours alone. I simply never imagined I would feel this way for a woman. So I never considered this outcome in my life's plans."

He knelt before her and grasped her hand in his. His hands shook. He was nervous. The warmth and the sincerity in that alone cut through her fears. She smiled. Alistair was so very much the kind of man she desired; both sexually and intellectually. "I believe you, Alistair. As completely unexpected as this event is, I do not believe you would lie to me as Quinton did."

"Sophia. No one can predict what our life will be. All I know is I need to be with you. Feeling that way, I know I will do all I can to protect you and cherish what we shall build and share. So please take pity on me, Sophia. Wed me, my love."

Sophia glanced to her aunt, who sat with a huge smile on her face and tears running down her cheeks. She nodded her head at Sophia.

Sophia looked at the man before her. A man she truly did not know all that well. He knew all she was capable of and what her fears were and still wanted her, and she wanted him. She closed her eyes, a smile of joy turned up her lips

"All right, Alistair. Yes, I will wed you."

Alistair released her hand and scooped her up into the air. He spun her around and kissed her harsh on the lips. "*Ah, Sophia you shall never regret you said yes.*"

LACY DANES made a New Year's resolution to write a hot historical romance. A year and a half later, she achieved her goal. She lives in Seattle, Washington, where besides writing she enjoys horseback riding, gardening, and savoring a good glass of wine while watching the world go by. Visit Lacy at her website: *www.LacyDanes.com*.

Lacy Danes

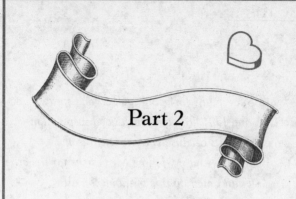

Part 2

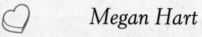

Get There

by

Megan Hart

To Superman, for being such a good sport.
To JRA and JTP, for being such good inspiration—
yes, it IS because you are so awesome.
To the Bootsquad and my fellow Mavericks for the crit:
I can't ever do this without you all.

I could get there by bus. Watch the country go by in ribbons of brown and green as we pass by towns the names of which don't matter, because they're not yours. The clatter-clack will lull me to sleep and I'll dream of you. The mountains will become your breasts, the hills the slope of your hips, and the valleys . . . the valleys will turn into that sweet valley between your thighs, and I'll wake with an erection hard enough to bore tunnels. And then, when I get there, all I'll have to do is lay you down and fill you up with all of me.

Because you've already filled me with all of you.

Edie Darowish folded the note card closed and pressed it to her smile for a second before putting it aside in the "keep" pile. That one was twice the size of the "toss" pile, but she couldn't bear to throw away even one of Ty's letters. It didn't matter that in just a couple weeks they'd be together again, this time for good. Having Ty in person would be infinitely better than having only his words, but these letters were important, too.

He always said his strength was with drawing and not prose. He sent her lots of sketches, sometimes cute and funny cartoons and other times breath-stealing sensual line drawings, so the rarity of his written communication was doubly precious. Not to mention sexy as all get-out. Ty might claim he was better with pictures than with words, but reading over what he'd written to her just a few months ago, Edie disagreed.

The file box in front of her was still half full as she sifted through the memorabilia she'd collected over the past two years. She pulled out a handful of receipts from restaurants and hotels, places they'd gone on vacation. Each was a memory and a story all its own, but she tossed most of them in the trash. There really was only so much she could take with her all the way from California to Pennsylvania, and living with Ty would mean she didn't have to keep every scrap any more.

Edie worked until her joints ached from sitting cross-legged on the floor, but when she was done, she ended up with a bulging manila envelope of letters and drawings and a garbage bag stuffed with the rest. Not bad for a few hours' work. She got up, stretching, and looked around at the stacks of file boxes she'd seal with tape and ship to the new house.

She'd already sold her furniture except for the Art Deco Waterfall armoire, dresser, and vanity that had been hers since childhood and had already been shipped off along with most everything else. The rest hadn't been worth much. She'd lived in this apartment for seven years and hadn't ever bothered to do more than make it a place to sleep and eat and work. She had a truck from the local thrift store scheduled the day before her flight to come for all that was left and an appointment at the car dealership to sell her car, too. She'd buy a new one in Pennsylvania. Ty planned on driving a moving truck, his car towed behind, from Maine. They were going to get there on Valentine's Day.

Edie's stretch turned into a little dance as she thought of it. They'd been officially a couple for two years but had never managed to spend a Valentine's Day together. Christmas and New Year's, yes, and once a memorable Fourth of July, but February was a bad time for both of them to get away. Not this year, though. This year she'd be with him, and no matter what they did, it was going to be romantic because they were together.

She'd stripped her apartment down to bare walls and floors, but she hadn't yet dismantled her office. She'd gotten rid of the desk and boxed up most of her paperwork and binders, but she wouldn't be able to completely pack up her laptop and her current projects until she was ready to move. A glance at the clock told her it was time to talk to Ty.

A scan of her instant messenger friends' list showed her he hadn't yet logged on, so she checked through her e-mail and visited the *Runner* message board just to keep herself updated. As usual, the new threads had accumulated during the day while old ones got bumped to the next page. Edie didn't read all the messages, most of which were squeals about the show's longtime star, Justin Ross, and this season's new costar, Tristan Winsam. The boys got most of the attention at the board with only a handful of threads dedicated to the show's other aspects, but one header caught her eye.

Runner Wedding, did you hear?

Her cursor hovered over the thread, but Edie hesitated before clicking. She liked checking in to keep up with what the fans were saying, but she ignored most of the board's messages because reading about how stupid her plotlines were when they didn't involve Justin taking off his shirt, or how much fans hated the episodes she'd written solo wasn't exactly great inspiration. Finding the threads that praised her and her work on the show's long-running mythology, or the fact she was the one to introduce the love story into the plot, were a thrill, but she'd been burned a few too many times to risk wading through the less-than-complimentary reviews just to find a nugget of squee.

Curiosity won out, and she clicked.

And laughed.

And blushed.

The facts weren't exactly spot-on, but that was all right. She didn't really want the *Runner* fan community knowing exactly where she and Ty were moving or when they were getting married. She might not be as popular as Ross and Winsam, but she'd learned her lesson about the lengths fans would go in order to get close to their idols. Some of them wouldn't hesitate at trying to get close to one of the show's writers in hopes of getting an introduction to the stars.

The comments following the initial post were full of congratulations and speculation, but one thing stood out. All the posters knew that Edie, one of *Runner*'s senior writers, and Tynan Murphy, illustrator of the first three *Runner* graphic tie-in novels, had met on this very message board during a promotional discussion about the novels before they were released. Which of course led to the inevitable rumors that Ross and Winsam actually read and posted on the message board and had even asked one of the fans out on a date last year.

When she got that far into the conversation, Edie, who knew for a fact neither of the boys bothered reading the boards, logged off. She'd never thought she and Ty would make gossip headlines, but it just proved again how rabid the show's fan base was, that they'd grab up and tear apart any scrap of *Runner*-related information. Not that she really minded, in the long run. The show had been her bread and butter for four years, after all. And it had introduced her to Ty.

See the latest? Ty's message window popped up with a familiar *doink* sound. *We're big news on the board.*

I saw. I didn't know we were getting married on set, or that Justin and Tristan were going to be your dual best men. When did you plan to tell me that?

Ty's smiley face emoticon could never replace the sound of his laugh, but seeing it, Edie smiled, too. Typing couldn't replace the sound of his voice, either, but they'd agreed daily instant message sessions were better than expensive long-distance phone bills or staticky cell-phone calls. Maintaining a long-distance relationship would have been impossible without the Internet, but then without the Net, they'd never even have met.

Can't wait to wake up with you in the same bed, she typed.

Can't wait to wake up with you in the same time zone.

With Edie in California and Ty in Maine, their conversations were never long enough. The time differences had always played havoc even though they were often able to set their own schedules. Even when they were able to get together physically, adjusting to the time changes had been interesting.

Her fingers flew over the keyboard. *No more falling asleep on me when I want to get frisky?*

No. I promise.

Just a couple weeks.

Seems like forever.

And it did, though not compared to how long it had been during the six months between the night Ty had slipped the diamond-and-emerald engagement ring on her finger and the day she'd finally learned the network had decided this would be *Runner's* final season, or the month following that before she'd found a new job. Writing for a popular spoof-news show based in New York wasn't going to be anything like writing for a popular sci-fi program, but the location had sold her. Not quite midway between them, but close to her family in Pennsylvania. When a prominent Philadelphia newspaper had expressed interest in running Ty's work on a semi-exclusive basis, the move had been a no-brainer. They'd bought a house in suburban Philly. It was going to happen, at last!

Everything work out okay with the realtor?

Edie could type almost as fast as she could talk. *Yep. She got my stuff delivered and will have the keys waiting for us at the office. All utilities will be on, too.*

You mean we won't have to make our own heat?

Perv.

You like me that way.

I love you that way, Edie typed.

They chatted a bit longer about their work, about the new house, and the wedding plans. All the sorts of conversation any engaged couple had, the only difference the distance still between them. Too soon it was time for them to log off.

But Edie had one more question for him before she did.

So, she typed, *how are we going to get there?*

We could get there by train.

And then he was off line.

Edie tapped her finger thoughtfully on her computer mouse as she read over Ty's last message. Train? She tried to think if she'd ever been on a train aside from the one at Disneyland.

"You bugger," she murmured.

The blue glare of her computer bathed her desk. She stared so long her screensaver, a slideshow of pictures pulled from her photo library, kicked on. She watched Ty's familiar grin fade into a stock shot she'd used while writing the time-travel episode. The couple in the picture were now somebody's grandparents, but back then they'd been young and in love, their attraction palpable even through the layers of time and digitization. He wore a World War II–era navy uniform and she perched on his lap, one hand on her head to keep her hat in place.

"Train, huh? All right, buddy. Here's your train." With a grin of her own, Edie bent over her keyboard and began to type.

"All aboard!" The conductor walked up and down the platform, shouting the words over and over.

Edie stood as the gust of wind buffeted her skirt around her legs and threatened to take her hat, that cunning little number with the half veil. She'd bought it because she knew Ty would like it. But now she was here, and where was Ty?

"All aboard! Miss, the train is boarding. If you mean to be on it . . ." The conductor gave her a thorough looking-over, the sort a gal couldn't miss.

Edie looked up and down the platform once more. She saw a couple soldiers being kissed and wept over and a single sailor in white slinging a duffel bag over his shoulder. But not the right sailor. Not Ty.

"The train—"

"Yes, yes, thank you," she said, and climbed aboard with her ticket clutched in one gloved hand.

She'd booked a sleeper car. The tiny compartment had a bed that folded up along the wall, two small seats facing each other with a minuscule table between them and a few hooks where she could hang her coat. The floor vibrated as the train pulled out of the station. Through the window, Edie watched the gray gravel turn to green grass as the train picked up speed.

Tears threatened, and she lifted her chin, determined not to cry.

Her mascara would run. But, oh, what did it matter if Ty wasn't there to see it?

And then, he was.

The door bumped open and she turned as Ty stumbled in, hat in one hand and hair askew from the same wind that had tugged her skirt. Panting, he pushed the door shut behind him and took her in his arms. Then his mouth was on hers and her arms were around his neck.

"Thought I wasn't going to make it, huh, doll?" Ty drew back from her mouth just long enough to grin before diving back in.

Edie pushed him away, just a bit. "That was awfully mean, Ty. I was worried!"

"Aw, honey. You know I'd never miss this. Not our honeymoon."

He looked so handsome in his uniform there was no way she could be angry with him. Not when his mouth was on hers again and his hands had begun roving so deliciously on her back. Edie ran her fingers through his hair, which was much too short for her tastes, then clung to him with her face buried against the crisp white front of his shirt.

"Hey, hey, doll, don't cry." Ty lifted her chin with a fingertip. "Aw hell, honey. You were really frightened, weren't you?"

"All I could think of was what if you missed the train? Then you'd go off to sea and I'd have to wait—"

"I'm sorry." Ty stopped her with another kiss. "I had to stop and pick up something special for my best girl. Don't be sore, honey."

His fingers drifted up her sides until his thumbs rested just below her breasts, and suddenly all that mattered wasn't where he'd been, but that he was here, now. Ty's eyes flashed, and the mouth she so loved parted, giving her a glimpse of his tongue between those straight, white teeth.

Suddenly, all Edie could think about was what Ty could do with that tongue.

"Let's see what we can do about this bed, what do you say?" Edie glanced over her shoulder at the latch keeping the bed held tight against the wall.

Ty grinned. "Now you're talking."

He studied the mechanism only a moment before figuring out how to undo the latch and lower the bunk. It creaked and wouldn't quite go into place until he shoved it, and Edie eyed it dubiously. The wrinkled coverlet looked clean, at least.

"It's not very big," she said.

Ty, sitting, held out his arms. "We'll have plenty of room."

She let him take her onto his lap. He kissed her, his mouth gentler now. His lips teased hers open, and when his tongue swept inside, Edie sighed. She wanted to capture every moment so she'd have something to hold onto in the long, lonely months ahead.

"Touch me, Ty."

He did, his hands running over the soft fabric of her new skirt and blouse, purchased especially for this trip. His fingers cupped her knee, then moved higher over the smooth nylon stockings—a gift from him that had made her the envy of all her girlfriends, who had to suffer with old stockings or none at all. When his hand reached the band of her garter, he stopped to trace the line where flesh and fabric met.

Edie shivered. Her thighs parted. "Put your hands on me, Ty. Please."

Ty groaned and slid his hand higher until his palm cupped her heat. He toyed with the lacy edge of her panties and then, oh yes, he slid a finger inside to touch her. He groaned into her mouth as his tongue stabbed her. His finger moved along her folds, slick with desire, and found the secret places that made her feel so good.

"Baby, I want you naked." Ty shifted her on his lap so she could feel his hot, hard length pressing her hip. "Get naked for me."

Edie stood. The train clack-clattered and she shifted with the motion. Her hips swayed as she unpinned her hat and tossed it to the chair and as she unbuttoned her blouse. She shrugged out of it and tossed that at Ty, who grabbed it with a laugh. His eyes shone, reflecting her. She'd never felt so beautiful.

Her hand went to the button and zipper of her skirt, and she eased out of it until she stood in her brassiere and panties and garter belt, wearing the stockings he'd bought her and her nicest shoes. Ty's tongue slid along his lips and again, Edie shivered. Her nipples peaked and she cocked a hip forward as she favored him with a saucy grin worthy of Lana Turner.

"Well, sailor. Like what you see?"

"I love what I see."

Edie let the train move her almost in a burlesque dance, a dirty little bump and grind. Her hips moved side to side. Ty's grin encouraged her and she added a little shimmy-shake.

"You're so beautiful," he told her.

She had fallen in love with his smile, but she'd stayed in love with him because of his words.

"Come here," Ty said.

She took the hand he offered. Ty pulled her closer until she stood between his legs. He pressed his face to the narrow stripe of her belly between her bra and panties. His breath, hot, gusted over her skin. She squirmed at the wet flicker of his tongue.

Ty's hands cupped her rear as he kissed each hip. He tipped his head to look up at her and she ran her fingers again through his hair. He smiled before ducking back to nuzzle her.

With careful hands, Ty unclipped her garters and rolled her stockings down, one at a time, lifting her feet to take off her shoes, too. Then he unhooked the garter belt and laid it aside. When he put his hand between her legs, the thumb pressing her in the front and his *fingers stroking the softness of her panties, Edie had to put a hand on his shoulder to keep herself from falling.*

"So pretty," Ty murmured as he eased her panties over her hips and helped her step out of them, too.

Next came her bra, tossed without fanfare, and Edie stood naked in front of her husband.

"You're still dressed," she said with a shake of her head. "That won't do at all."

Together they undressed him. His clothes mingled with hers in the pile the way their bodies would soon join in the flesh. Naked, Edie stood between Ty's thighs and looked down at his body, so lean and finely muscled.

His penis begged for her hand. When she curled her fingers around his length, not yet as familiar as his mouth, he let out a low, whispering sigh that sent thrills all through her. *This is what it means to be a woman,* she thought. *This is what it means to be a wife.*

With his hands on the backs of her thighs and her hand on his shoulder, she stroked him and watched, fascinated at the way his skin flushed. She twisted her hand around the head of his erection, and he jerked under her touch.

This is power, she thought. *This is love.*

"I need to taste you," Ty said. She bent to give him what he wanted, but though he kissed her mouth, Ty shook his head. "Not that way."

When he laid her back on the narrow bed and parted her thighs, Edie had to close her eyes. When his mouth slid over her body, teasing her nipples and wetting her belly, she arched into the touch of hands and mouth. And finally, when Ty kissed her **there** she let out a long, slow cry of desire.

His tongue moved against her flesh, circling in a way that had her lifting her hips within seconds. Edie wanted to cry out at the sound of his breathing, so loud even above the noise of the train on the tra ks.

She did, unable to keep her ecstasy silent when Ty slid a finger inside her. Then another, stretching her deliciously. Her hips rocked upward to his feasting mouth. Tension spiraled in her belly, her thighs twitching as Ty's tongue and fingers moved in tandem with the train's rocking.

Edie cupped her breasts, found her nipples and rolled them. Ty's hair, too short for fashion, was barely long enough to tickle her thighs and belly as he licked and suckled. He added a third finger and the first spasm of pleasure shook her.

She cried out his name and he eased off. He moved up her body, replacing his tongue with a fingertip but keeping up the same maddening pressure. He reached between them to guide himself inside her welcoming body. He paused, his penis just inside her, and took long, slow breaths.

Edie shifted and hooked her ankles over the backs of his calves. "Make love to me, Ty."

"Give me a second, honey." Ty kissed her, hard, his mouth tangy from her arousal. "I don't want to go off like a cannon first thing."

She laughed softly, surprised she could when desire had stolen nearly every other reaction. She held his rear tightly and urged him forward. He opened her with his body, each delicious and indescribable inch. She gasped into his kiss and he took her breath, then gave it back with his moan.

"I can't wait," she said against his mouth.

Ty pushed forward and seated himself inside her. He bent his face into the curve of her shoulder. He trembled, and Edie stroked her hands down his back, holding him tight to her.

The spirals of tension had faded a bit, but when he moved, they flared again. Bright sparkles of pleasure radiated throughout her entire body as Ty thrust. Pleasure mounted. He moved faster at her urging.

The train rocked them together. Ty moved in her slickness and her heat, and he filled her completely. Edie brought his mouth to hers, and kissing him, she burst the first time.

As her body bore down on his, Ty said her name over and over. His hips pushed forward. He slid his arms beneath her to hold her closer as the bed rattled beneath them, and Edie no longer could tell or cared if it were the train or their bodies making it shake.

Ty slid a hand between them, his fingers pressing each time he thrust, and pleasure, unexpected, built again. Her fingers clutched his back, scratching, but Ty only moaned and moved faster. Harder.

He shuddered and thrust once more, collapsing on top of her just as Edie exploded into another climax.

The train rocked them both to sleep after that, and when Edie awoke, the first bright pink strands of morning streaked by the window outside. Ty sat in one of the chairs by the window. He'd been watching her.

"Another hour or so," he said quietly, "until we get there."

Edie sat without caring the blankets had bunched around her waist. The bed hadn't been too small, after all. She reached for him and he came to her. They made love slowly and in silence, mindful they had only so much time.

Later, as the train slowed and prepared to stop, he pulled the box from his pocket. "This is why I was late. It's not much, I know, but—"

Edie kissed him into silence, and she put the ring on her finger. It was more than she'd expected. "It's beautiful."

"I wanted you to have one for the wedding, but—"

"It's enough I have it now." She didn't ask him how he'd afforded it. She didn't tell him a diamond chip on a band of gold wouldn't

replace him beside her. She just kissed him again and again until the
train pulled into the station and it was time for them to go.

"How about this one? Can I have this one, too?" Ham held up an
early-'80s issue of *Pandaman*.

Ty, hands full of slippery comics trying to slither from his
grasp before he could wrestle them into the packing box, looked
up. "You want that one? Why?"

"Some of your best work," Ham said seriously, flipping the
pages. "Totally underrated. Worth a mint someday. Trying to get
in on the ground floor."

Ty laughed. "Right. Fine, take it. One less thing I have to pack."

Pandaman had been his freshman foray into the world of in-
dependent comics. A critical but not financial success, he'd managed to put out only a dozen issues before the small press that'd
taken a chance on him had folded. It was possible, Ty supposed,
that those issues might be worth more than a buck or two someday, but hell. His parents probably had a few boxes of them in the
garage.

Ham set it in the box of stuff he was liberating as part of his
"fee" for helping Ty pack for the move. He looked around the
living room, mostly bare now. He shook his head.

"What?" Ty stretched, all his joints popping in protest at
kneeling for so long.

"You sure about this, man?" Ham, self-proclaimed bachelor-
for-life, said. "Really sure?"

"Do I have to punch you?"

Ham laughed. "Don't get me wrong. Edie's a great girl, but–"

"She's a woman," Ty interrupted. "Maybe if you went out with
a woman instead of a girl once in a while, you'd understand."

"Touché, mon frère." Ham couldn't keep his look of pretended

hurt for long. "Seriously, I'm happy for you. I just wish like hell she lived in Maine. Or would move here, so you didn't have to move to Bumfuck, Pennsylvania."

Ty used the tape gun on the box he'd filled. "Could be worse. I could be moving all the way to California."

"Now that wouldn't be so bad." Ham grinned. "I could visit in L.A. You could introduce me to all the starlets."

"In your dreams, buddy."

Ham shook his head again. "I'm just saying."

Ty held out the tape gun. "Less talking. More packing."

Later, after a few beers, some ordered-in hot wings and a hockey game on the tube, Ham had finally gone home. Ty, glad for the help and the company, had nonetheless been glad for his friend to go.

The time difference meant Edie would just be getting home from work. Some days, like him, she worked from her apartment, but with finishing the final season and the move, she'd been spending more days in the office.

Already grinning with anticipation, Ty slid into his desk chair and clicked open his e-mail and instant message programs. A small box popped up immediately: "ontherun327 is offline." It was the same screen name she'd used forever on the *Runner* message boards, and it never failed to make him smile.

She'd sent him an e-mail saying she'd been invited out after work for a going-away party with the postproduction crew. She'd *ping* him when she got home, if he could stay awake that long. Ty couldn't blame her for going, but he did miss her. She'd left him something else, too: a story about a train that got him hard and a prompt of his own.

We could get there by magic carpet.

Ty laughed aloud at that and sat back in his chair, spinning it while he thought. She was paying him back, was she? He'd thought a train was easy, and from the story she'd sent him, it didn't look as though Edie'd had any trouble writing it. But then, she never did. It was one of the first things he'd learned about her—give her any scenario and she could come up with something. He, on the other hand, was better with pictures to illustrate his words.

Well. He'd just have to see what he could do.

It's woven of threads in many colors. Blue, black, green. Red. A hint of yellow, like sunshine, that reminds me of the scarf you wore the first time we met. It's a rug, really, not a carpet, but it's big enough for two, and that's all that matters.

I know the words to make it rise and fly, but I haven't used them yet. I'm waiting until we've both stepped on. When we're both ready to go.

When I lay you down on the soft threads, your hair spreads out like part of the design. It weaves into the vines and flowers, those living, growing things. You make them beautiful.

Naked, your skin is softer even than the woven silk. The carpet cradles us, silk on skin. Skin on silk. And then, when I've covered your body with mine, I say the words.

And we go up.

The sky isn't bluer than your eyes, the breeze not sweeter than your breath. The sun shines warm and yellow on my back, but it's not nearly as hot as your kiss.

I kiss you. I touch you. I taste every part of you, there in the sky with a carpet of silk beneath us, carrying us to the place we'll be able to stay together. Always.

* * *

"Always."

Edie echoed the last word of Ty's letter as she clicked the printer icon.

She'd missed him last night, gotten home too late for him to wait, but this morning when she'd checked her e-mail she'd found this. It wasn't as lovely as one of his handwritten notes or drawings, but she wanted to save it forever with the others. The printer whirred into life, spitting out the document. She read over it again at her desk, while outside her office the murmur and mumble of people passing tried rudely to remind her she was at work and wasn't supposed to be reading love letters.

"Knock-knock."

The rap on the doorframe drew her attention and she looked up. "Hey, Billy."

With a grin, Billy lifted a pizza box. "I brought a pizza."

Edie gestured for him to come in. "I'm starving. How'd you know?"

"I know how you get when you're concentrating, sweetie. I figured if someone didn't bring you sustenance, you would starve." Billy set the pizza on the edge of the desk and looked around her stripped-to-the-essentials office. "Wow. You're really going."

Edie looked at the blank walls, where once she'd hung framed promotional posters for the show and awards she'd won. All packed up and shipped off already. "I'm really going."

"Seems like just yesterday you were ordering me to bring you coffee," Billy said in a faux-nostalgic voice, with a flutter of his lashes. Billy had started as her intern and moved up to assistant before nabbing a place on the writing team. He knew her better than anyone else, other than Ty. "Now look. You're abandoning me."

Edie stood and gave Billy a squeeze. She drew in the delicious scent of sauce and cheese. *"Mmmm,* what am I going to do without you?"

"Be taken care of by another handsome man," Billy said matter-of-factly. "Ty will be happy to make sure you're fed and clothed appropriately, I'm sure. Pennsylvania gets cold you know, sweetie. No running out for the mail in your tank top and shorts in February. Hell, no sitting in your living room in a tank top and shorts in February."

Edie looked down at her outfit, a tank top and cutoff jeans. The *Runner* office, unless they had some press function to attend, was always casual. "I guess not."

"Ty will keep you warm." Billy grinned and wiggled his brows. "But damn, sugar, I'm going to miss you."

She squeezed his arm. "Me, too. But you'll visit. And I'll be back out here for meetings once in a while, I'm sure."

Billy grabbed a slice and bit into it with a sigh of pleasure. "You couldn't pay me enough to move all the way across the country."

"I'm not doing it for the money, Billy." Leaning on the edge of her desk, Edie took her own slice and sighed with satisfaction at the first bite.

He used his thumb on the corner of her mouth to clear away an errant glob of sauce. "I know, sweetie. You're doing it for the fabulous mind-blowing sex."

Edie's laugh hurt a little bit at the sight of her dear Billy's face. "That's part of it. But I'm going to miss you, too. You know that."

He grabbed her hand and squeezed. "You'd better. And you'd better write me a Pulitzer."

"Somehow I doubt any of the *Runner* novels are going to hit the *New York Times*'s best-seller list, much less win a Pulitzer, but

I'll see what I can do." She paused, thinking of how different it would be, working on a new show, in a new city. "Anyway, we'll see if they even contract any new books."

"Honey, this is the show that wouldn't die. You know they're going to want movies and books and comics."

"Doesn't mean I'll be the one they ask to write them."

"Worried?"

Edie bent to hook open the dorm-sized fridge where she kept her stash of diet sodas. She handed him one, then cracked the top of hers and drank before answering. "Maybe."

"About what? The work? The new show?" Billy wiped his fingers with a paper napkin and tossed it into the trash before snagging another slice that wouldn't dare add a fraction of an inch to his lean frame.

Edie nodded, sipping.

"Ty?"

After a minute, she nodded again.

Billy chewed and swallowed, then put down the pizza to gather her into his arms for a full-on, full-frontal, patented Billy hug. "You can write circles around every other hack out there, honey."

Edie leaned against him for a minute, then pulled away with a sigh. "Tell me something. Do you think I'm doing the right thing?"

Billy laughed. "Honey. I don't think you could do anything else. You're crazy about that man. And he's absolutely head over heels for you."

"Yeah, I know." Warmth flooded her at the thought, countered only with regret he wasn't going, too. "I'm sorry you can't come."

"I'm not. I'm not made for the cold." Billy shuddered. "Besides, I've still got a job and I have dibs on your office here. Sure, it won't be the same as working on *Runner*, but *Distant Shores* is a good show, too."

"It will be even better once you're on staff."

"Flattery will get you everywhere." Billy grabbed up his pizza again, folding the slice in half to fit it into his grin.

They finished the pizza and drinks, but then it was back to the grindstone. Edie had only two more episodes to finish before the move, but they were for the finale, and had been giving her fits. The show's fifth and final season had to end in a way that would satisfy the fans while tying up the final threads of the story arc the writers had built over the past two seasons and setting the show up for the anticipated movies.

Piece of cake.

Two hours later, it was stale cake with sour icing.

Edie sighed and pushed back in her chair, rubbing at the small of her back to ease the ache from sitting hunched over for too long. Her eyes burned from staring at the computer screen. Hell, even her fingertips hurt from pounding away at the keys.

Twilight was still toying with the sky when she forced herself to shut down the computer and head home, though she knew she had another few hours of work waiting there. That was the life of a writer, and one she loved, but, oh, how nice it would be when she could come home to Ty instead of an empty apartment and an e-mail message!

It would be late for him, and she didn't blame him for not waiting up for her, but Edie couldn't hold back the sigh of disappointment when she logged in and found an e-mail from him instead of a bouncing instant message icon signifying he was online and ready to talk to her.

Only another week. One more week. She could last a week, couldn't she?

Babe. Lots to do tomorrow morning (potential buyers coming to look at the house in the a.m.). Going to bed now. Love you. T

She sighed again. She'd been able to get out of her lease without much complication, but Ty was having a harder time selling his house. "Good night, Ty," she said.

P.S., she read. *We could get there by rocket ship.*

"All systems in lockdown, Captain." Commander Murphy waved toward the control console, where all the lights had gone green.

"The crew, too?" Captain Darowish turned from the console to stare at her first mate, hard. "I don't want any accidents, Murphy. Not like what happened to the Delta crew."

The Delta crew hadn't been in full sleep when the ship went through the Surge. They all lived. It would have been better if they'd died.

Murphy faced her, his deep green eyes glinting in the light from the console. Clad in his regulation black sleep suit, his honed body looked slight, even weak. But Darowish knew from experience there wasn't a damn weak thing about Tynan Murphy, and there was no other man she'd rather have at her back. Or her front, she mused, watching as Murphy gave a last-minute inspection of the controls.

Once upon a time she'd had him there, and as often as she'd wanted. She'd thrown it all away then, and there was no use wishing for it now. No matter if this was the last half hour she'd ever remember.

"We're clear," Murphy said.

It wasn't his job to do this. Under normal circumstances, the ship's engineer would have overseen putting the ship in lockdown, while the medical officer would have taken care of the crew. But the Gamma had lost her engineer and four other fine crewmen to a midspace virus brought in by one of the survey teams. A virus couldn't jettison half their cargo or sabotage the ship's water and food sup-

plies, but infected crewmen could, and had. The infected, driven to madness by the virus acting on the hypothalamus, had also damaged the android medical officer beyond repair.

Murphy and Darowish had managed to get the infected under quarantine and forced into the comatose state required for the Surge. The rest of the crew had also been settled into full sleep, but with the medical officer out of commission, the only one left able to pilot the ship through the Surge was Captain Darowish herself.

"Time to power down, Commander," she told Murphy. "Get into your bunk."

"No, Captain."

It was the first time he'd ever refused a direct command. Murphy had argued with her in the past. He'd discussed and offered opinions. But he'd never outright refused.

Darowish, her mind already on the next steps of the journey, faced him. "This isn't a matter for discussion, Commander. Power down."

Murphy shook his head. The military cut did nothing to flatter the dark hair she knew would be like silk against her fingers if he allowed it to grow. He didn't move out of her way, either. "No."

"Commander. Are you refusing a direct order?" Darowish stood as tall as she could, though Murphy still topped her by a good six units. "I don't have time to fool around. We're nearing the Surge. We've got infected on board and—"

Murphy kissed her. No slow slanting of mouth on mouth, his kiss was hard. Harsh. Utterly without mercy.

Darowish leaned into it, her arms going around his neck as his hands, those big hands, slid beneath her ass and lifted her. Murphy pinned her to the smooth plazmetal wall of the control room, and Darowish hooked her ankles around his waist. The sleek material of his sleep suit might have disguised his very firm muscles, but it did nothing to hide his erection.

"I won't leave you to face it alone," Murphy said into her mouth.

Darowish pulled away and caught her breath before she spoke. It was important her voice didn't shake. That she didn't lose her nerve. "You don't have a choice, Murphy."

His hands held her up and she had no fear he'd drop her. Murphy had never dropped her. When his fingers flexed, Darowish felt the imprint through her own sleep suit. The suit she wouldn't need.

Murphy pressed against her, his cock thick and hard. He put his face into the curve of her shoulder, where his breath stole along the curved neckline of her suit and warmed her chilled skin. Again, he shook his head. Again, that single word.

"No."

"Murph—" Her warning tone sounded choked, and Darowish swallowed hard before trying again. "Put me down."

He kissed her again. Softer this time. The gentle pressure of his lips on hers urged them to open. When his tongue swept inside, tasting her, Darowish wanted to weep. This would be the last time of last times. Why had she fought this for so long, only to accept now what he'd have offered her a thousand times over?

Because of the Surge. Without the medical officer, human in appearance but nonetheless only a replica, someone else had to man the ship through the Surge so it didn't shake itself apart, or worse, reassemble in occupied space. And without the medical officer, the captain was the only person able to do it.

"Thirty minutes until Surge." Gamma's soothing female voice echoed from the speakers.

Darowish pushed away from Murphy until he set her on her feet. "I'm giving you a direct order, Commander. Get to your bunk and power down, or I'll—"

"What? Put me in the brig? Keelhaul me? Bring me up on

charges?" For a fourth time, Murphy shook his head. His hands en-
circled her wrists as he pulled her closer. "No, Edie. You won't. And
I won't let you go through the Surge awake. Not alone."

She could have taken him down with a few well-executed moves,
no matter how much bigger he was. Or stronger. They'd worked out
together often enough she knew his strengths and weaknesses.

But he knew hers, too.

When he kissed her again, his hand moved over her body to undo
the stick-seam closing the front of her sleep suit. It parted under his
fingers. When his bare skin touched hers, Darowish shuddered at the
wanting she'd been pushing aside for so long. When his hand moved
over her belly and down to the heat between her thighs, she put her
hand over his wrist to stop him.

But again, Murphy disobeyed her. His fingers slid along her curls
and inside her before she could more than murmur his name. Wet
with her arousal, his finger stroked her clitoris in small, tight circles.
Her hand clamped on his wrist hard enough to grind the bones, but
Murphy didn't flinch. He didn't stop, either.

"I will not let you go through the Surge alone," Murphy told her.
"And I won't spend the last thirty minutes of our lives wasting any
more time."

Her bunk wasn't as fancy as she could've had as the Gamma's captain, but Darowish had never yearned for creature comforts. All she'd
wanted was to command her ship, to earn the respect of her peers, to
work hard. And to love Tynan Murphy. She'd only failed the last.

She'd wanted this for so long the wanting had become as much
a part of her as the mote in her eye, the length of her limbs, the
number of her teeth. She'd wanted Murphy from the first moment
she'd seen him, had slept with him as cadets in the academy and left
him behind when her first chance at an off-world assignment meant
she had to choose love or career.

She hadn't told him then why she'd been afraid to choose him, or why she'd been so cowardly she hadn't told him she was going. And for years she hadn't had to face that leaving him had been the worst mistake she'd ever made. Not until she was assigned the Gamma and the mission to the outer reaches of the sixth inhabited galaxy and Murphy had shown up on her crew list. Even then, she hadn't told him. They'd worked together. Eaten side by side. Guided this ship through space and kept it safe from harm as best they could. And she'd never told him she was sorry she'd left him.

Murphy stepped out of his sleep suit and didn't wait for her to finish getting out of hers. He pushed her back onto the plain-sheeted bunk. His mouth moved on hers, then over her jaw. Down her neck. To the swell of her breasts, over nipples sensitized by his kiss. Over her belly. When he settled his mouth on her center, Darowish lifted her hips and pressed herself into his kiss. They didn't have enough time for this, but she couldn't give it up.

His tongue slid along her skin. When he suckled gently at her clit, her body leaped. It surged. She bit her tongue at the thought and pushed away the knowledge they were reaching the Surge point. There'd be no turning back.

When Murphy pushed a finger, then two inside her, curving them to find the sweet spot inside her, Darowish groaned. Her fingers fisted in the regulation-weight blanket, finding no purchase. She had to put them in his hair to find that, and Murphy had cut his hair too short.

His mouth moved on her cunt as mercilessly as he'd kissed her minutes earlier. Her orgasm built without hesitation. It filled her, and then it emptied her, too.

"Don't wait." She urged him with her hands and mouth to cover her with his body, clutched at his back and ass to hold him closer as their mouths met. She moaned at the taste of herself on his tongue. "Don't wait any more."

They'd both waited too long. Now their time was short, but Ty was right. She didn't want to spend her last conscious minutes with regrets.

They weren't Captain and Commander any longer. Not even Darowish and Murphy. She was Edie to him again, after all these years. She was Edie, and a woman in his arms.

He slid inside her with a low cry she echoed before capturing his mouth. Their kiss was familiar, even after so long. His tongue stroked, his lips nibbled. His cock stretched her, and Edie clasped him tight.

"Five minutes until Surge." Gamma's voice made the alarming words soothing.

Ty's broad shoulders tensed under her hands, but Edie urged him to keep moving. "Don't stop."

"I won't stop." Ty kissed her again.

"I love you, Ty," she gasped out as orgasm swept her.

"I've always loved you, Edie."

They didn't have time to make it slow, or to bask in the afterglow. They barely had time to slip back into their clothes and take their seats at the controls that would guide the Gamma home. In minutes the ship would hit the Surge. Their molecules would be disassembled and shot miles through space and put back together on the other side. Nobody had ever made it through awake and come out sane.

Their chairs had always been next to each other, close enough for them to touch, but they never had. Not until now, when Ty leaned to kiss her as she punched in the final coordinates that would keep them safe.

Lost in pleasure as the ship leaped, Edie didn't notice the dark-

ness. There was no pain. She and Ty were in each other's arms, and they merged. Joined. No more waiting, they were together at last.

Forever.

"Gruesome," Ty said into the phone. "They didn't make it through the Surge? They got all . . . mashed up together, or what?"

Edie laughed. "That's up to the reader to decide."

"I'm the reader. I say they got out of it alive." Ty lay back on his bed to stare at the dark ceiling. It was late and he was tired, but he'd held onto the anticipation of this conversation for hours.

"Okay. And then what happened?"

"You're the storyteller, babe."

Edie sighed into the phone. "But I like to hear you talk, Ty. I like the sound of your voice."

"I can talk about a lot of things." He stretched out a hand to the unseen above, wishing she were close enough to touch. Soon. Not soon enough.

"I know you can." Her low chuckle crept over him and tickled the back of his neck.

So they talked. For an hour, then longer. It beat the hell out of typed conversations, some of which in the past he'd had to manage with only one hand. It was easier on the phone, sexier when he could hear the sound of her breathing shift instead of only imagining it.

"I wish you were touching me," Edie murmured.

"Close your eyes. I am touching you."

He knew she liked him to talk, though just as he claimed to be better with drawing than writing, so he'd said the same about speaking. But because he knew she liked it, hell, needed it, Ty was willing to make the effort.

"Where?"

"All over."

"Ty." Edie gave an exasperated sigh.

He laughed. "Your hips. I'm touching your hips."

Her sigh sounded more contented this time. "*Mmm.* Go on."

He spoke. She listened. He tried to weave a picture with his words and he must have done a fairly decent job, because after a while he heard the pattern of her breathing change. Heard her low moan. If he strained his ears, Ty could hear the shush and shuffle of her body moving against her sheets.

His own hand moved on his prick, up and down. He stopped for a minute to add a palmful of lube, and Edie murmured encouragement. She was close, she said. Was he?

"I'm close, babe. Thinking about you." He cradled the phone against his shoulder so he could use both hands, one on his cock and the other on his balls. It took some work to imagine the press and squeeze of his palm as Edie's body, but he was trying his best.

When they made love, Ty liked to wait for Edie to finish first, sometimes more than once. He'd never been with a woman whose body responded so well to his. The fact she could come two or three times seemed like a miracle to him, a gift he wasn't stupid enough to take credit for. But on the phone, without being able to see and touch her, Ty could concentrate on his own pleasure and know she would get hers, too. Her hand never faltered on her body the way his sometimes did.

"Are you close?" She asked in a low, sweet purr that told him she'd come and was waiting for him, maybe still toying with herself the way he knew she liked. Trying for round two.

"Close." It was harder to talk now, not because he had no words but because forming them took too much effort.

Ty, fist slick, pumped his cock slowly, then faster. His back arched a little, head pressing into the pillow, and he closed his eyes. He had a stable of stock fantasies to call on during times like this, when the sound of her voice was enough to tease and tantalize but he wanted more. He thought about Edie and the first time he'd seen her for real, not a photo on a website or an icon on the message board.

Edie Darowish, for real. They'd talked for months online and a few times on the phone, business at first and later . . . pleasure. But the first time he saw her he hadn't been sure what he'd think when faced with the real woman. The meeting had been set up for them to talk about the *Runner* graphic novels, and though they'd been flirting online, Ty wasn't willing to bet Edie felt about him the way he'd started feeling about her.

Until he saw her for the first time.

She'd worn a simple dress patterned with flowers and low sandals that showed off her long, tanned legs. Her long blond hair had fallen over her shoulders, begging him to touch it, and at her throat, the scarf, a wispy scrap of sheer yellow. Later, he learned it was silk. He'd come from snow-covered and frigid Maine to California, but the sunshine he most remembered hadn't come from the sky. It had been in the sight of Edie's scarf.

It still smelled of her when he drew it across his nose now, and whether it was because he made her wear it sometimes when they were together, or because he only imagined it, Ty didn't care. He buried his face in the silk, imagining it was her skin. His fist slid along his cock, palming the head and down, and his balls tightened.

"Oh, Ty, I'm going to . . . I'm . . ." Edie's small cry sounded through the phone's earpiece.

Ty couldn't speak. His orgasm jetted from him and all he

could manage was a strangled, muffled moan. The scarf brushed his face as the phone slipped sideways into the pillows. Heat and pleasure shot from his balls and out his prick, and he fell back, spent.

"Ty?"

A minute had passed and he realized Edie was still on the line. "Yeah, babe."

She laughed, low and sweet. "I miss you."

"I miss you, too." He yawned and tucked the scarf back into his nightstand drawer, then reached for the box of tissues to handle cleanup.

"You know I'm not really into the whole Valentine's Day thing. . . ."

He laughed. "Riiiiight. This from the woman who wrote an entire story arc around Cupid?"

It had been three of the most popular episodes and had directly affected the first graphic novel he'd been contracted to draw. Ty knew how Edie felt about Valentine's Day. Nonchalant didn't describe it.

"Well, I'm just saying that I understand if this year it's not as extravagant. Since we'll have just moved into the new place and all. And if you don't sell your house . . ."

"Babe. Don't worry. I have buyers coming tomorrow, and a nice royalty check coming, according to my agent." Ty yawned again, bone-crackingly. "We'll be together on V-Day this year, and we'll celebrate it. I promise."

Neither had planned the move to coincide with the lovers' holiday. It had just worked out with *Runner*'s shooting schedule. The people they'd bought the house from had been able to move out earlier than expected, too, which meant Ty and Edie could take ownership before they'd thought possible.

"Valentine's Day together. Oh, *mmmm.*" Edie made what Ty always thought of as one of her "yummy" sounds. "I can't wait. I wish we had a time machine so we could just skip ahead."

He didn't want to fall asleep on the phone, no matter how much he wanted to drift off to dreams with her voice in his ear. "Me, too. Babe . . . I gotta get to sleep."

"I know you do. Sleep tight, honey."

"You, too."

Ty thumbed off the phone and turned on his side, facing the empty spot where Edie would have been—and would be, in just another week.

We could get there by time machine.

In it, we could skip the days ahead. Inside, not even minutes would pass. Outside, all the hours keeping us apart would vanish as if they'd never existed. And when we reached our destination, we could take out the key and throw it away and stay there, just like that, while time passed us by and the world moved around us, but we stayed the same.

I have some bad news. Call me.

Edie's smile at Ty's latest addition to their fanciful game faded. Bad news? What bad news? Her finger was already stabbing the numbers on the phone. Whatever it was, it had happened hours ago, before she woke and had time to get onto her computer.

Outside her door, people carrying boxes and pushing trolleys loaded with more boxes passed. The entire office was abustle with the move, some of the staff packing up entirely and others staying behind. Still more were trying to prep rooms for the incoming group who'd be taking over the space. She'd spent the last four years in this place, with these people. She'd been so focused on getting out of here to be with Ty, she'd been ignoring what she was leaving behind.

Edie pressed the phone to her ear and turned from the door, not wanting to give in to the sudden waves of melancholy and anxiety. Bad news from Ty was bad enough, without her getting all fertootzed about the move, too.

He wasn't answering, and Edie checked the time. Early morning for her, just before lunch for him. Ty worked from home and always had his cell phone with him. Where was he?

She'd logged in to her instant message program first thing, but his name was grayed out. She typed in a quick message, anyway. He didn't answer that, either, not even when she buzzed him.

What could the bad news be? How bad could it be? Her mind whirled with a thousand possibilities, each worse than the last, and Edie cursed her overactive imagination. She tried to focus on the work, instead. Her phone rang as she was halfway through a scene she'd been halfway through for an hour.

Edie, who'd been looking at the screen but not really seeing the words, flipped open her phone and replied before Ty could even speak. "Are you all right?"

She could tell she'd caught him by surprise. "I'm fine, babe."

It felt as if she'd been holding her breath for an hour, and now it sighed out. "Oh, thank God. I was worried. You're okay?"

"I'm fine, really." Ty's voice soothed her. "I'm sorry to worry you."

"You said you had bad news, and then you didn't answer the phone, and . . ." Edie took another shallow breath and let it out. "I was just worried."

"No. I have good news, too. Not just bad."

She could see his face, the half smile and the way his green eyes would crinkle at the corners. Good news, bad news, whatever it was, so long as he was fine. That's all that mattered.

"Good news first," she said.

"I sold the house."

"*Whoo-hoo!*" Edie punched her fist in the air and spun around in her chair. "That's not good news, that's great news!"

She sobered a little. "What's the bad news? They didn't give you what you wanted?"

"No. Not that. They made a good offer on the house. With everything else going on, it's enough to cover the realtor's fees and what I owed. I won't come out a prince from the deal, but I'll have some cash in pocket for the trip."

"So . . . ?" Edie chewed her bottom lip and stopped her chair spinning.

"They want to settle next week."

Her heart sank, but she tried optimism first. "So . . . you'll have to leave a day or so later?"

"I won't be there for Valentine's Day, babe."

Ty sounded so forlorn she couldn't be angry with him, but disappointment splintered her voice. "Oh."

"Yeah. I'm sorry." Ty sighed, and she imagined him running a hand through his shaggy dark hair. "The realtor and the lawyers have to do their thing . . . they can't meet until the Monday after. I'm really, really sorry."

Edie had been running on close to empty for the past month, trying to wrap up all her work, say good-bye to friends and plan the move, too. She was putting aside everything she'd known for the past seven years since she'd taken a long shot and moved to California to pursue a dream, but none of that had mattered compared to not being with Ty. Missing him had been an ache, soul-deep, that she'd only managed to put aside with knowing she'd see him soon. Valentine's Day had never been meant to be such a big deal. Not until they weren't going to have it.

"There will be other Valentine's Days." Maybe if she convinced him, she could convince herself.

"There will." Ty didn't sound any more convinced than she had. "I'll make it up to you."

"Oh, Ty." Edie sighed. "You don't have to make anything up to me. It's not like that. I'm just glad you sold your house. And a few more days won't matter, really. Right?"

"Right."

It didn't feel right. It felt all kinds of wrong, but Edie wasn't about to lay a guilt trip on him. "It's only a few more days."

"And I'll leave right after the settlement. Be packed and ready to hit the road. I can be there in eleven hours if I drive straight through."

"As much as I want to see you, I don't want you to be too tired," Edie cautioned. "You were going to take two days."

"I'll be ok."

Tears filled her voice, though her words were meant to sound upbeat. "It's just Valentine's Day. What's more important is that we'll be together after that. For good. Right?"

"Right." But he felt bad about it, she could tell, and Ty feeling bad about it made Edie feel worse for being a silly girl who'd let herself get all wrapped up in an image of red ribbons and boxes of candy.

A rap on the door turned her in her chair. To her surprise, it was Justin. He'd visited her office only a few times in the entire time she'd been writing for the show, both times by happenstance and coincidence on his way to meetings with someone else. She'd seen him on set the few times she'd gone, but it wasn't like they'd ever gone out for drinks or hung out. She didn't get invited to the parties he did. He spoke her words every week, but it was his face the fans wanted to see.

"Ty, I have to go." Too late, she'd sounded more abrupt than she meant to. "There's someone here."

"Babe, I'm really sorry."

His apologies only made her feel worse for being upset. "I'll call you later, okay?"

"Sure. All right." Ty hung up and Edie, stomach churning, turned to face the doorway.

"Hey . . . Edie." Justin leaned against the doorframe, one long leg crossed over the other. Today he wore a button-down shirt left untucked from faded jeans, an outfit completely different from what he wore on the show. It made him look younger. "How's it going?"

"Oh, hey, Justin. It's going." Edie waved at the computer, where her cursor squatted like a fat, blinking spider, mocking her with its lack of web.

"That good, *huh?*"

She wasn't about to tell him she was stuck on the finale or that her fiancé wasn't going to be with her on Valentine's Day, after all, and she was about to burst into hysterical tears better suited to a television show than real life. "How's it going for you? Looking forward to wrapping the season?"

"Oh yeah." He shot her a lower-wattage version of the grin that had set fandom on fire. "I'm going to take a long vacation."

"Sounds good." She paused, her fingers brushing the keyboard, and gave him a curious look. "Is there something you wanted?"

He'd asked her, once, to give him "smarter" lines. That had been back in the beginning of season two. Edie had just come on board and taken over some of the secondary story lines, most requiring him to come out of the bathroom in a towel or have a short-lived, angsty romance with a guest star. Edie, new to the gig, had been stuck between the senior writers and wanting to prove she could really write. She'd come up with one of the show's most popular story lines, given Justin something meaty to work with, and earned the position of senior writer for the next season.

"I was wondering if you wanted to have lunch with me? Today? Erm . . . now? To talk about the finale. I had some thoughts."

Normally he just shot her an e-mail or had his agent bring up points at the beginning of the season, but this was the last season. There'd been changes all over the place, more than in any other season. Suggested arcs had been dropped to concentrate on tying up the long-term threads and new ones devised with wiggle room for the inevitable movie follow-ups. Aside from that, Edie was one of the few writers who'd made it clear from the start she valued actor input, if for no other reason than she believed if someone were going to give life to the people in her head, she wanted it to be done right.

Edie looked at the keyboard. This wasn't going anywhere, and the next writers' meeting wasn't until tomorrow. She needed lunch, preferably something chocolate.

"Sure. Okay. I can do that."

As she got up from her desk, another figure loomed in the doorway. Shaggy-haired *Runner* newcomer Tristan Winsam had only been on the show one season, but his pre-built fan base had followed him from his previous show. There'd been some trepidation about how he'd get along with Justin, but the pair, though they played rivals on the show, akin to *The X-Files'* Mulder and Krycek, got along famously in real life.

"Hey, Edie. Ready to go?"

She'd been half out of her seat but now stood slowly, looking from one to the other. Neither was smiling. "Hey, Tristan. What's up?"

"Not much." He clapped Justin on the shoulder. "We've got some things to talk about with you, that's all."

This didn't bode well, especially when Edie caught the glance Justin shot the other man. Trouble brewing? *They'd better hope neither one of them pulled a diva,* she thought as she grabbed her bag and followed them out into the hall. She wasn't in the mood.

Her mood changed five minutes later when they took her down the hall to the conference room instead of out the door to the parking lot. Justin and Tristan parted in front of her so she could enter first, but Edie already knew what she'd find inside by the way they both were grinning. She didn't need to worry about anyone playing diva. They'd been trying to surprise her.

"Surpriiiiiise!" The word rang out in the small room, and Edie turned in a slow half circle to take it all in. All her cowriters, the production staff, the director . . . several of the show's stars, and even the head Foley guy, all there with grins as bright as the California sunshine.

"Hey, sweetie." Billy help up one end of the banner reading "Good Luck, Edie and Ty!" in huge red letters. "Surprise!"

Edie shook her finger at him. "You can never keep a secret!"

"That's why we didn't tell him until fifteen minutes ago." Tristan gestured at the sign. "It wasn't easy keeping it from him, but we managed."

Billy made a face and handed off the banner so he could enfold Edie into a crushing hug. "Thank those boys. They had a lot to do with this."

Edie squeezed and kissed Billy and looked toward Justin and Tristan, who'd already moved to the table laden with food. "They did?"

Billy nodded. "Yep. They're going to miss you, too, hon. Not just us. Imagine that."

Edie managed a smile. "Don't start with me, Billy. You know I'll cry, and I hate that."

He started to reply but then held her off at arm's length and studied her face. "What's wrong?"

In the crowd pushing forward to wish her well and offer hugs and congratulations, Edie didn't want to be a downer. Not when all her friends had gathered to give her a send-off that included catering from her favorite restaurant and—

"Gummy worms!" Tristan showed her the tin from a swanky gourmet candy shop frequented by the sort-of rich and trying-to-be famous. He grabbed up a handful and dangled one into his mouth, grinning.

"Such a boy," Billy said as he steered her toward one of the seats in the back. "C'mere, sweetie. Tell me what's wrong."

"Later," Edie said. "Now it's time for lunch."

Suddenly starving, she loaded her plate with fresh deli rolls, sliced turkey and cheese, and a handful of chips, then grabbed a can of diet cola from the cooler and headed for the seat Billy had picked out for her. The ones to her left and right were immediately occupied by Sandy from payroll and Debbie from legal, who gabbed away and saved Edie from having to say anything at all.

There was another surprise, too. A wedding shower, all the gifts small enough to pack in her suitcase. She got a lot of gift cards and a few skimpy, lacy things they all expected to make her blush but which she instead insisted on holding up and showing around.

The party didn't last long, but by the end of it, Edie had been hugged, kissed, and squeezed by just about everyone. She'd even had her picture taken between Justin and Tristan, their long arms slung around her shoulders. She'd be the envy of the Internet as soon as these hit the message boards, but though both men were well built and handsome, neither of them was Ty.

When the room had cleared out, leaving behind only scraps and crumbs and shredded curls of wrapping paper, Edie tossed her trash in the can and grabbed up another diet cola. Before she cracked the top, a tap on her shoulder turned her. It was Justin.

"Hey." She touched his arm briefly. "This was great. Thanks."

Justin shook his head. "No thanks necessary. I wanted to thank you. And wish you luck. Wish you were hanging around here."

"We've had a great run, *huh?*" Edie's grin wasn't forced, this time.

He shot her a smile at her deliberate play on words. "You know I almost quit after season one. I would've had to stick it out for season two for my contract, but . . . then you came along. Thanks."

"I just wrote the words, Justin."

He shrugged, and Edie thought everyone who loved him so much based on his face and the character he played on TV would love him even more if they knew what a nice guy he was, too. "Couldn't have done any of it without them."

She held out her hand. "Let's agree to call it a joint effort, shall we?"

He took her fingers and squeezed them gently. "Sure we can't convince you to stay here? I can think of a dozen shows that would die to get you on board."

It hadn't been that easy, no matter what he thought. She'd had offers, sure, many worse than what she was leaving and none better than where she was going. "Thanks, but . . ."

"Yeah. I get it." He laughed. "You and Murphy are getting married. It's true loooove."

Edie knuckled his arm the way she'd done to her younger brother long ago. "Yes. It is."

"Good for you."

Tristan appeared in the doorway. "Justin. You coming?"

Justin nodded. "Yeah, man. Be there in a minute."

Tristan, hand full of gummy worms, waved. "Good luck with the movie script, Edie. Give me better lines than this douche."

"If they let me write it." Nothing was ever set in stone in this business.

"They'd better." Justin laughed and held out his hand again.

She shook it. "See you, Justin."

Alone in the conference room, Edie looked around. In this room she'd had the beginning of a career. It seemed fitting it would see the end of one, too.

"Chill, dude." Ham ducked as Ty threw the basketball at him.

It had been meant to be a pass, but somehow his frustration had ended up erupting. "Sorry, man."

Ham tossed the ball back and forth in his hands before dribbling but didn't shoot. The indoor gym echoed with the squeak of sneakers on the wood floor and shouts as men and women played. Ty and Ham had been coming here for years. Since they were kids, as a matter of fact. They played racquetball or a game of pickup basketball at least once a week, and Ty had always counted on the exercise to work him out of whatever funk he might've been in.

Not today.

He held up his hands for Ham to make a pass, and Ty took the ball down the half-court to the basket. He laid it up but instead of a slam dunk, the ball bounced off the rim. Ham grabbed the rebound and set up a perfect, sweet shot. *Swish*. But, unusual for Ham, he didn't razz Ty about how easy it had been.

Ty took the pass from Ham back to center court and then up to the basket again. Another failed shot had him cursing, and Ham took the ball to the hoop without hesitating. Ty, sweat stinging his eyes, bent to put his hands on his knees.

"You up for it?" Ham bounced the ball near Ty's feet, caught it, and bounced it again. "Gonna take it?"

Ty looked at the basket, then hooked the ball from Ham's grip and took another shot. This time, the ball swished through the hoop and Ty grabbed it on the rebound, sending it through the hoop again. Ham didn't even try to go after it that time, and they both watched it bounce away toward the bleachers.

"Your concentration's for shit," Ham offered.

"Yeah. I know."

"You want to quit? Go for a beer?"

Ham, Ty's friend since the sixth grade, shifted on his worn sneakers. Ty straightened and went after the ball, cradling and not dribbling it. Ham had barely broken a sweat, but Ty's entire shirt clung to him and he had to swipe at his eyes.

"Beer would be good," he admitted reluctantly and waited for Ham to mock him.

Miraculously, Ham didn't take that chance, either. "C'mon."

They showered and dressed and headed out into the frigid February air. Ty's hair froze into the spikes left as he ran his hand through it, and he looked at the sky for a hint of sun, but all he saw were clouds scudding across the darkness. He'd lived here his entire life, and he doubted he'd miss the Maine winters. It would be worse for Edie, his California Girl, moving from the land of oranges and oceans back to suburban Philadelphia.

"Lenny's?" Ham jerked his chin in the direction of the beer and pizza joint they frequented.

"Yeah. Meet you there."

Ten minutes drive was all it took, but in that ten minutes, all Ty could hear was the sound of disappointment in Edie's voice when he'd spoken to her earlier. Even over the sound of his favorite local classic rock station. Even over the sound of the sudden gust of wind that rocked his car.

By the time he got out in the parking lot at Lenny's he'd lost his taste for beer, but there was no way to admit that to Ham without coming off as a total pussy, so Ty just pulled his scarf tighter around his neck and put his head down against the wind. Inside, the heat from the pizza ovens and the scent of sauce and cheese and beer hit him like a living thing. He breathed in, deep.

Ham waved him over to a booth, where their regular waitress, Tammy, had already put out a basket of breadsticks with a small ceramic bowl of tomato sauce.

"Getcha?" she asked, pen ready to scribble.

"Pitcher of the usual. Large pie, half sausage. And I want two dozen wings, hot, with extra blue cheese." Ham grinned and turned to Ty. "What'll you have?"

But Tammy, who knew Ham too well, had already turned to go. Ham shrugged and dug into the breadsticks. He pushed the basket toward Ty, who grabbed a few, not because he was especially hungry but because Ham tended to eat the whole basket before asking "did you want some more?"

They had food, they had beer, and they didn't have conversation about anything more important than the score of the game on TV, the possibilities of bad weather and the tightness of Tammy's ass, and the probability of her ever agreeing to go home with Ham. Ham thought it was a question of sooner rather than later, Ty didn't much care, and Tammy, when asked, was of the opinion that hell would feel much like Maine did at the moment before she went anywhere with Ham.

"She's crazy about me." Ham said this with the same enviable confidence he'd had since high school, when he'd shot up over everyone else and had been the first to grow armpit hair.

"I can see that." Ty'd only sipped on one beer and eaten two slices of pizza.

Ham looked at the food still laid out in front of them. "Dude. You sick?"

"No."

"*Ah.*" Ham leaned back in the booth, his hands behind his head. "Something up with Edie?"

Ty lifted his mug and looked at the circle of wetness it had left behind. He picked it up and put it down four times and made the Olympic rings. Then he swiped them into blurred ovals with his fingertips.

"Yeah," he said.

"Talk to Uncle Hammy. She finally wise up and decide to dump your ass for some hot younger stud?" Ham reached across the table to poke Ty in the ribs.

Ty didn't feel like laughing but it was almost impossible not to when Ham started in with the "Uncle Hammy" business. "I sold the house."

"Great." Ham goggled for a minute, his familiar grin faltering only when he saw Ty wasn't joining it. "What's the problem?"

Ty outlined the situation quickly. Ham frowned. "Sucks, man."

"Yeah. Big-time."

"Was she pissed off?"

"No. That would have been better. She cried."

Both men fell silent at that. Playboy Ham knew what it meant to make a woman cry, and even he wasn't immune to it. Ty sipped morosely.

"A lot?"

"She tried not to, but I could tell she was."

Ham winced. "Ouch. That kills."

"Yeah, tell me about it." Ty turned his glass in his palms until the beer sloshed. "It's Valentine's Day, man. The first we were able to be together for. I told her I'd make it up to her, but . . ."

"Yeah. I know." Ham looked sympathetic. "V-Day is big shit with chicks."

"You can be so charming."

Ham gave Ty an unapologetic grin. "You know it, fool."

"It's just bad timing. I know Edie understands that. But I still feel like crap." Ty fixed his friend with a look, daring him to mock. "I wanted to be there with her."

Ham had shown remarkable restraint so far, but now it broke. He cracked an imaginary whip in the air, nearly clipping Tammy's elbow as she passed. She whirled on him with a glare undimmed by Ham's returning smile.

"I think it's beautiful Ty wants to be with his fiancée on Valentine's Day," Tammy said with a sniff. "You could take some lessons, Hamilton Parker."

Ham watched her flounce away and turned back to Ty. "What did I tell you? She wants me."

"She wants to slap you, maybe." Ty looked at the pizza on his plate, but didn't want any more. "I'm going to head out."

"Dude." Ham didn't reach to grab his arm or anything girly like that, but he did lean forward as Ty got up. "I'm really offended."

"About what?" Ty frowned as he tossed a handful of crumpled bills on the table. Ham could be a pain in the ass, but he was still a friend . . . unless he was ready to give Ty shit about the thing with Edie, in which case Ty was probably going to tell him to fuck off.

But then Ham spoke, and for the first time since getting the call from the realtor, Ty's stomach unloosened from the skein of knots it had become.

The flight was late. The rental car Edie had reserved had gone missing, mysteriously. Though the clerk at the desk knew she was supposed to get one and had her confirmation number and everything, the car itself could not be found. By the time they figured out what to do, she'd already spent half an hour on the phone with the realtor, trying to find a time to get the keys. The realtor had sounded as though she had a bad cold and agreed to leave the keys in the lockbox on the front door and give Edie the combination, rather than having her come to the office. By the time she got to the new house, night had fallen and she didn't have a remote to open the garage door, so she had to park in the icy drive. All in all, it had been a pretty lousy day.

So when Edie opened the door to their new house and found herself wading through a sea of red and pink balloons, all she could do was look around in surprise. Then she laughed. A few of the balloons floated through the door and into the February winter beyond, and Edie quickly shut the door to prevent further escapes.

Her feet kicked balloons with every step down the short hall toward the kitchen. He must have had a couple hundred delivered. It was such a Ty thing to do. . . .

And then there he was, standing in their new bare kitchen, a bottle of champagne in one hand and two long-stemmed glasses in the other.

"Happy Valentine's Day," he said.

Balloons flew and a few of them popped as she ran to throw herself into Ty's arms. The glasses clattered, sloshing Moët, but Ty's mouth on hers was sweeter than any wine could ever have been. He set the bottle on the counter as he kissed her, then used his free arm to lift and spin her. The taste of him filled her and oh, it had been so long.

"Too long," Edie murmured against his lips as he set her down. "Oh, God, Ty, how did you get here? I thought you weren't coming!"

"And miss our first Valentine's Day in the new house? No way." Ty handed her a glass from which half the contents had spilled onto his arm and shirt. "I drove. Ham's going to road-trip the moving truck down here, and I'll pay for him to fly back. I promised him an introduction to some starlets, though, if you can help me out with that."

After all the long months and all the stories, having the real Ty here in front of her was almost too much to handle. Edie drew in a deep breath, willing herself not to cry. "I'll see what I can do."

Ty took her in his arms again, settling her into that place where she fit just right. Edie closed her eyes and breathed in deep, the familiar scent of his soap and his skin. Ty's chin rested on the top of her head and he squeezed her gently as they rocked to silent music.

"But what about the paperwork and settlement?"

"Well, as Ham pointed out to me, I could give him power of attorney, since he is a lawyer and all. He's going to sign off on the papers for me."

Edie tilted her head to look at him. "Wow. That's . . . you did all that just to get here?"

"You're not upset, are you?" he asked softly against her hair. "I could leave if you want. Go to a hotel—"

She pushed away far enough to punch his chest. "Don't you dare!"

Laughing, Ty kissed her again. More champagne spilled when

he lifted her onto the counter and stood between her thighs. His mouth, hot and wet, stole her breath as his tongue darted in to stroke hers.

"We're making a mess of the kitchen," Edie whispered into his kiss. "Champagne's for drinking, not spilling."

"I beg to differ, babe," Ty whispered back. "Champagne is made for spilling if it means I can lick it off your body in all the places it drips."

"I like the sound of that." Edie's hand went to the top button of her blouse, then the others all in a row as Ty stepped slightly back. "You mean like this?"

She tipped her almost empty glass toward her skin, bared by the open shirt. Golden liquid surged to the glass's edge but didn't spill out. She watched Ty's face, his eyes glowing, tongue swiping over his mouth as though he were already tasting her.

Edie leaned back to let her shirt fall open wider. The champagne hovered at the rim of the glass. Ty, his gaze locked with hers, reached out and used the tip of his finger to bump the glass.

"Oops."

Edie's gasp turned to a giggle as the chilled champagne hit her skin and spattered her bra. She had a moment to wish she'd known Ty would be here so she could've worn the red lace demi-bra she'd bought, but in the next moment she had no more time to care because he'd bent to press his mouth to her collarbones. His tongue swiped away the champagne, and his mouth moved lower, to the swell of her breasts. He put his hands behind her, holding her so she didn't have to support herself on the countertop.

She cupped the back of his neck, her fingers twining in his thick, dark hair. Ty's mouth brushed her breasts softly, his tongue flickering. Wet heat pressed her through the bra's lace, and when he closed his lips over her nipple, Edie sighed. She closed her eyes, leaning back into Ty's steady embrace as he nuzzled her.

Ty pulled away to take the champagne glass from her and held it to her lips, then kissed her wet mouth. "It tastes better on you than from the glass."

Edie raised a brow. "I'm going to need a shower."

"You're going to need a shower, anyway." He tipped the glass for her to drink again, then drained and refilled it. He set it on the counter and touched the button of her jeans. "Take these off."

Edie looked to the French doors leading to the deck, then to the window over the sink. "Ty, the neighbors—"

"Can't see a thing. I stood in the yard and made sure."

That, like the balloons, was such a Ty thing to do that Edie had to laugh. She flicked open the button at her waist and toyed with the zipper as Ty stood back and watched her. She shifted on the slick counter, but there was no way she was going to get these off without help.

She didn't have to say a word.

Ty, his mouth anchored to hers in another scorching kiss, hooked his thumbs in her waistband and pulled so hard he scooted her entire body against him. They laughed, kissing, as Edie wrapped her arms around his neck and her legs around his waist, using the leverage to lift her ass so Ty could slide the denim down to her thighs.

"Cold!" she cried when her mostly bare skin settled back on the marble.

Ty, busy pushing her jeans off her legs, looked up. "You okay, babe?"

Edie, bare legs dangling, kicked lightly at the cupboards below and spread her legs, leaning back with her hands supporting her weight. "Oh, sure. I always sprawl naked on my kitchen countertops."

Ty tossed her jeans to the floor and kissed both of her knees. His hands circled her ankles as he moved between her legs. "I'm going to insist on it."

"Might make for some interesting," he kissed her, "dinner," she kissed him, "conversations."

Ty grabbed her ass and moved her to the edge of the counter, her satin panties making the motion effortless. Edie wrapped her legs around him again, shivering at the soft flannel of his shirt and the harder denim of his jeans as it rubbed her bare flesh. Ty's kiss was harder this time, and when his hand fisted in her hair to tip her head back, Edie no longer gave a rat's ass about the neighbors.

"I love it when you moan like that." Ty nipped at her throat and licked a path over her shoulder, then back to her breasts again. With one finger he flicked open the catch of her bra and helped her shrug out of it.

When her breasts fell free, he reached for the glass and tipped it over them again. Edie bent her head to watch the champagne ease over her skin. The golden liquid diverted around her tight nipples and dripped, splashing, onto her thighs and belly.

With a mouthful of champagne, Ty bent and took her nipple in his mouth. The cool liquid sloshed around her hot flesh as he tongued her, and the overflow cascaded over her skin. He swallowed, then licked the underside of her breast, suckling again on her nipple until she writhed and moaned.

Her fingers loosed his buttons as he kissed her mouth again, and Edie slid her hands inside over Ty's bare chest. His heart thumped beneath her palm, laid flat, and she curled her fingers slightly to dig her nails into his skin. With the other hand, she eased the fabric off his shoulders and down his arms.

Their kisses had become harder but not yet frantic. Edie tugged Ty's belt to pull him closer so she could kiss his chest, and when he moaned, she looked up at him with a smile. "I like it when you moan, too."

She undid his belt buckle, then the button and zipper beneath. When she slid a hand inside, Ty's hips bumped forward. Edie rubbed the front of his silky printed boxers. "*Oooh.* Someone was prepared."

"You like 'em?" Ty pushed his jeans down, pausing to toe off his sneakers so he could get the denim past his feet. He stood up straight, grinning, to show off the boxers.

"Kiss prints. Nice." Edie laughed softly as she stroked the outline of his cock through the soft satin. "This is nicer."

Ty moved between her legs again to kiss her. His cock nudged her through his-and-hers layers of satin, but that was almost as delicious as bare skin. For now.

"I wanted to make everything special, babe."

"You," Edie said as she kissed his throat and nuzzled just under his ear, "are made of awesome."

"I'm not done yet."

"Not more champagne." It was only half a protest.

Edie watched as Ty took the glass, only a few dribbles left in it, and held it over her belly. When the champagne splashed on her skin this time, she arched into it, already anticipating the swipe of Ty's tongue. She wasn't disappointed. He moved over her belly, then lower, down to the satin covering her cunt. He pressed his mouth there, blowing hot breath through the fabric, and Edie parted her legs with a small sigh.

Ty put a hand on each side of her, close enough that his fingers brushed her hips. He kissed her panties, then her inner thighs until Edie spread them wide. She slid on the counter, easing toward the edge, but didn't fear falling. Ty would catch her before that happened. She let her head loll back, her eyes closed, as she concentrated on the pleasure of him pressing her clit.

The rasp of his tongue on the satin, the sound of him licking her, urged her hips to rock under his touch. Her panties blunted the sensation but took away none of the pleasure as Ty moved from her inner thighs to her cunt and back again. The hot wetness of his mouth moved away, replaced a second later by more coolness as he poured a bit more champagne, the last, she guessed, onto her panties.

Edie giggled, then gasped when Ty's mouth pressed her again. His finger slid beneath the elastic, pulling her panties away from her skin. Heady seconds passed as he used the motion of the fabric to further arouse her.

"Ty," she said finally. "I can't stand it any more. Use your mouth on me, please."

"Gladly."

In seconds her panties had followed the rest of her clothes. Edie opened her eyes to watch him put his mouth on her, at last, without the barrier of anything between them. The muscles in her thighs and belly leaped when he leaned to brush his lips across her swollen clit. When Ty kissed her there, Edie arched her back again, giving up to the sweet sensations flooding her.

Ty's big hands gripped her hips to keep her in place as he feasted on her. The counter was big enough for Edie to lay back, her elbows propping her. Her head just cleared the raised edge of the bar between the kitchen and family room, and though the lip of wood made a hard pillow, she couldn't quite bring herself to care just then.

"God, it's been so long." Ty said it low, but Edie had no trouble hearing him.

His hair tickled her belly and thighs as he settled into licking her cunt, back and forth, up and down. He circled her clitoris with his tongue, then paused to suckle gently, tucking it between his lips while he slid one thick finger deep inside to nudge her G-spot. Edie clutched at smooth marble, her mouth open in a silent cry. She bit down hard on her bottom lip as Ty's stroking finger urged her pussy to bear down on it. His tongue flickered gently against her clit as he added another finger, twisting them as he fucked in and out of her.

"You're so wet for me."

It always moved her how awed he sounded, how grateful. It was one more thing about Ty she adored. How much he loved her body's reactions to him.

"I want to make you come, Edie."

"I'm close," she murmured, concentrating, and her voice trailed off into the moan he loved so well.

He was the only man she'd ever been able to talk to like this during lovemaking. With Ty she could say what she felt, she could scream or cry out, or moan. She could be as loud as a porn star or give him her pleasure in near-silent groans and the twisting of her fingers in her hair. With Ty she never worried how she looked or sounded when she was coming. She didn't have to be anything but what she was.

It began as it always did, with a burst of warmth concentrated in her clitoris. Edie drew in a breath, long and slow, and let it out again as her body tensed. Ecstasy sparkled, tiny lightning flashes, and she rolled her pelvis up to meet Ty's questing mouth.

His fingers hooked upward inside her and heat exploded. Her

cunt spasmed, and she cried out as her climax washed over her in one, two, three waves of pleasure so strong they left her limp and wrung out.

The aftershocks rippled through her as Ty, breathing hard, kissed her pussy again and withdrew his fingers. He pulled her close to kiss her mouth, and Edie was already reaching for his cock between them.

"I want you inside me." It wasn't a request.

She stroked him first, but not to get him hard. He already was. She ran her hand up and down his shaft, using the satin of his boxers to tease him, because she needed a couple seconds to come down from her orgasm. And because she wanted to tease him as he'd teased her, she thought with a grin as Ty's hips jutted forward under her touch.

"You like that?"

"It's good." Ty wasn't as vocal when it was his turn. He'd told her once it was because when all the blood went to the head below, he wasn't much good with the one above. "Really good."

Smooth satin stroked over his cock, but that wasn't good enough. After months of nothing but long-distance loving, Edie craved Ty's skin against her. She pushed the boxers down and took him in her hand, loving the heat of cock in her palm. She weighed his balls with her other hand, loving the way he shivered as she ran a fingertip along the seam between his cock and sac.

Edie scooted to the edge of the counter, which was just the right height for what she planned. Marble squeaked under skin as she moved. With one hand gripping Ty's shoulder for balance, she used the other to guide his cock to her well, where she dipped the head into her folds. She teased them both, nudging his cock head half an inch inside her, wetting him, then pulling him out.

In again, an inch this time. Her body opened, embracing him. Wet from the orgasm he'd already given her, there was nothing but slick acceptance. Only delicious friction.

In. Out.

Ty bent his head to press against her shoulder, his breath caressing her breasts and nipples, still sticky from the champagne. Edie, her fist gripping his penis tightly at the base, eased him in almost the entire way. This time she didn't urge him to pull out. They stayed that way for a moment, both breathing hard.

"I love you, Ty," she whispered against the side of his face.

"I love you, babe. Missed you so much." Ty shifted his hips, pushing, and Edie released his cock so he could fill her.

Ty didn't move right away, but he did kiss her. A gentle slanting of mouth on mouth, tongue on tongue. He cupped the back of her head, his big hand cradling it. She locked her ankles behind his back, holding him to her.

This was a moment she didn't want to forget, not ever. Not when they were old and gray. Not tomorrow, or next week. Not the next time they had an argument. This moment, this joining, was meant to stay with her forever, just like this.

"Make love to me," Edie said into his mouth, and Ty moved.

So much about sex, real sex, was different than in stories. The wet sound of their bodies slapping, the rub of marble on her ass, the way her hands slipped on Ty's sweat-slick skin and made it hard to keep hold of him. How her body would ache in strange places after this coupling. But there were other things mere words had never been able to replace. The smell of him mingled with the tang of their sex. The thick softness of the hair on his head, the matching crinkly crispness of his chest hair and the thatch between his legs. The way her body bloomed under his touch, easing his way so when he moved inside her each stroke of cock in cunt sparked a thousand electric impulses all over her. The heat of his breath on her face as he kissed her.

The sound of his voice, murmuring her name.

Edie slid a hand between them to touch herself, and Ty let out a low grunt of desire. She wasn't sure she could come again, but he loved it when she tried. Her clit, still sensitive from before, came to life under her touch and she had to do little more than let Ty's thrusts rock her body against her hand.

"So close." Ty bit his lower lip, eyes closing briefly.

Edie leaned up to lick the sweat from his upper lip. Her fingers dug into his shoulder. Every thrust rocked her harder on the countertop. When she leaned back to give Ty a deeper angle, he shuddered. He was close, she could tell, and that more than anything else tipped her closer to another climax. He thrust harder and faster.

Then Edie was slip-sliding into another burst of pleasure. Ty echoed her cry, his voice gone hoarse. He moved inside her once more and slowed. His arms, propping them both, trembled, and when she slid her feet over the backs of his thighs she felt his muscles leaping there, too.

"Not like it is in the movies," he said, head bent, then lifted his laughing face to hers.

"Oh, it's better than in the movies," Edie told him. "In the movies they have to do it twenty times just to get it right."

Ty kissed her slowly, holding her close. "I wouldn't mind doing it twenty more times."

"*Hmm.* But you got it so right the first time," she teased and squeezed his fine, firm ass.

"Practice does make perfect."

His sweet sentiment was slightly ruined by the rumble of his stomach. Edie pushed him gently away so she could hop off the counter and make her way to the sink, where she grabbed a tea towel she didn't recognize and ran it under the faucet so she could do a hasty cleanup. She turned to see Ty watching her as he leaned against the counter, his arms crossed and a smile tipping his mouth.

"What?"

"Just thinking," he answered. "About how I'm going to get to see this every day for the rest of my life."

"Me, naked at the sink?" She rinsed out the cloth again and wrung it damp, and tossed it to him.

Ty did a neat one-handed catch. "If I can get it. But just you, naked or not, at the sink. In our kitchen. Every day."

Edie stood on tip-toe to kiss him. "Just in the kitchen?"

He pulled her snug against him. "All the rooms."

Edie put her head on Ty's chest, content for the moment to stand in his warm embrace. "That sounds good to me."

His stomach grumbled again, and they both laughed. Edie kissed his chest, then the Celtic knot tattoo on his bicep before she bent to retrieve her clothes. She stepped into her panties and pulled on Ty's T-shirt without bothering with the bra. Ty pulled on his jeans, and shirtless, went to the fridge.

"Hungry?" He pulled out a tray laden with cheese, sliced fruit, and chocolate and set it on the kitchen's center island. He disappeared inside the fridge again and returned with a handful of plastic-wrapped potatoes for the microwave and a platter of thick steaks so juicy her mouth watered just looking at them. "These will only take a few minutes on the grill."

"We have a grill?" Edie clapped her hands. "In February?"

"We have a grill," he confirmed with a grin. "On the deck. And I will gladly brave the weather to cook these steaks."

"My hero." She kissed him again, giddy with being here, with him.

* * *

Ham and the moving truck wouldn't arrive for a few days, but Ty had found a local superstore and stocked the kitchen with paper plates, plastic ware, and napkins. He'd even bought a plaid blanket, which Edie set out on the family room floor for their picnic.

It wasn't the first meal they'd shared, but it was the first in their new house and it deserved attention. Ty lit some candles and brought out the bouquet of roses he'd hidden inside a cupboard. The balloons were now sneaking into the rest of the house.

"I left my present for you in the car," Edie said when he handed her the small gift bag. "Darn it, Ty. This is too much."

"It's not too much," he told her. "You can give me your present later. Open it."

He held his breath as she pulled out the small velvet box. He'd bought her a ring months ago, but these earrings had had Edie's name all over them. He'd spied them in the window of the small antique shop he'd passed on the way to the superstore. Small oval emeralds set in gold with a pair of wee diamonds at the top and bottom, they should have been too small to have caught his eye from a moving car, but when he'd slowed to stop at the light and turned his head, there they'd been, glinting.

He loved how she bit her lower lip when she was trying not to grin and give away her excitement. When she lifted the box's lid, her bit-back grin faded. Ty sat up, concerned.

"You don't like them?" To his surprise, tears glittered in her eyes and he reached for her automatically. "Babe?"

She waved a hand and shook her head, but let him gather her into his arms. She nestled her face against his chest. Her shoulders shook. Ty stroked her hair in silence. He didn't know much, but he knew the best move a man with an armful of weeping woman could make was to keep quiet.

"They're beautiful. All of this is incredible," she said. "Perfect."

"It's Valentine's Day. I had to do something special."

"If I'd known you were going to be here, I'd have done something special, too." Edie said, and looked up at him with wet eyes, but with the smile back on her face.

"You can make it up to me."

"Oh, really?" She leaned to kiss him, and her lips tasted of salt. "However shall I do that?"

"Do the dishes."

Laughing, Edie punched his chest lightly then gathered up the paper plates and put them in a pile. "Done. You're easy to please."

Ty snagged her wrist and pulled her closer, leaning back to pull her along with him. When she'd settled on top of him, he pushed her hair off her face and looked into her eyes. "Let's go to bed."

Since he had a king-sized bed and she'd only had a double in her small apartment, they'd agreed to use his. It was on the moving truck along with everything else. He had, however, found more than earrings at the antique store.

"I thought we'd have to camp out here. I sent a sleeping bag and inflatable mattress in one of these boxes." She waved at the stacks and piles in the den.

Ty linked his fingers through hers and shook his head. "You don't want to sleep on the floor our first night in the new house, do you?"

She narrowed her eyes, studying him. "Ty? What did you do?"

He grinned but would say nothing, only tugged her to her feet and led her up the stairs. Their fingers still linked, he took her to the room at the end of the hall and nudged open the door. Then he stood back and did as his mama had always said he should. He let Edie go first.

She let out a low, breathless gasp and whirled. "Ty!"

He had no question about if she liked his present this time. He'd known she would the moment he saw the matching twin beds in the back of the shop. Curved blond wood with an inlaid pattern, they matched Edie's Art Deco waterfall-design armoire and dresser almost perfectly. And, pushed together and attached with a couple handy bolts and screws, they were just the right size to hold a king-sized mattress and box spring.

Edie touched the curved footboard. "How? I've been looking forever for a matching bed frame. They didn't make them king-sized back then."

He explained, even bending to show her the places he'd attached the frames. Edie sat on the bed and pulled him down with her, catching his chin to bring his face to hers. Ty stopped his description of the size of the bolts he'd used in mid-syllable.

"You are the most amazing man." Edie smoothed her fingertips over the simple white flannel sheets he'd bought.

"Anyone could have put them together," he said.

Edie shook her head. "But not everyone would."

He still almost couldn't believe she was really there with him, after all the months stealing moments on the phone or online. Her mouth tasted real. Her skin, soft beneath his fingertips, felt real. Her hair, when it brushed the back of his hand, was real too.

She put her arms around his neck, drawing him down onto the soft, clean sheets. His body settled naturally into the space she made for him between her legs. Her shirt had ridden up, so her bare knees nudged his hips above his jeans, and Ty wished neither of them had bothered getting even partly dressed.

She pushed his shoulder to roll him over and ended up on top, her hands flat on his chest. Her fingers curled in his chest hair and she leaned forward to brush her lips on his. Before he could capture her mouth, she'd moved down, over his neck and to his chest. When she slid her tongue over his nipple, Ty tensed.

Edie looked up at him with a wicked grin. "*Mmmm.* Did we miss dessert?"

"I sort of thought you had a box of candy for me in the car."

She gave his nipple another experimental lick, and his cock started to fill. "Would you like me to go get your present now? Or can you wait a bit longer?"

She bared her teeth and took his flesh between them as Ty drew in a hissing breath. His prick thickened in his jeans and Edie smiled at him again as her hand wandered down to give him a squeeze through the denim. In the next moment, she'd unzipped him and moved her body down the length of his.

"No waiting," Ty managed to say just as she reached in to take his cock in her hand.

"I didn't think so." Edie stroked him, then urged him to lift his hips so she could push down his jeans. She made a happy noise low in her throat when she was able to free him.

Ty made a happy noise of his own when she took him in her mouth. She sucked the head of his cock gently for a minute, then left him to pull his jeans off the rest of the way. The T-shirt went over her head next, tossed to the floor, and Ty groaned at the sight of her gorgeous breasts. Edie licked her mouth, her gaze fixed on his, then she took his prick in her hand and stroked upward, slowly.

With her other hand she toyed with her nipples, pinching and stroking. Her tongue crept out again to swipe along her lips as she looked down at his cock in her curled fingers. She licked her fingertips and painted her nipples with wetness, then did the same to the head of his cock. She bent her head to blow hot breath along the wetness, and his hips thrust upward toward her waiting mouth.

Edie gripped him at the base and shook her head. "Not so fast."

Her tongue came out to taste him, flicking the rim of his cock-head, and Ty bit back a groan but stayed still. Edie, still wearing her panties, straddled his leg. The heat of her cunt pressed his calf as she rubbed herself along him and slid her mouth once more down the length of his erection.

Ty closed his eyes for a moment as pleasure swept over him but had to open them in a second. He wanted to watch her. He loved to watch her, and Edie knew it.

Down, down, the wet heat of her mouth engulfed him. Up and up, her hand following as her pussy moved against his leg, driving him crazy with the urge to reach for her and give her the same pleasure she was giving him. Yet when he shifted, reaching, Edie shook her head again and gave him a mock glare.

"No," she said firmly. "Lie still."

"But I want to touch you—"

"Ty," Edie said, and licked his cock the way she would a lollipop. "I want to do this without being distracted."

He fell back on the mound of new pillows with a groan. In her hand his prick leaped as she stroked a fingertip down the seam of his balls. When her light touch brushed his anus, Ty clutched a double fistful of sheets. His back arched, hips thrusting up, and this time Edie didn't tease him. She took him in again, all the way, and then slid up, sucking gently as her finger pressed lightly.

He wanted to feel her, bare on his leg, as she rocked against him. Instead, all he got was the whisper of the soft cotton along his skin. Watching as Edie's mouth released him, as her tongue circled his prick and flicked the divot just under the head, Ty imagined how soft, how wet she was. How good she would feel around him when he pushed inside her. Her mouth, her hand. Her cunt. He wanted to sink inside this woman and bury himself.

They'd made love only a few hours before, and he was ready for her again. Nobody had ever affected him the way Edie did. Nobody, he was sure, ever would.

She glanced at him from the corner of her eye, then slid her hand into her panties and drew out her fingers, glistening with her arousal. She ran them along his shaft and down over his balls. Then again, dipping her hand into her slickness and covering him with sweetness he wanted to taste.

Touching and kissing Edie always got Ty hard, but knowing doing the same to him got her wet turned his cock into a steel shaft. Her fingers, still slick with her sweetness, feathered over his prick and down, circling just long enough on his perineum to tighten his balls. Now his cock shone with her wetness and he breathed in the heady, sweet scent of her sex.

Edie, stroking his cock, shifted to ease her panties off. When she switched hands, Ty gasped and thrust upward into the new angle made by her other hand. Edie smiled and slowed her stroke, teasing him.

"You're so hard for me," she murmured. "I love that."

Ty couldn't manage to corral the words tumbling around in his brain and force them out of his mouth, but Edie didn't seem to mind. She kissed his lips as she straddled him, her hand still gripping him firmly. She lowered herself over his cock, the head nudging at her opening. She didn't let go, didn't let him push inside her the way he wanted.

"Slow," she whispered in his ear and grazed the lobe with her teeth.

Though his muscles clenched and shook with the effort of holding back, Ty didn't push again. His hands gripped her hips, but he waited. Edie used her hand to slide him back and forth along her slick heat. She opened for him, easing the head of his cock an inch inside her, then pulling away. Then another inch deeper and out again.

The twist of her hips urged a groan from him. Her breath puffed in small pants, hot on the side of his face. Her tight nipples brushed his chest, and Ty couldn't hold back from running his hands up to pinch and rub them.

Edie shook at his touch and sank onto him the whole way. Her sweet ass, so perfectly round, settled onto his thighs. She engulfed him. Her knees clutched his sides as she pushed up, her nails scoring faint lines down his chest and belly.

They moved at the same time, her body lifting and coming back down as he thrust deep inside. *Ah,* fuck, it was heaven, it was glory, it was too much.

He could never get enough of her smile, her laugh, her scent. Her heat. He filled his grasp with her breasts, tweaking her nipples, and she cried out and arched into his touch.

He was close, but she needed more. Ty's fingers crept between them. His thumb settled on the hard button of her clit. Edie's immediate cry of satisfaction sent ecstasy rippling through his balls and up his shaft. He wanted her to come first.

Edie had never been shy with telling him what she liked or wanted, and Ty had never been afraid of listening. Now, though, Edie gave him no encouragement but the rolling of her hips and her clit getting harder under his touch. When she came, he felt it in the pulse of clit and flutter of her pussy. He heard it in her low shout and watched it on her face as her head tipped back. Later, maybe pain, but now only sweet pleasure shot through him as her fingernails dug into his skin. He shifted his hand, taking away the direct pressure that would be too much for her right now.

Edie leaned forward to kiss him. Their mouths met, tongues stroking, and she pulled away, breathing hard. She looked into his eyes, and Ty's whole world became this woman.

"Slow," she murmured again, and Ty let out a muffled laugh.

"I can't hold out much longer, babe."

"You can." Edie traced his mouth with her tongue but pulled away when he moved forward to catch her mouth. "Let me do it."

It was too hard not to move when she did. Desire blinded him to anything but her pussy bearing down on his cock. It deafened him to anything but the sweet sound of her saying his name, telling him how good he was making her feel. Ty's entire world had become Edie.

She moved on him, slowly, as she'd promised, lifting her body and twisting her hips as she slid back down his length. Again she did the same agonizing motion. Her inner muscles clenched on the downward stroke. He imagined the head of his cock sliding over the tight knot of nerves just behind her pubic bone, and when Edie groaned, rocking and twisting a little faster, he knew that's exactly what she was doing.

She shook her head when he made to move his hand between them again. Her eyes opened, pupils dilated, and she drew in a quivering breath.

"Slow," she repeated.

Up. Down. Twist. Ty lost himself in the inferno of her body. His cock throbbed with each slow thrust, and he tasted sweat on his upper lip. When Edie rocked forward again, he took one sweet nipple into his mouth. Her entire body jerked as he suckled, and she twisted her body on him again.

Now there was no room or need for words. Their bodies spoke. Edie put a hand on his shoulder to brace herself, and Ty held her ass, his fingers slipping around to slide against her from the back.

"Now." Edie's voice skipped on that one syllable. "Oh, God, Ty. Harder!"

Unleashed, he did as she said. He thrust up inside her, moving her entire body as she cried out. Her pussy convulsed and her heat spread over him. She'd been slick before, but now his cock slid inside her on the flood of her orgasm.

Their bodies slapped together. Edie went stiff and shaking, her head falling to his shoulder as her hips pumped to meet each of his thrusts.

Climax boiled up from his balls and tore through him. His cock jetted, each pulse an explosion of ecstasy that left him briefly mindless but for one thought.

"Edie!"

Bright pleasure brightened the back of his eyelids, and when he opened his eyes, she was there. Edie. The woman he loved.

She collapsed on him, breathing hard. Their bodies merged and melted, softening in the aftermath of their ecstasy. Ty held her closer, happy never to move if he didn't have to. Happy never to let her go again.

Good sex could knock a person brainless, but it was still only a few minutes before Edie noticed the goose bumps prickling her. She lifted her head and brushed a kiss on Ty's mouth. He opened his eyes and smiled, and she kissed him again simply because she could.

"I'm cold," she said.

Ty lifted his head and looked to the right. "Blanket."

She followed his gaze and found the folded comforter. Plain

white like the sheets, it was thick but light. Down, maybe. It would be warm, too. She tented it over them, blocking out the light. In moments their breath and body heat had made a warm cave of the space.

The hills and valleys of their bodies aligned, Edie pillowed her head on Ty's chest. His heart thumped beneath her cheek, and she pressed her fingers to the inside of his wrist to feel the pulse. He curved his fingers through hers, holding her hand to his lips before tucking it against him.

"Happy Valentine's Day," he said after his slow, deep breathing had already convinced her he was asleep.

Edie kissed his warm skin and let her lips rest there a moment before she answered. "Best I ever had."

"For now."

Ty's arm tightened around her. Outside, a dog barked. Edie's eyes drifted closed. She should get up and go to the bathroom. She should at least make sure the doors were locked. At the very least, she should turn out the light. Instead, she did nothing, drifting to sleep in the cradle and comfort of Ty's arms.

She'd taken a plane and a rented car. Ty had driven for days to surprise her. They'd spent the past two years dreaming of the ways they would find to reach each other, and now they no longer had to dream about how to get there.

They were here.

MEGAN HART has been writing since she could grip a pencil in her fist. Published in nearly all genres of romance, perhaps most notably erotic, she intends to keep writing stories that make her happy. She lives in the deep, dark woods of Pennsylvania with Superman and two monsters . . . *erm* . . . children. Readers may learn more about her at www.meganhart.com or drop her a line at readinbed@gmail.com.

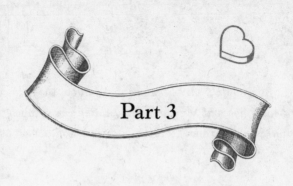

Part 3

Hell Is Where the Heart Is

by

Jackie Kessler

This story wouldn't have been possible without the following people: May Chen and Miriam Kriss—thank you so much for the opportunity to write about a little (okay, a lot of) demon nooky.

Tom Knapp—
thank you so much for the awesome barometric pressure line.

Caitlin Kittredge and Richelle Mead—
thank you for keeping me sane and spurring me on.

Renée Barr—
thank you, once again,
for reading every single version of the first chapter.

Heather Brewer—
thank you for helping me figure many things out
way before (and when) the deadline loomed.

And most of all, Brett—
thank you, thank you, thank you for running all those errands
with the kids and leaving me alone to finish the story.

You guys are the best!

NOW:
VALENTINE'S DAY

♡ *Chapter 1*

Daunuan

I smelled her before I saw her—this immediate, irresistible scent of cinnamon and sex that hit me like a witch's curse. Closing my eyes, I inhaled deeply, drew her aroma inside of me and savored her.

Jezebel was nearby.

A memory flashed: my face buried between Jezebel's strong thighs, my lips on hers, my hands squeezing her ass as my tongue worked her clit. I remembered how her hands fisted in my hair, how her hips bucked as I sucked her, how I teased her to the point of ecstasy. . . .

The woman under me moaned her pleasure, loud enough to pull me from my reverie.

Whoops. Focus, Daun.

I crooked my fingers again, just so, and she gasped. She tightened around me, and I could have nudged her over the edge right there—she was so close. Instead, I slipped my fingers out of her, smiled at her breathy protest.

I'm nothing if not an evil bastard.

Besides, if I finished her too soon, there was the slight possibility that I wouldn't leave her craving me, making her almost delirious from the thought of me finally fucking her. I could have happily taken her right now, pounded her until she screamed my name and I burst inside of her. But that wouldn't be tonight. No, tonight it was all about her pleasure. Her desire.

After all, clients always come first.

Look at her, sprawled on the bed beneath me, here in this tiny room in a tiny apartment. See her chestnut hair on the pillow, her tresses dark against the white cotton. Drink in the soft curves of her flesh. Feel how all she wants is for me to bring her to rapture.

My lips pulled into a hungry smile. But damn, I do so love my job.

She cooed as she watched me suck her juices from my fingers. Her flavor filled me—tangy, delicious.

Just not my Jezebel.

Licking the last of her from my fingers, I said, "Think I can make you explode in my mouth?"

Her eyes lit, the promise of passion making them sparkle. "*Ooh*. God, yes . . ."

My smile slipped before I froze it into place. Fuck me; why did they *always* have to mention Him? It's such a blessed buzz-kill. . . .

"You make me feel so good," she babbled, "make me come so hard. No one's ever made me feel like you do."

Aw. Flattery. That perked me up again. "You think you feel good now, doll? Wait until you feel my tongue on you."

She shivered from anticipation, murmured her *ooh*s and *ahhh*s.

It should have made my balls throb to see her spread out naked before me. Her entire body was an offering, so very flushed with need, her lust all but dancing over her limbs. And nestled within her fragile human shell, her soul silently beckoned me, taunted me. Between how her body was responding to my attention and how the evil within her soul was responding to my presence, it should have been impossible for me to think of any other woman at the moment.

But instead of imagining how I was about to make her squirm and squeal, how she would be sticky sweet in my mouth—how her soul would taste on my tongue—I kept picturing Jezebel. Smelling her.

Wanting her.

Even after almost twenty years, I still wanted her like a submissive wants to be dominated.

Soon, I told myself. First the client. Then go find Jezebel.

My smile stretched into a wicked grin, and I dove down.

Jezebel

Normally, I don't have to worry about my clients dying on me before I finish the job. After four thousand years, my timing's down pat. Sex, like dancing, is about the timing. And passion, of course. Without passion, it's all just going through the motions. (Okay, granted, enjoyable motions. I'm certainly not complaining.)

This client was different. Too huge to settle for massive, he was a wall of flesh, with mere suggestions of musculature beneath all the fat. Me, I have no objection to obesity. People are a turn-on, no matter how they're shaped—big, small, short, tall,

flabby, trim, hang-nailed, well hung, you name it. Their bodies
are unique art forms, and I appreciate them all for what they are:
human and inherently beautiful. But my current client was a
heart attack waiting to happen. And if he died before I killed him,
I'd never hear the end of it.

I'd also be tortured, but that's just a given. When you live
forever, never hearing the end of your failures really sucks angel
feathers.

"I don't know about this," my client said as I closed the door
behind us. "Maybe it's not a good idea."

"*Aw,* don't be like that." Smiling, I reached out to touch his
shoulder, and with that contact I pushed a smidge of my power
through him. Just a hint of lust—enough to turn the "maybe not"
into "do me now." No, it's not cheating; it's part of the job.

But even if it *were* cheating, I wouldn't lose any sleep over it.
I'm not exactly a saint. Neither was my client—after all, there was
a reason why he was next on my Bag Him/Tag Him list. Good
people are strictly off limits in my line of work. But people like
him, who spent their lives lying about others, with no other purpose than to cause pain? They're cruel. Heartless. Evil. In other
words, perfect.

My client let out an adorable gasp as his body shuddered
with desire. Bless me, I love the noises that humans make. Their
sounds, their smells, the way they taste . . . *ah,* bliss!

Pitching my voice to warmth-inducing levels, I said, "We'll
have fun. You'll see."

"Fun," he breathed. "Okay. Fun."

Beneath my hand, his shirt was damp. He'd sweated through
most of the material, so now dark patches plastered the light blue
button-up to his body. I was making him nervous. No, more than
nervous: I saw the unease in his eyes, understood his building dread

that maybe I was leading him on. That maybe I'd laugh at him. Over his sweat and his liberal use of Old Spice, he reeked of fear.

Yum.

Inhaling his personal terror, I brightened the wattage of my smile. "If you want, you can undress me." Putting a purr into my voice, I added, "I don't remember if I'm wearing a bra. Care to find out?"

"I . . . I . . ." Perspiration beaded on his forehead. "I don't know. . . ."

"Not a trick question." I winked and stepped forward, which made him take a shuffling step backward. The office was cramped—between the desk, the bookshelves, and the filing cabinet, there was barely room for the two of us. Not a problem. I've seduced men (and women) in smaller spaces than this closet-sized room. I liked being creative, and part of my job was to be flexible. And double-jointed.

His ass hit the desk, and he let out a startled squeak.

Slow it down, Jezebel. Don't scare him to death.

"I—"

"*Shhh.*" I brushed my fingers over his shoulder, up to his chins, lingered behind his ear. "No need to be so nervous. I promise I'll make you feel good."

"I'm not nervous," he lied. "It's just—what if a customer comes in?"

"It's past closing time. Store's locked tight."

"I don't know if I remembered to lock the front door. . . ."

"I'm sure you did." I found a sensitive spot on the nape of his neck and stroked him there. He shuddered, leaning into my touch.

Yes. That's right, sweetie. Go with the feeling. It's okay to let yourself enjoy it.

Almost as if he were shocked by my thoughts, his eyes popped open and he pulled away. "But it's Valentine's Day."

"So?"

"They'll be banging on the door, begging for just two minutes to get a card."

Banging and begging? Sounds like my kind of place. And there's a lot I can do in two minutes.

Tracing the folds of his skin, I said, "So they want to . . . take advantage of you?"

"They do." Something ugly passed over his face, and he pulled his lip into a sneer.

Obviously, my client was not a people person. Dancing my fingers along his collar, I asked, "What do they do?"

"I'm already keeping the store open later than the Hallmark across the street. But can people bother getting here during business hours?" He snorted. "Hell, no!"

"Poor guy."

"And they're rude! Make me work late, and they yell at me when they can't find what they want, as if I told them to wait until close of business before shopping for a freaking holiday card!"

He was getting all worked up, and not in the way that I preferred.

I leaned against him, making sure my double-Ds pressed into his chest. My client was a boob man, so I'd accommodated the fantasy when I'd dressed for the occasion: specifically, I'd magicked up a luscious body with supersized tits. (Human women needed bras or silicone to have their breasts defy gravity. I, however, didn't have to worry about things like natural laws. Or lower back pain.) A low-cut, tight black shirt called even more attention to my Dolly Partons. A black patent belt cinched around my tiny waist, emphasizing my hourglass figure. And my ability not to breathe. Vampira, eat your heart out.

"And then they never leave," my client said. He was babbling now, even as my hands explored his chest. "It's always like this on Valentine's Day. Always, always."

"Sweetie . . ."

"And all the chocolate! And hearts! And those stupid kissing bears! I hate this holiday, hate it!"

"It'll be over soon," I promised.

"Valentine's Day." He closed his eyes again and shuddered— and not from how I was rubbing my chest against his. "It's just a candy-coated hell."

"So angry," I murmured, feeling my body respond to his fury. Wrath wasn't nearly as much fun as lust, but human ire was still enough to make my nipples ache with need, enough to heat my blood. I grabbed him by the back of his head, yanked his face to mine. He squawked his surprise, but then I sealed my lips against his and kissed him hard, and his protest turned into a moan as I tasted the rage on his tongue.

Mmm.

I felt him melt and go with the kiss for a moment, then he stiffened against me. He pulled away from my mouth, but not my embrace. Pressed against his body, I felt his heartbeat dancing in either anticipation or panic.

He whispered, "Why're you doing this?"

"It's called kissing," I said, kissing his sweaty cheek. Salty. Sinful. Scrumptious. "It's part of the sex."

"But why me? Girl like you could get any guy she wants."

"Told you before, when I saw you behind the counter." I nibbled on his earlobe, grinned as I felt him squirm against me. In his ear I whispered, "I like 'em husky." I put extra breath into the last word, let him know with my voice just how much I liked him. He was slated for Hell; he was my current client. What's not to like?

"But I'm . . ."

"Big. Powerful," I said, reaching down to touch his crotch. "Huge."

He let out a squeak.

"*Mmm.* Enormous," I crooned, stroking him.

He started to pant, and his sweat glands kicked into overtime. Eyes glazed, he said something close to "*ahhg.*"

My fingers slowly worked their magic—strictly from experience, no infernal power needed—and his shaft swelled in response. My, my. Big Boy here was clearly a big boy where it mattered most. Excellent. I increased the pressure, but kept the movement slow, languorous. *Cock tease,* thy name is Jezebel.

"*Ahhg . . .*"

I mused aloud, "I wonder if my mouth is big enough to take you all the way inside . . ."

"*Ahhg.*"

"I agree. Let's find out." I yanked the snap of his jeans, pulled down his zipper.

And that's when a man's voice called out, "Hello? Anyone here?"

Crap.

Daunuan

One of the rules of Seduction is you always leave your clients begging for more. Unless you're killing them, that is. (Then you just leave them begging.)

Leaning down over the bed, I kissed my current paramour on her breast, a small press of my lips to the heavy underswell of her flesh. She murmured something nonsensical and then sighed, a smile lingering on her mouth as she rolled over.

Smiling in return, I watched her settle deeper into sleep. She was a beautiful thing—soft where it mattered, and smooth, and altogether sexy. Mortals wouldn't see the greed marring her soul, staining her nicotine-yellow and condemning her to the Abyss. She was an entrepreneur of sorts: a white-collar criminal who had a knack for creating fake identities and collecting their salaries. Her file said that she'd amassed enough embezzled money over the years to either retire in style or buy herself a private island.

Shame she wouldn't be doing either. She'd be too busy dying with my name on her lips and her scream in my ears. I could hear it now: the terror in her voice, the lust in her eyes giving way to fear. . . .

Mmm. Shivers.

But that would be in two more weeks, according to the schedule. Until then, it was all about pleasuring her to insensibility. Fine by me. The way I look at it, a lifetime of sin deserves *some* reward.

Besides, if I had to fuck her to death now, I'd have to drag her soul Below as soon as I was done. And Hell knew, the last thing I wanted to do was wait on line to get admittance into the Abyss. Because after that, I'd have to escort my client to the Heartlands of Lust, where I'd watch her be judged for her mortal crimes. And *then* I'd have to wait on an even longer line to file the soul claim. Infernal red tape truly sucked bishop balls. I wasn't in the mood to wait for weeks before my paperwork was processed.

I smiled as I traced the planes of my sleeping client's face. What I *was* in the mood for was about two blocks away, based on the strength of our psychic Seducer connection. All creatures of Lust shared the bond. Unless we were distracted—say, entertaining a client—we could sense another of our ilk roughly within a thousand paces. Useful trait when we were looking for a quick fix between assignments.

And in my case, even when I was otherwise occupied, I still sensed Jezebel. It's been that way for me since . . . well, since the beginning. (No, not *that* Beginning.)

I gently brushed a lock of hair away from my client's brow. Her profile was a vision to behold; her steady breathing was hypnotic to watch as her breasts bobbed up with her inhale, then slowly back down as she exhaled. She was attractive, certainly; desirable, without a doubt.

But she just wasn't the one I wanted.

Well then, time to go find my favorite succubus. Maybe I could catch her before she finished her client and had to mosey on Downstairs. If I timed it right, she could do her job *and* we could have some fun before she had to get her affairs in order.

As I rose from the bed, one of the framed posters on the wall caught my eye. My current client was either a movie buff or a Matt Damon worshiper, based on all the ads and stills littering the walls. *Ocean's Eleven, Good Will Hunting, The Talented Mr. Ripley* . . . numerous others. But *Dogma* stood out in particular. Maybe it was the pseudo wings the actor sported, or maybe it was just the tagline. "Get 'touched' by an angel," indeed. *Hah.* As if angels knew how to give good touch. They were so fucking frigid they made nuns look like streetwalkers.

Matt Damon, *huh?* Well . . . why the Hell not? Jezzie loved to play dress up. So did I, although I much preferred to play doctor.

I let my power wash over me, transform me from a skinny artistic type—my client's preferred male—to something that would have gone well on her wall: shorter side of tall, short sandy hair, hazel eyes that hinted at blue. Cleft chin. Trim body, with the muscles well defined. Black-on-black clothing, from trench coat to boots. Cute dimple. Killer smile.

Boom: *Bourne Identity*, infernal style.

Before I left, I magicked up a piece of paper and wrote my client a love note, telling her I'd see her in two weeks. A little something for her to hold onto over the next fourteen days, and a promise of things to come. I didn't sign it. She knew who it was from; besides, only stupid demons actually sign their names on anything. (All it takes is one time for a wannabe mage to come across your name. Next thing you know, you find yourself in the middle of a protected circle, and some asshole in a dress is demanding that you make him immortal, or some shit like that. Which would be amusing as Hell, except (a) sometimes the mortals actually have a limited magical ability, which is annoying, and (b) magicians tend to repeat on me.)

Folding the note, I released it with a flick of my fingers. The paper landed on my client's pillow, the corner close to her rosebud mouth. She kept sleeping, dreaming the dreams of the sexually sated.

See you, doll.

Thinking of Jezebel, I headed to the door.

Jezebel

Even as my hands started working on Big Boy's big boy, I turned my head and listened. Yep, sure enough, there was a person walking around in the main store. Looked like my client was right: he hadn't locked up. Terrific.

"AHHG!" This in a strangled whisper. How humans can shout when they whisper is their own sort of mortal magic.

Turning back to my client, I arched a brow as I took in his purpling face, the sheen of perspiration flowing on his forehead and cheeks. "Oh, relax. Well, no, don't *relax*," I said, giving him a squeeze where it counted. "Don't worry."

"Ahhg?"

I stroked his cock slowly, a counterpoint to his building terror. "It doesn't really matter, now, does it? A little exhibitionism never hurt anyone."

"AHHG!!!"

From outside the office door: "Hello? Is someone in the back room? Can you ring me up, please?"

Big Boy groaned and screwed his eyes shut.

I heard the erratic thump of his heart, smelled the sour odor of his sweat mixed with the heady scent of his terror. *Yum.* Even with the annoying person outside, I would have blissfully given my client a blow job before getting to the bump and grind, but it was clear that his sheer panic was affecting his ability to enjoy our encounter. Proof of that was softening in my hand.

The infernal Seducer's creed: The client comes first. Always.

"No worries, sweetie," I said, patting his dick. "I'll go out there and tell the mean old customer that we're closed. Would you like me to do that?"

"Aggh," he wheezed.

"Okeydokey." I kissed him on the lips, just a quick peck to let him know that we weren't done yet. "When I return, I'll make you feel so good that you'll scream my name, and you won't give a shit who hears."

He smiled weakly, then dropped his head as he clutched the edge of his desk for support.

"Back soon." With that, I left the office.

The customer—a guy in an off-the-rack suit and ill-fitting wool coat—was all but dancing with impatience as he gripped a card in one hand and a small red box with the other. He spotted me as soon as I sauntered into the main room of the store. "About time," he said, clearly exasperated. "Thought no one was going to help me."

"Store's closed, sweetie," I said, walking up to him. I smiled to let him know that if it were up to me, I'd happily fuck him for his inconvenience. "I'm afraid you'll have to come back tomorrow."

His face crumpled. It was the cutest thing to watch. "But it's Valentine's Day."

"So I hear."

"You can't kick me out."

"Not my rules."

"But she'll *kill* me if I don't give her a card!"

Ooh. "Really? Would she stab you, do you think? Or would she be more subtle about it, maybe poison you over a few weeks?" Murder in a fit of passion would be one for Lust. But a slow, calculated death would probably go to Wrath. Maybe I could get a twofer . . .

His eyes swam in misery. "Please," he said, his voice breaking. "*Please.*"

Something in my chest tugged, and I blew out a sigh. "Fine. Just this once, though."

"Thank you! Oh God, thank you so much!"

Heh. "I'm not Him, sweetie. Come on, let's take care of you. I've got business to attend to."

He was already at the counter, turning his card just so. Okay, so I had to let him pay for the items. I had no idea how the cash machine worked, and I also didn't care. As I took the card and the small box with the big piece of chocolate, my fingers brushed his. I pushed my power into him, and he gasped, closed his eyes.

I watched the bliss work its way onto his face. Hey, no one should be so frantic on a day meant for love and lust. Smiling at his reaction—and hello, his erection—I tucked his items into a paper bag from beneath the counter.

"You're all set, sweetie."

His eyes popped open. "What? Oh . . . thanks," he said, blinking. He looked confused, and somewhat caught in the afterglow. A dazed smile on his face, he took the bag and floated to the door.

I brushed my hands together and nodded. Now, back to—

"You're open! Oh, thank God!"

This from the skinny woman who just marched through the door . . . along with two other people.

"Hey," I said, scowling. "We're closed."

"I saw you just ring up that guy," the woman said, "I'll just be a second . . ."

"Miss? Is this on sale?"

"Excuse me, do you have any of those huge Hershey's kisses?"

"Miss? Did you hear me?"

"Oh, look," the first woman said, "this mug is perfect, but there's no box. Is there a discount for a display item?"

"Hey! Are you deaf? I want to know if this is on sale!"

I closed my eyes as I debated whether I could get biblical and do a little pre-holiday smiting. Or maybe just hit them all with my magic, make them all drop to the floor in a puddle of ecstasy.

But slaughtering humans without the proper paperwork meant I'd be up to my chin in Wrongful Termination forms. Ditto for unleashing too much infernal power on mortals who weren't scheduled clients; one or two people could be explained as collateral damage, but more than that meant forms out the wazoo. Bad enough I'd missed most of the 1990s and the turn of the current millennium, thanks to a little demonic misunderstanding. I didn't want to spend the next ten or so years in another administrative nightmare.

In the time that it had taken me to come to the conclusion that I couldn't just bedazzle everyone (let alone kill them), five more people had scampered into the store, visions of candy hearts dancing in their eyes.

Fuck this.

"You all have two minutes," I growled. "Then I lock the door and shut the lights, whether or not you're still inside. Ready? Scurry!"

They scurried.

Daunuan

I slipped into the greeting-card store just as Jezebel finished threatening the customers with imprisonment. Me, I would have threatened dismemberment. Then again, she always did have a better understanding of how humans thought and felt outside of the bedroom than I did.

Pit and Paradise, look at her standing there behind the counter, frustration blotching her cheeks, rage simmering in her eyes. Her lips, painted a wet fuck-me red, were pressed together in an angry line, and her arms were crossed beneath her ample—my, my, *very* ample—bosom. I couldn't see her foot from here, but knowing my little succubus, it was tapping erratically. (Jezzie was about as patient as a cat in heat. And about as loud, with the right encouragement.)

Whatever form she wore across the ages, whether swimsuit-model gorgeous or next-door quiet beauty, she was always immediately recognizable to me. Perk of our Sin's psychic bond. She'd know me for who I was as well; if she were a second-level Seducer, like me, she would have sensed me before now.

Hmm, maybe not: she was rather distracted at the moment, too busy huffing at the customers and intimidating them in her adorable way. I could have announced myself to her, but for now I preferred to watch her. To bask in her.

Oh, Jezzie. Look at you.

The very sight of her was enough to make me hard. But more than just seeing her, I *sensed* her—this seductive presence, a maddening scent of cinnamon and sex . . . a sound, low and lush, that I heard in my mind and felt in my groin: her voice, her breath, the memory of her laughter.

Her. Jezebel.

Grrrrowl.

It took all of my control not to leap over the counter and slam her against the wall and thrust into her right there. My hands clenched as I watched her carelessly brush a tendril of black hair away from her eyes. I wanted my cock inside of her, surrounded by her, filling her. *Now.*

But creatures of Hell have rules—ten of them, to be precise—and one was to keep mortals unaware of our true natures if we weren't taking them to the Abyss for judgment. And my true nature was to fuck everything in sight.

In other words, now was not the time to think with the wrong head. So . . . control. Deep breath, Daun. (This was a mortal trick, and it usually worked. The infernal don't need to breathe, but the act of breathing was somewhat relaxing. Rather like meditation, or eating a yoga instructor.)

Besides, I'd gone for almost twenty years without her, all because she'd screwed up an assignment back around 1990. I could wait a few more minutes.

Exhaling slowly, I grinned, allowing my fangs to slip through my false human teeth for just a moment. Soon I'd be inside of her. Soon she'd be writhing on top of me, her claws sinking into me, digging into me with my every thrust.

Soon.

As Jezebel glowered at the various customers scuttling around the store, I quietly scanned them. A few of the humans looked like candidates for future collections, but none of them were clearly marked as Jezzie's current client. Given how she was trying to kick everyone out, that meant her squeeze toy was somewhere else. Another customer, perhaps, tucked out of sight behind the counter?

No. She wouldn't have taken someone here in the store if they were just passing through—so that meant the person was a store employee. Jezebel liked to pounce on a person's home turf. Made them more comfortable, she said. Just thinking about that made me roll my eyes. Like I gave two shits about where I screwed someone's brains out.

I let out a quiet laugh, shaking my head. Women. Whether mortal or infernal, they always focused too much on the atmosphere. On setting the mood. The only mood music I needed was my client's heavy breathing.

Stuffing my hands into my coat pockets, I strolled around the store, throwing looks at people's chests to see if they sported name tags (and just admiring the view if they didn't). Heeeeere, person, person, person. Where are you hiding? Did Jezzie get you too worked up to come work?

As I walked up and down the aisles, I took in all of the sickeningly sweet terms of endearment emblazoned on the thousands of cards and toys and candy. Leave it to humans to turn messages of the heart into a commercial opportunity. Rather insidious. I had to admire that.

"One minute," Jezebel snarled to the store at large.

At least three people groaned. One woman whimpered as she pawed through a stack of cards. A man, clutching a stuffed cat in one hand and two embracing bears in the other, looked like he was either going to vomit or maybe have a bowel movement right there in his pants.

All of this, over which gaudy display of token affection was just right. Humans bemuse the Hell out of me.

"All right, people," Jezebel said, her voice deadly soft. "If you leave before I say it's time, whatever you've got is free of charge. If you can carry it out of here, it's yours. Free. Sixty seconds, starting now."

No one moved.

"Fifty-nine," she singsonged. "Fifty-eight."

The customers bellowed their glee, and then in a human stampede they proceeded to clear the shelves.

Heh.

As I laughed silently at the display of mortal greed, I noticed a sign by the back of the store. "Employees Only." Sounded promising. Ignoring human rules and physics, I ghosted through the back door and followed my nose down a narrow hallway to a tiny office.

And what I saw there, lying in a heap on the floor, made me grin.

"My, my," I said aloud. "Jezzie always was bad at writing her name on her toys. And she's worse about putting them away when she's done playing."

The obese man's mouth opened, closed, opened again, but only a strangled breath emerged. His face was a rather alarming shade of purple. He reeked of sweat and fear, and something else—a more pungent odor, much more toxic. Impossible to ignore.

"And her timing is pretty lousy today," I said. "Wouldn't you agree?"

He whispered something and tried to get up from the floor, but his body didn't seem to work properly. Poor man. Someone should put him out of his misery.

Happy Valentine's Day to me.

I hunkered down on my haunches and flashed my fangs through my grin. "Tell me, Trigger," I said to the terrified man, "what does 'gift horse' mean to you?"

Jezebel

"Five seconds!"

Everyone let out a squawk, like chickens about to meet the business end of a hatchet. As one, they stared at the goods in their hands (and dangling from their arms, and tucked under their armpits, and stuffed into their bags), obviously wrestling with the notion of getting something for nothing. Time froze as they considered the implications. Stealing, after all, is a sin—and deep down, they knew what I was letting them do was wrong.

Then they all bolted out the front door.

After the sounds of the mad rush faded, I took in the damage to the store. And I let out an appreciative whistle. Not bad for two minutes of work. Entire shelves had been cleared of their inventory, and at least two racks were broken. Discarded envelopes and second-rate cards carpeted the floor, their messages of forced cheer and love and happiness trampled into the ground. Amid the candy and knickknacks left behind on the higher shelves, a lone teddy bear sat awkwardly, perched between a sampler box of chocolate clusters and a hideously ugly silk-flower arrangement; the bear's oversized paw seemed to motion to the trail of litter on the ground and that led out the door, as if it were pointing out the avarice that now stained the customers' souls.

Well, maybe that was overstating it a little. I had invited them to take whatever they could, so that canceled out any technical wrongdoing on their part. They weren't thieves, no. But they had all acted out of greed, which nicely planted the seeds for future sins—ones they might commit without any such invitation. Ones that would eventually lead to a very hot seat for a very long time.

Hey, one could always hope. I might not be a creature of Covet, but at least I'm a team player.

I made a beeline to the front door, my mind whirling as I stomped over the debris on the floor. That little delay only cost me about five minutes, start to finish. Not too bad. Big Boy was probably soft as a kitten by now, but that wasn't anything I couldn't fix. Maybe I'd start him with a blow job, let him get hard and huge in my mouth. There's nothing like feeling a man's pride swell from the way you worked your tongue and teeth. Yes, I decided—a little cock sucking, a little teabagging, and then I'd take him for the ride of his life.

Smiling, I slid the master lock into place. There we go. No more unexpected interruptions—

The telltale stink of rotten eggs, just for a moment—enough to make my nostrils flare and to signal that one of my infernal brethren had arrived. Brimstone gave way to a heady musk, heavy with the promise of sweat and sex. And then a man's strong arms wrapped around my waist.

Hey now . . .

Breath on my neck, the hint of a smile as lips pressed against the curve of my throat. "Well, well." The voice was deep, and exceptionally male, and went right between my legs. "Alone at last."

Even as he spoke, I felt his presence slide into my mind, all satin sheets and scented oil. *Been thinking of you, babes.*

My heartbeat quickened, and not just from the way his hands were brushing against my breasts. *Daun?*

In the flesh.

I felt a smile bloom on my face, and my shoulders relaxed even as a different part of me tensed in delicious anticipation. Any incubus worth his horns could make a succubus climax (repeatedly). But Daunuan could make me come with just a look. Over the millennium, I've worked with—in the "working girl" sense— thousands of other Seducers. No one, not demons or gods or any entity in between, made me feel like Daun did. He was a very talented, very attentive creature of Lust. He had a wicked sense of humor, which isn't as commonplace in Hell as you might think. And he was the best lay in all of the Heartlands.

He was also a demon, which meant he was here for a reason. The nefarious aren't known for their social skills.

This is a surprise. I rested my head against his chest, allowed myself a moment to enjoy how his fingers traced my curves. *What're you doing here?*

You.

I chuckled softly. "Cocky bastard."

"Always."

He was playing with my nipples now, rolling the buds slowly, maddeningly, until they nearly burst through my shirt. "How'd you find me?"

"Finished with a client. Felt you nearby." One of his hands moved down the curve of my belly, down more, dangling now by the juncture of my thighs. He brushed against my crotch, a whisper kiss of the pads of his fingers against the gauzy black material of my skirt. Just that hint of a caress, and already a liquid heat stirred in my core; just that unspoken promise, and that was enough to make my body hum with desire. He said, "Wanted to feel you in person."

I sucked in a breath as his strokes grew bolder, teasing me now with lingering touches. "I'm flattered," I said, my voice thick, heavy with lust. I moved beneath him, rolling my hips, angling to coax his fingers to go deeper. Longer. Harder.

"I'm encouraged." I couldn't see Daun's face, but I heard the grin in his voice. He nudged me *just so*, and like that, the simmer between my legs transformed into a raging boil.

Oh unholy Hell, what he does to me . . .

I felt Daun inhale deeply, his body pressed close to mine, and a shock worked its way up my spine as he rumbled his pleasure. "Jezebel," he whispered, rolling my name on his tongue, turning it into something erotic. "You smell good enough to eat."

Eat.

Unbidden, my mind flashed on the image of my client, his flesh overflowing his clothes, his huge shaft softening in my hand.

Oh, fuck me with a fork. My client. My trans-fat-gorging, ticking-time-bomb *client*.

"Babes? You just stiffened. That's *my* job."

"And my job's the problem." I snorted, completely exasperated, and more than a little frustrated. "I'm working."

"I noticed." His hand nuzzled between my thighs, his fingers probing, dancing. My sex pulsed to the rhythm of his fingers. "Every part of you is in fine—"

His magic licked my vulva, and I squealed.

"—*fine*—"

Another lick, slower this time, serpentine, and my squeal melted into a moan.

"—working order."

My breath was coming in hitches. I could have stopped breathing, of course; demons don't need oxygen, not unless we're setting something (or someone) on fire. But cutting off my breathing would have also cut off some of the fantabulously wonderful sensations shooting through my body.

Life is a series of compromises. I kept breathing.

His magic nuzzled deeper, and suddenly my clit was throbbing from his invisible touch. I let out a very undemonic mewl as I sagged against him. He was cheating, the bastard—clients always come first. What he was doing was absolutely breaking the rules.

Sweet Sin, how I've missed him.

"Daunuan," I panted. "Naughty demon. I'm on the clock."

"Take a break."

Bless me, how I wanted to. How I wanted *him*.

My hands reached back and around, cupped the swells of his ass. "Would love to," I said, rubbing against him. The bulge of his erection pressed into the small of my back. "But my client's waiting."

Kisses now, sizzling on my neck, his lips blazing a trail to my ear.

"Checked on him," Daun said, punctuating his words with his tongue. "He'll keep."

Oh, the temptation. If it were any other incubus, I would have sent him away with a slap and a tickle. But this was Daun, and my body was addicted to his like a miser was to money. No matter what forms we wore, we always fit together like a plug in a socket. However else things changed across the millennia, that was a constant. As was our incessant sex drive.

But no matter how much I wanted Daun inside of me, my client was waiting. And being a succubus is all about providing excellent customer service. (Not to mention lip service.)

I sighed. A demon, about to do the right thing. What was the world coming to?

Turning around to face Daun, I did a double take. "Why do you look like Matt Damon?"

His lips—his beautiful full lips—quirked into a bemused smile. "This from Elvira?"

"Hey, it's what my client wanted."

"And the customer is always right." Daun had moved his hands when I'd turned, and now one of his arms was wrapped around me. His other hand was planted over my crotch.

"So I've been told," I said, my voice husky.

Now his fingers were working on me, teasing me, turning me into a puddle of ooze and eroding the little control I had. I felt my knees weaken, and I wondered if I had time for a quickie . . .

No, no, no. Bad succubus. You can screw Daun any time.

Well, any time we happened to find the time together. How long had it been since we'd last had a heat-filled moment to spare for each other? Ten years? Twenty?

"But the clothing doesn't make the woman," he said as he fingered me. "You could've appeared in a hair shirt and ashes, and your client still would have begged you to fuck him."

"You're a sweetie," I said, or tried to say, but the words came out more like "Youhhhhhhhh." Not my fault. Daun got my sweet spot. Daun *always* got my sweet spot.

Panting, I spoke through our psychic Seducer link: *My client's skittish. I've got to get back to him before he bolts. Or expires. Which would be totally unacceptable.*

"He's not going anywhere," Daun said, as insistent as his fingers.

Normally, his tone would have given me pause; Daun was acting much too confident, even for him. But then a knowing smile unfurled on his face, and he stroked me again . . .

Eeeeee!!!

. . . and who really gave a shit about one measly client, anyway?

"Besides," Daun said with a chuckle, "it's Valentine's Day. And I have a gift for you."

Ooh. "A prezzie?"

"For Jezzie."

"A rhyme! How inventive!" I squeezed his ass, then stretched my hands enough to skim my nails against his balls.

He let out a sound of pure animal intention, a growl that echoed in my breasts and my belly and my clit, and as that delicious sound skimmed over my body I decided that just this once, I'd put my own selfish needs before my client. Really, Big Boy was a stone-cold liar in life. So what that I'd lied to him when I said I'd be right back? What comes around goes around.

And I'd make him come around. Eventually.

"Okay," I said. "I'm yours."

Daun's smile bloomed into an evil grin, all poison and poppies. "Don't I know it."

"Why, Daunuan. You sound as possessive as a Coveter."

"One of my many vices," he said, his voice the satisfied rumble of a tiger's purr. "I've waited such a long time for this."

I shivered with anticipation. "Daun?"

"Yeah."

"I've missed you."

He paused, then his hand moved away.

For a moment, I thought I had insulted him—demons don't have feelings, not in the way that humans do, and to admit that I'd missed him was akin to an anathema, like the L-word. Then again, demons lie, so maybe he thought I was just teasing him.

I shouldn't have cared about what he thought. But bless me for an angel, I did. I cared about him. And that was the biggest anathema of all.

All of this, in a heartbeat. Then the moment passed as he wrapped his arms around me in a tender embrace, and I felt something loosen in my chest.

"Babes," he said, "I've missed you, too. I've been thinking about you. And now I'm going to show you just how much I've been thinking about you."

I smiled. Daunuan was such a horny little devil.

Some things never change.

THEN:
THE GREAT FLOOD

♡ *Chapter 2*

Daunuan

There's nothing quite like the acoustics of the Abyss.

Listen: sounds carry over the polished stones of the Great Wall that presses against Hell's periphery like a monolithic anaconda. Background noises, first—the lamentations of the damned, their screams slowly unraveling until they're nothing but sighs in the hot breeze over the Lake of Fire. Next, the clinking of metal on metal as the Coveters stockpile their gold. The Gluttons now, smacking and belching as they gorge themselves on meat and gristle and bone.

But those aren't the sounds that get under your skin, the ones that burrow deep and fester.

Over the Wall, the buzzing snores of the Lazy saw through the acrid air. Louder than that is the inane boasting of the Arrogant as they swagger and preen, their asses so tight you'd think there's a sinner wedged between their cheeks. Worse still is the incessant yammering and yowling and of the Envious, whining about wanting what they don't have. And then there's the thunderous crashes of the Berserkers, bashing one another into pulp and roaring their victory and pain.

Those sounds don't matter, either.

Go beyond those background noises of unimportant Sins. Delve into the heart of Hell, and you'll feel its beat working its way through you, boom, *boom*, boom, *boom*, dancing over your limbs and seeping into your pores until your heart beats with it. That's Lust pounding through you, seducing you, shaping you.

Now, listen the way a Seducer does: the squeals of delight that tickle their way up your spine, the grunts of exertion that coil your muscles tight. The moans of pleasure that set your blood aflame. Hear them? All the sighs and the *oohs* and the growls of desire, blending together in a symphony of sex? *Those* are the sounds that matter: the sounds of demons fucking like rabbits terrified of extinction.

Those are the sounds of an orgy surging through the Heartlands of Lust—the music of flesh on flesh, hypnotic, insistent.

And I was missing it.

I slammed my fist against my thigh, snarled my rage. Here I was, an incubus, missing the biggest fuckfest that Lust had seen in more than a millennium, all because it was my turn at the Gates. The afterlife just wasn't fair.

Grumbling, I rubbed the sting out of my leg. All right, fine, it was completely fair, which made it even more unbearable. All demons had to pull a stint as Gatekeeper, and it just happened to be my turn. So instead of getting laid, I was standing on the mouth of Hell, picking my fangs.

Not like there really needed to be a Gatekeeper in the first place—really, who was going to try to break into the Pit?—but the mortals doomed to an eternity of torture and despair seemed to expect there to be someone checking them in. And so, we obliged, like it or not. And I definitely didn't like it.

I snorted, pawed my hoof over the hard-baked clay of the ground. The whole thing was just so pointless, and never more so than right now. For the first time in longer than I could remember, there was no line of sinners and demons outside of the Wall, waiting for admittance into Hell. That alone would be considered a minor miracle, except (a) our side didn't do miracles and (b) there was a major catastrophe responsible for it.

Things were running amok Above—from what I heard, the waters were still flooding the Earth, drowning beasts and babies and all manner of living things. But none of the infernal or the celestial were out collecting souls, even though almost every human in the world was dying or already dead, good and evil alike. The supreme ruler of the Pit had declared an embargo: none were to travel between the planes until further notice. All of the creatures of the Abyss, from the most minor infernal entity to all the major deities, were slumming deep within the boundary of Hell, their tails and other assorted appendages tucked between their legs and other body parts.

And that meant it was party time Below . . . all except for yours truly, stuck on guard duty.

I once heard a mortal exclaim that if you can't complain to someone who can change your situation, don't complain at all. Demons follow a similar notion: if you complain, you'll get drawn and quartered, then thrown into the Lake of Fire, so don't complain at all. So I silently bitched and moaned, and counted the various ways I wished I could slaughter whoever had called up my name for standing watch at the Gates, and I waited for my shift to end.

Demons are very good at waiting. But waiting with no real purpose drives me bat-shit insane.

Folding my arms across my chest, I leaned against one of the wrought-iron Gates that separated Limbo from Hell and closed my eyes. If I couldn't exercise my favorite muscle, I could grab a little sleep. A smile quirked my lips as I thought about the possibility of the Almighty still wringing out the water from the skies when I got off duty. If that came to pass, I'd be able to partake in the celebration of Sin.

But I couldn't sleep. Maybe it was all the noise from beyond the Wall keeping me awake, or maybe it was knowing that if the King of Lust happened to find one of his Seducers asleep at his post, that Seducer would be publicly castrated.

Hell isn't big on sympathy. Or second chances.

Time passed. Ball-breakingly slowly.

I was so lost in my own boredom and resentment that I almost didn't hear the lighthearted voice say: "Heya, sweetie. Come here often?"

Female demon. Another Seducer, based on the salutation. Creatures of Lust usually greeted one another; we understood the concept of the more, the merrier. Thus, the orgy that I was missing right now.

I mentally kicked myself. She'd caught me off guard. Normally, the psychic link all Seducers shared would have announced her presence before she'd bothered to speak, but I'd severed my connection about three hours ago. That's a huge no-no, but today all of the Lower Downs of Lust were too busy fucking to notice that one of their minor brethren wasn't part of the group mind.

It wouldn't be in my best interest to show that she'd startled me, so I acted nonchalant. Keeping my eyes closed, I gave the standard Seducer reply: "Every chance I get."

"Looks more like you sleep every chance you get."

Ooh, she was a sassy one. I pried my eyes open. And then I grinned.

Hellooooo, sexy.

Like me, she was a satyr, but like all of her sex, she didn't sport horns or hair. Her skin was cherry red, and the pelt than covered her from hips to hooves was curly and black, begging for me to run my fingers over it. One of her hands was planted on her hip, and she stood with her tits thrust out, as if she were offering them to suck. I took in the swells of her breasts, the curve of her thighs, the concave turn of her belly . . . *ah,* I wanted to run my hands over her body, trace her shape and memorize her form.

Fuck me, she was so beautiful.

Remembering where I was, I said, "Where're you off too, sweetness? Above's still off-limits."

She laughed—this rich, musical laugh that went right to my balls. Her black leathery lips pulled into a grin, and she said, "My back needed a break."

"*Aw.* Poor little succubus. Is your bottom all bruised?"

She batted her lashes. "Wouldn't you like to know?"

Unholy Hell, absolutely. I wanted to caress that sweet flesh, nuzzle my fingers between her cheeks and probe the puckered hole nestled there. I wanted to slide into her and feel her contract around me. I wanted to hear the sounds she made when I nudged her sweet spot.

But I'd be blessed if I'd ever admit that. I had a reputation to uphold.

So I shrugged, acted bored. "Screw one succubus, screw them all."

She barked out another laugh. "Charming."

"I can be," I said, waggling my brows. "For the right reason,

I can be a silver-tongued devil." I let out a dramatic sigh. "But why bother? You're just another succubus. You've got nothing I haven't seen before."

"Look who's pompous enough to be one of the Arrogant."

"It's not pompousness if it's true."

"Pompous *and* rude."

"You're not worth good manners."

She eyed me, and I found that I liked her penetrating gaze, how her luminescent green cat's eyes shone as she looked me up and down. Then she chuckled. "Poor little incubus," she said, "stuck out here when all of the other Seducers are fucking their brains out. Someone must really hate you."

I clucked my tongue. "Just happens to be my time to serve as Gatekeeper."

"Of course it is."

She was good; she put just the right amount of sympathy into her words to make them stab. If I weren't fascinated by her, I probably would have been annoyed. "Nothing more to it," I insisted.

"Of course there isn't."

"I'll get off duty soon enough," I said. "Plenty of time to dip my wick."

She glanced between my legs, her gaze lingering over my most prominent feature. Her mouth quirked into a bemused smile when my dick twitched its own hello. "Quite the muscle control you've got there," she noted.

"You should see the things I can make it do."

She shrugged, her green eyes gleaming. "Nothing I haven't seen before."

Hah—touché. I quashed the urge to laugh. "I guess you'll never know."

"And I must be all the poorer for it. So you can make it do tricks?"

Grinning, I said, "I thought it's your kind that does tricks."

"He speaks! How adorable. What else do you do? Do you come when called?"

Oh Gehenna, I liked her. Most succubi were good for the brief sally, and then they let their bodies do the talking. They didn't flirt, because they didn't need to; everyone knew that a succubus could never say no to sex. But this creature, with her impertinent gaze and her wicked grin, had substance.

"I come when I'm good and ready. And yes, I can make it do tricks." To illustrate, my shaft moved in a slow circle.

She smiled at my erection. "Most of your kind would grudgingly admit their cocks have minds of their own."

"And most of *your* kind would be too busy offering their cockpits to notice or even care."

"*Ooh,*" she said, a smirk tugging at her sensual lips. "Is that the silver tongue you mentioned? I think the polish is too greasy for my liking."

"I don't need grease to get my lovers slippery. One touch of my fingers gets them wet. One thrust of my cock ruins them for all other incubi."

Her eyes sparkled with mischief. "I'm sure you'll have all the succubi just begging for a piece of you. Unless," she added thoughtfully, "they're completely sated before then."

I snorted my derision. "No such thing as a sated succubus."

"No?" She ran one taloned finger up her inner thigh, over her mound and skimming her stomach, now tracing the outline of her breast. "Maybe you've just never been able to fully satisfy one before."

I couldn't help it: I laughed. "Oh, sweetness, you have no idea who you're talking to."

She arched a brow. "Oh, really? Enlighten me."

"I'm Daunuan."

The briefest of pauses before she replied, "Never heard of you."

Heh. "If I cared, I would be insulted."

"I can't decide which is bigger," she said idly, "your ego or your attitude."

"My ego," I said, wrapping one hand around my erect cock. "I tend to get a swollen head."

A longer pause now as she smirked at me, considering. She kept playing with her tit, circling it with her long fingers, tweaking the nipple. Taunting me. Daring me to have a little taste. She said nothing as she stood in the Gateway, but lascivious thoughts danced behind her eyes.

I pumped my shaft slowly, grinning as I watched her watch me, imagining that it was her hand on me instead of my own.

"Well, Don Juan," she finally said, slightly mispronouncing my name, "why don't you show me just how well you can satisfy a succubus?"

"Would love to," I said, meaning it. "But I'm working."

Her lips pulled into a luscious grin. Oh, how I wanted those lips around me, sucking me, swallowing me . . .

"I can see that," she said. "You're working so hard, you're going to chafe."

Hah. "I'm on guard duty."

"Take a break."

I laughed softly. "Is that an invitation?"

"A suggestion."

"And what happens," I asked, "if I take you up on it?"

Her eyes widened into a parody of innocence. "Well then, you get to have your wild, wicked way with me."

Jezebel

He was all swagger, even just leaning against one of the Gates—completely full of himself, like all of his ilk. Utterly confident in his ability to seduce. That was delicious in a fleeting sort of way, but unremarkable by itself. He was an incubus; I would have expected no less.

It was also exactly what I'd needed to take a break *from*; there's only so much posturing this one succubus could take, no matter how excellent the sex. (My sister succubi always said I was odd.)

If that had been all there was to him, to this Daunuan, then I just would have appreciated his form and then moved on. He certainly was pretty enough to look at, with his well-muscled body and appealing blue skin, its hues shifting from sapphire to indigo. And that said nothing of his enticingly long yellow hair. His pelt was the light brown of desert sand; his erection, a monument to carnality. But even with his glorious mane and impressive dick, he was just another incubus. From horns (red) to hooves (polished), he was like the other male satyrs of our Sin.

I eyed his jutting cock again. All right, maybe not *just* like the other male satyrs. *Yum.* If all the other incubi were as endowed as he was, I wouldn't be able to walk right. Or sit down. Ever.

But there was more to him than good looks and evil intentions. It was in the sparkle of his amber eyes, in the quick smile that transformed his face from merely handsome into something magnificent. I didn't know what it was, but it kept me outside of

Hell, loitering with him instead of working out the kinks in my shoulders before diving back into the orgy within the Wall.

"Wild and wicked," he said, his voice a low rumble that did interesting things to me way down low. "Now there's something I've never encountered here in Hell."

I shrugged my indifference. "If you prefer, I can play the impenetrable virgin."

"*Mmm*. Virgins. Very tasty."

"I don't know," I said with a smile. "I find them a bit too raw."

"I prefer raw to rare."

"Agreed. Too rare, and there's little to enjoy."

He laughed softly, and I found myself enjoying the easy movement of his broad shoulders. "Virgins are overrated," he said. "I prefer the aggressive, experienced sort."

"How lucky for me." Grinning, I sashayed over to him, putting an extra wiggle in my walk. "I just happen to be very experienced. And I can be very aggressive."

"How lucky for *me*."

He stayed where he was, leaning against the wrought-iron Gate, one of his hands working on his penis while the other was loosely fisted by his side. Watching me. Waiting for me to make the first move.

Happy to oblige, sweetie.

I leaned in close, ran one of my hands over his bicep. *Ooh*, very strong. Very nice. I reached out mentally, but I couldn't read him. *Huh*. He must have cut himself off from the psychic connection all Seducers shared. Maybe he'd gotten tired of listening to the sounds of a million demons fucking.

"So, Daunuan," I said, pitching my voice low, "tell me how you want me."

The smile on his face stretched wide. "How? Is this where I start quoting mortal poetry? Something from *Gilgamesh*, perhaps?"

"Are you going to shove me against the Gate?" I asked, entwining my arms around his neck. "Throw me to the ground and mount me? Take me from behind?"

"Decisions, decisions . . ."

I nuzzled against his jaw, inhaled his aroma—all pumpkin spice and musk, and a deeper, more primal scent that was purely male. My nipples tightened as I breathed him in. Exquisite. In his ear, I whispered, "Maybe I'll just throw myself on you."

Lifting myself up, I wrapped my legs around his trim waist. The tip of his cock rubbed against my inner thigh, sending all sorts of tingles straight to my core. Shifting to the left, I positioned myself over him and dropped down.

A moment of utter bliss as he glided over my clit and into me—

(he slides into me slides deep deeper now and he's so long and thick and filling me he's filling me so completely and oh yes I want him in me just like this just like)

—and then a sudden pressure under my armpits, just before I was hefted up. And off.

Hey. . . !

My eyes opened—when had I closed them?—to see Daunuan grinning at me, his fangs gleaming. He settled me down on my hooves, but kept his hands under my arms, just over my breasts.

Move them southward, sweetie. Put those big old hands of yours to use.

"Slow," he said, amusement and lust deepening his voice. "Slow. What's the rush?"

"No rush. Just want to get to the good part." Get *back* to the good part.

"It's all good, sweetness."

My gaze dropped to his shaft. "Some parts are better than others."

"See, that's the thing about you succubi." His amber eyes glistened, and his lips pulled back into a predatory grin. Bless me, I wanted to suck his lips off of his face. He said, "You go too fast."

That made me blink. I've seduced scores of men, fucked hundreds (*er,* thousands) of demons. I've felt the pull of lust more times than I could count. And never, not once, have I ever been told I was going too fast.

Frowning, I said, "We're *supposed* to go fast. That's what we *do.*"

"But going slow can be so much more fun," he said, lifting one hand to stroke my cheek. "Slow," he said again. "Anticipation."

"Is a kind of torture."

He laughed softly. "That, too." His hand traced the lines of my mouth, and I closed my eyes, went with his touch. Now his fingers were moving down the curve of my throat, playing now over my collarbone. My heartbeat quickened as his fingers dipped lower, brushing the very tops of my breasts. Between my legs, my sex pulsed with desire.

I wanted him back inside me. Right now. I wanted to feel how deep he could go, move with him hip to hip, my hands on his ass and his hands on my . . .

Biting my lip, I told myself to stop acting like the virgin I'd offered to be.

"You know," he said, "you have the most adorable blush when you're aroused. Your cheeks burst into this dark crimson, like drying blood."

"Such flattery. You *do* have a silver tongue."

"I can do more with it than speak the right words." He darted his tongue out, licked his way across my jaw.

"This is different," I said, my voice ragged. "Other incubi are less about the foreplay and more about the actual fucking."

"With succubi?" He chuffed laughter, his breath hot on my neck. "Of course they are. With you, we can rut like mindless animals. You want to be fucked hard. We don't have to seduce Seducers."

That was true. Sex with a Seducer—whether male or female—was a given.

"But with mortal women, we go slow." As he spoke, he punctuated his words with kisses, his lips wet on my throat. "We draw it out. We tease. We please."

I closed my eyes as he sucked on my neck, feeling myself become wet from his attention. My pussy tingled, aroused, eager for his cock.

But this wasn't an all-consuming need to copulate—no, this was a slow burn, a gradual fire heating me, flushing me. This was more intimate than simple lust. And far more insidious. He kissed me, and my body hungered for more.

"With mortal women," he murmured, "we put off our own pleasure until the very . . ."

His fangs grazed my ear, and I shivered.

". . . very . . ."

A nip on my lobe; a small suck to take away the sting.

". . . end."

I wasn't a creature of Envy, but at this moment, I was obscenely jealous of those mortal women.

He whispered in my ear, "You asked me before how I wanted you."

My throat had gone dry as he'd used that fabled silver tongue on me. I had to swallow before I could reply. "Yes."

"I want you slowly," he said around his kisses. "I want you

like this, standing here before me, naked and ready for me. I want to explore you with my hands and mouth and tongue. I want to probe inside of you and discover your sweet spots."

His hand snaked down my body, touched me so very briefly where it mattered most, just enough for sparks to fly behind my closed eyelids. I let out a groan as his fingers brushed over my vulva, whisper soft.

"And after I make you come so hard that you drench me in your juices, then I want to fuck you raw. And then we'll see how well I can satisfy a succubus."

It took me three tries before my mouth worked properly.

"Well," I said, my voice a high-pitched squeak, "if you insist."

Daunuan

"Keep your eyes closed," I said, drinking in her features. Succubi, like incubi, could shift their appearance the way the Almighty could shift the weather to His liking, but here Below, most wore their natural forms. Her face was heart shaped, with full cheeks and a small chin. Her lips, black as Evil itself, shone wetly.

She opened her eyes. They were the green of emeralds, with a vertical slit of a pupil. And at the moment, they were narrow with suspicion. "Why should I?"

"So I can better surprise you, sweetness."

Her nose wrinkled. "As far as monikers go, I loathe that one."

Heh. Opinionated, wasn't she? "Then tell me what to call you."

She stared at me, her cat's eyes shining brightly, her thoughts hidden, and for a moment I thought she'd give me a pet name, pretty but meaningless. (In any harem of succubi, at least five of them will call themselves "Chastity.")

Instead, she said, "Jezebel."

It resonated in my mind, in the manner of all true names. The epitome of who she was, who she would always be—all wrapped up in those three syllables, strung together like a necklace of gems.

"Jezebel," I repeated, rolling her name on my tongue. I liked the way it sounded, liked the way my lips formed those specific sounds.

I liked *her*.

"I could use my magic," I said, moving my hands up her back. "That would tell me what you like, what pleases you best. But I think it's more fun to discover it the mortal way."

She thrust her chin up, an impertinent move that was utterly adorable. "I like sex."

"That's a given. But there are so many paths to pleasure."

"Are you going to talk me to orgasm, incubus? Or just bore me to death?"

I laughed softly. "Impatient thing, aren't you?"

"Patience is a virtue."

"That doesn't mean it can't also be a vice. Close your eyes, Jezebel."

"Fine, fine," she huffed, snapping her lids closed, acting annoyed, as if I couldn't smell her arousal.

I started at the crown of her head. My fingers massaged her scalp, moving in small circles and slowly framing her face. Back now, featherlight over the tips of her ears, and down, my claws tickling her lobes.

"You're too high up," she said.

"*Shhh.*"

My fingers trailed down her neck, swooped over the curve of her shoulders. As my tips brushed against her collarbone, she let out a soft moan—tiny, almost inaudible, but I noted it. Just as I noted how her nipples hardened as my fingers dabbled by the hollow of her throat.

Over her arms now, teasing the insides of her elbows, enjoying the smile that quirked her lips. The pads of my fingers ghosted her wrists; the edge of my claws whispered over her palms. Her moan was louder now, and I grinned.

"Like that, don't you?"

"Just clearing my throat."

"*Uh-huh.*" I took her by the wrist, lifted her hand to my lips. Kissed her palm, then slowly traced the lines there with my tongue.

Her hips twitched, but then she blew out a breath and stood still, her lips pressed into a thin line.

"You're allowed to enjoy this, you know."

"Just waiting for the good part."

Oh yes, I liked her.

I licked her index finger slowly, then took it into my mouth. Sucked it gently. Watched her lips part as she said, *"Oooh."*

And you like that, don't you?

Keeping suction on her finger, I stepped closer, until her arm was trapped between her chest and mine. Moving my hands behind her, I rained small touches down her spine, and back up, flowing outward so that the next cascaded down her back, tripping over her shoulder blades and ribs, stopping just over the start of the black pelt on her hips.

She captured her lower lip with her fangs, bit down as her breathing grew more ragged—a nice touch, since demons don't have to breathe. Her brow had smoothed, no longer set in determined lines. Despite herself, she was going with my touches.

Yes.

I released her finger, and her hand fell to my chest, quivering. The points of her talons tapped a beat on my flesh, all staccatos and sharps as I kept rolling my hands, up and down, moving now to her sides, the indent of her waist and up to the fur beneath her armpits.

"You hone your body as a weapon," I said, my voice a low purr, my hands traveling to the jut of her hipbones. "And you dangle it as a prize." Up again, slower, over the indents of her ribs, stopping just under the slopes of her breasts.

She was panting now, her lips wet with her saliva. And her smell, *ah,* her smell was drenching her, all cinnamon and musk and swirls of peppermint bubbling through her.

Cupping the swells of her tits, I let them rest in my hands as a shudder worked through her. Smiling from her reaction, I said, "But your body is meant to be worshiped."

Small moans escaped her as I caressed her twin mounds, moving in the slowest of circles, tracing their shape. Testing their weight. Feeling them bob as she breathed heavily. Claws now— gently grazing her sensitive skin as I trailed my way to the deep crimson of her areolas. I whispered over the outermost edges, and she cried out, thrusting her hips against mine.

"And I haven't even gotten to your nipples yet," I mused aloud.

"Suck me," she panted.

"No."

"Suck me!"

Back to the pads of my fingers as I traveled over the dark circles, pressing more firmly. "Patience."

She snarled, "Shove your patience up your ass!"

Heh.

I jerked my hands away from her breasts, stepped back to let the acrid air outside of Hell blow over her body.

"Hey!"

"Patience," I said again.

Her scowl was a thing of malefic beauty, a war between passion and ire. She said, "You sound like a high priest."

"*Ooh.* Cut to the quick." Walking behind her, I sank to my knees so that her bottom was in front of my face. Her buttocks were magnificent: tight but amply padded, promising to be both meaty and juicy.

But instead of licking her crevice, I skimmed my hands down the outside of her firm thighs. Back up now, this time over the backs of her long limbs, all the way to the bottom of her ass cheeks. And down, trailing to the inside of her legs.

And up, so very slowly. And stopping just shy of the apex of her thighs.

Beneath my hands, her muscles tightened in anticipation. Her tortured groan was exquisite, and it made my balls throb.

And then I removed my hands.

She hissed her frustration, and I grinned as I sidled around her.

"Patience," I said again. Then I wrapped my arm around her waist and crushed her against my chest. "Just a little taste first."

I kissed her, hard, bruising her lips with mine, thrusting my tongue into her mouth. She kissed me just as passionately, attacking my mouth and serenading me with her moans. Lips locked together, our tongues danced, rolling and dipping, our fangs scraping as the kiss deepened.

Oh, unholy Hell, how I want her.

Breaking the kiss, I licked my way down her chin, traced the lines of her jaw, teasing her collarbone with my mouth. She arched back, shoving her tits up, telling me with her body exactly what she wanted me to do.

And I finally obliged. First one nipple, taking that succulent berry and sucking it until she was writhing in my arms, her aroused noises nonsensical and delightful, her aroma and taste filling me. Then the other nipple, that exquisite pearl, polishing it with my lips and tongue, blowing on it until it gleamed.

Her hands tangled in my hair, her talons slicing into the back of my neck. Her hips were rolling, beckoning. As I kept sucking her tits, I reached down, snaking over the curve of her belly. Down more, trailing my fingers through her pubic hair.

Stroking her pussy.

She let out a throaty growl, insistent. Demanding. So very hungry.

I slid my fingers between her wet folds, exploring her, testing her secret waters. And then I dived in.

Jezebel cried out as I fucked her with my hand, called my name as if I could save her soul. She was bucking wildly, pushing me in deeper. I stroked her harder now, faster, using two fingers and now three, stretching her. Probing her.

Rubbing her clit with my thumb.

She tensed around my hand, her body poised on the edge of rapture.

I crooked my fingers as I went deeper still . . . and found the spot that pushed her over the edge. She screamed as she came, slicking my fingers with her hot cream, shuddering against me as if she was about to die.

When her trembles finally stopped, I pulled my hand free. Releasing her nipple, I inhaled the scent of her cum, then slowly licked my fingers clean, relishing the salty sweet taste.

Mmm. Sensuous.

Jezebel was swaying on her hooves, so I wrapped my hands around her waist to steady her.

"See?" I couldn't keep the smug purr out of my voice. "Going slow has its merits."

She licked her lips before she replied, "I'll concede the point."

"Well then," I said, lowering my hand to squeeze her ass. "Do I have a satisfied succubus in my hands?"

She looked up at me, lust glazing her green eyes. A smile lingered over her kissable lips. "No, incubus. I'm not satisfied."

I arched a brow. She was lying through her fangs; even if her body posture didn't tell me so, her smell certainly did. She reeked of contented bliss.

Before I could open my mouth to call her on the lie, she grabbed my shoulders and shoved me backward. She leaped on top of me, riding my body down to the ground. I landed on my back with an unceremonious *"Oof,"* barely getting my arms down to take the brunt of the fall.

Straddling me, Jezebel grabbed my arms and pinned them over my head.

"You showed me your way," she said, her grin huge and altogether wicked. "Now it's my turn. I'm going to fuck you, Daunuan, fuck you fast and hard." Grinding her hips, she rubbed her pussy—still wet from her juices—over the base of my cock.

Rrrrr.

Oh, fuck me, I want to be inside of her so bad . . .

She leaned down until her mouth hovered just over mine. "And when you scream my name to Pit and Paradise as you come inside of me," she purred, *"then* I'll be a satisfied succubus."

Gehenna, I do so enjoy a woman who takes control.

Jezebel

Sweet Sin, no one had ever made me feel the way Daunuan did.

I've had orgasms before, of course. I pride myself (as much as any creature of Lust could acknowledge Arrogance) on my orgasms. Other lovers have done more to me than Daunuan did, and for longer. And in far more interesting positions. But none of them had ever made my heart pound like it would explode in my chest. None of them had ever made me go weak in the knees.

None of them had ever seduced me.

All of this went through my mind in a huge rush—a long stream of nonsensical thoughts haphazardly flowing together, this overwhelming mix of sentiment and sensation—as I threw Daunuan to the ground.

Now I was looking into his wicked eyes, watching them sparkle with intent, enjoying how they crinkled at the corners. This was a demon who enjoyed laughter. Who enjoyed being lascivious. Who tormented his victims with his deliberate touches and languorous kisses. Who made his lovers mad from anticipation.

Fuck that.

Straddled over him, I rocked my hips just once, a slow grind, feeling his cock beneath me, waiting for me, full and erect and eager for my cunt.

"I could just walk away now," I said, and he rewarded me with a flare of anger in his amber eyes. *Ooh,* pretty. I said, "I could just leave you to your post. Unfulfilled."

His face flushed to a dark blue, nearly indigo, and his red horns gleamed like hot coals. "You could," he said. "But then you wouldn't be sated, would you?"

I smiled at his response. "There's an orgy going on inside Hell. Or maybe you'd forgotten, stranded here at the Gates as you've been?"

He stiffened beneath me; my words had scored.

Heh.

I rubbed myself over him, getting him wet with my own wetness. "But I want to hear my name on your lips," I said, pressing my breasts against his chest. "I want to see the look on your face as you climax."

Leaning down, I nuzzled against his neck, inhaled his scent of musk and pumpkin spice. Delicious. Delectable.

Desirable.

My lips pressed against the meat of his throat as I kissed him, scraped him with my fangs. Licked away the small hurt. Nibbled the lobe of his ear. His groan of pleasure was like magic, making my nipples tingle and my sex throb with desire.

I whispered, "I want to hear you scream."

And then I slid down his shaft, taking him inside of me to the hilt.

Ahhh!

I held him there for a moment, relished how he filled me, how his hot length felt so fucking perfect inside of me. Reveled in the look on his face—how his eyes had both widened and darkened, how his mouth had opened in a soundless *O*, how his breath had caught in his throat.

How beautiful he was in that shining moment, with him below me and inside of me, with me about to send him spiraling to the brink.

And then I pivoted my hips up, allowed him to ease out of me until the only head of his cock was still blanketed in my folds. And back down, again, slow and deep.

Oh, how his eyes shone.

He arched up to meet me, thrusting with me. We moved faster, our bodies finding a natural rhythm together as I flowed over him and he pounded into me. He was grunting now, and so was I, our sounds mixing, blending into a primal song that beckoned us faster now, faster.

I crushed my lips to his in a burning kiss, stabbed him with my tongue. Even faster now, I rode him hard, harder, losing myself to the moment. My body rocked fiercely, caught in a punishing momentum of ecstasy that threatened to rip me apart. He slammed into me, and I took it, demanded more, clutched him as shook beneath me, his arms and chest and thighs almost humming with tension.

My lips peeled back in a feral grin as I impaled myself on him, took him as far as he could go.

He screamed out my name, a howl of victory as he burst inside of me, his hot seed blazing through me. My own orgasm broke over me, merciless, drowning me in passion as my scream joined his.

All too soon, our voices quieted, the sounds fading to soft echoes in the stagnant air, all but lost amid the backdrop of wails and screeches from the damned inside the Wall of Hell. Daunuan and I shuddered together, our bodies slick, tremors of pleasure rippling over us in small aftershocks.

"And now," I said, gasping my words, "I am a satisfied succubus."

He let out a hoarse laugh. "Duly noted."

I rolled off him, my sex already missing his warmth, aching for the way he'd fit so perfectly inside of me.

Toughen up, Jezebel. He's just another incubus.

I was about to kiss his forehead and thank him for the roll

before I sauntered away, but he surprised me by wrapping his arms around my torso.

For a moment, I froze, not understanding what he was doing. Did he want another go already? I'd be happy to oblige, but usually the incubi were more direct than this. They were more of the throw-them-against-the-wall variety than the subtle sort. They didn't just hold their lovers in an embrace and . . .

Oh.

Oh.

Smiling at the unexpected tenderness, I settled into his arms, pillowing my head on his chest.

A cuddly incubus. Who would have thought it?

We stayed like that for a while, neither of us saying anything. His heart thumped out a steady, soothing rhythm, and I closed my eyes. It was some time later before I opened them again, stunned to realize I'd dozed off in Daunuan's arms.

Screw me on Salvation Day, what was I, a mortal?

Shaking my head at my own foolishness, I started to untangle himself from his embrace.

"Where're you going?"

I planted a soft kiss on his lips, tasting the remnant of myself on them. "Heading back inside."

He made a playful pout. Bless me, he was just too adorable, trying to look cute when his face was a thing of superb demonic beauty. Beautiful creatures don't pout well; their faces aren't made for it. He said, "Leaving so soon?"

"Hadn't planned on falling asleep."

His mouth pulled up into a wicked smile. "I must have tired you out."

He had, but his ego didn't need the boost. "In case you haven't heard, there's an orgy going on." Smiling broadly, I added, "And I don't want to keep you from your job as Gatekeeper."

Daunuan chuffed laughter, the sound incongruously soft in the harsh air outside of Hell. "The succubus Jezebel is too kind."

"So I've been told."

"Careful. That's the sort of reputation you don't want to get."

"*Mmm.* Somehow, I'll manage." I leaned down for one last kiss. And we lingered there.

After a small slice of eternity, he broke the kiss and looked into my eyes. The smile on his face was still wicked, yes, but softer at the edges, hinting at something else. Something unreadable. He winked at me. "See you, sweetness."

Yuck. "Really," I said, wrinkling my nose, "you think I'm *sweet*? I'm a succubus. Succubi aren't sweet. Baby bunnies are sweet."

"Depends on how you cook them."

We shared a laugh, and I found myself enjoying the sound of our voices mingling. It faded slowly, until it was nothing more than a memory on the dry, hot wind.

"Well," Daunuan said, "I'm sure I'll come up with another name for you." He traced one clawed finger over my cheek, and I leaned into his touch. "Give me time."

"And here I thought one succubus was as good as another."

"They are," he agreed. "But they're not you."

Simple words, spoken plainly. They shouldn't have echoed in my heart.

I shouldn't be gazing at him, seeing myself reflected in his amber eyes.

"You know," I said slowly, "I'm not quite ready to go back inside."

He arched a golden brow. "No?"

"No." My hand slid down to his mammoth erection. "And you can't leave your post," I said as I squeezed him.

"True," he replied, his voice gruff.

Running my hand up his shaft, I said, "I suppose we'll be sharing each other's company for the time being. Unless you have something else to do . . . ?"

"Do?" He peppered my lips with small kisses. "There's no one I'd rather do than you."

Warmth flooded my breasts and belly and lower, the memory of bliss heating me. "Why, Daunuan," I said lightly, "flattery after sex? From an incubus? Unheard of."

He laughed, the sound soft and inviting, and altogether out of place here outside of the Abyss. "Oh, Jezebel," he said, my name a purr in his throat. "I'm looking forward to doing many unheard of things with you."

A delightful shiver worked its way through me as I imagined what he and I could do together, across the ages.

He'd lied when he said that there was no one else he'd rather fuck; I knew that. Demons lie. But that doesn't mean the lies aren't pleasing.

And the truly blasphemous thing was that a small part of me wanted his words to be true.

But I didn't let that bother me. Hell and blasphemy go very well together.

NOW:
VALENTINE'S DAY

Chapter 3

Daunuan

Jezebel. At long last, my Jezebel.

I inhaled deeply, took in the overt smells of perfume and soap that were part of her mortal disguise and, below that, the scent of cinnamon and musk that were all her. Her aroma rushed through me, flooded me, until all I could smell was her, right here in my arms. *Mmm.* Shivers.

"You're an addiction," I murmured, kissing the top of her head, tasting the shampoo that lingered in her tresses. Jezzie always does an excellent job when she dresses for a collection. I bet she even sported an interesting birthmark or two.

She lifted one hand to my cheek, stroked the side of my jaw. "You say the sweetest things. You'd think you wanted to get in my pants."

I slid my hands down to her bottom. "No pants for you today. And unless I'm mistaken . . ." Spreading my fingers, I cupped her ass, feeling her curves beneath the flimsy material of her skirt. ". . . I don't think you're wearing any panties, either."

Her eyes darkened as my hands traveled the swells of her cheeks. "One way to find out."

"Is that an invitation?"

She laughed quietly, and I watched, fascinated, as the features of her face softened, smoothed. Look at her—the way her chocolate-brown eyes sparkle with humor and something else, something warmer than mirth but gentler than lust. See the way her nose crinkles just so, how her lips shine from her lipstick and saliva. Listen to her laughter, rolling softly and hinting at the power deep within her, the sound like waves lapping the surface of the ocean. When she spoke, her voice was the rich purr of sex kittens and amused tigers.

"Daunuan," she said, and I shivered from the sound of my name on her red, red lips. "Would you please have your wild, wicked way with me?"

I grinned hugely, felt my false human teeth slip into demon fangs. "I thought you'd never ask."

She tilted her head up, and I leaned down to kiss her. Our lips touched, just that, and something surged through us, electric, magical, charging the very air around us as we opened our mouths to each other. She *ummmm*ed, and I ate the sound; she melted into me, and I drank her up. We kissed and kissed, and the world stood still.

Until some asshole banged on the front door.

With a growl, I broke the kiss. Jezebel and I stared at each other for a long moment, and I saw the humor in her eyes, even as I smelled her frustration.

"Hey!" This from the jackass outside of the store. His voice was muffled, but desperation made the words carry clearly. "You still open?"

I glanced over my shoulder, looked at him through the clear storefront door. Just another yahoo, banging on the glass, frantic to get last-minute proof of eternal devotion. I shook my head. Sorry, chuckles. You're shit out of luck.

"Come on," he shouted.

I shrugged—a "Hey, not my fault" sort of shrug.

"Please! It's Valentine's Day!"

"I know!" I shouted back. "And I'm trying to get laid!"

The guy blinked, then pounded on the door even harder.

"Oh, for fuck's sake, Daun." Jezzie sighed, then darted a glance at the mortal on the other side of the glass. "Just help him, or make him go away. Or ignore him and do me now."

Oh, I'll help him, all right.

I smiled at the guy, all "Oh, okay, you convinced me," down to my sheepish grin. I even took a step forward. He visibly relaxed as I reached out as if to unlock the door. But then I *flexed*, pushing my power into him. Nothing drastic; certainly, nothing to tip some cosmic balance against me. If the fellow was good, then no harm, no foul. But if he had even a touch of evil in his soul . . .

His eyes widened, and I heard his startled gasp through the door. Then he threw back his head. I grinned as I watched him fumble with the snap on his pants.

Heh. Gotcha, chuckles.

Behind me, Jezebel snorted. "That wasn't what I had in mind."

"He was too uptight for my liking."

"So now he's going to come all over himself," she said, "and then what? He's going to freak out and be even louder."

Everyone's a critic. "Fine," I grumbled, "I'll send him away."

"Wait."

"Make up your mind." I turned to face her and was surprised to see her looking at the bespelled man, pursing her lips as if she were going to blow him a kiss. "What're you doing, babes?"

She exhaled, and I felt her magic flow out of her and through the door. Outside, the man panted, his face flushed, sweat beading on his brow. A shiver rippled over him, then he spun on his heel and raced out of sight.

I arched a brow at Jezebel. "He suddenly remember he left the lights on?"

She smiled at me. "It's Valentine's Day," she said sweetly. "I just encouraged him to run along to the one he's so eager to impress."

"Without the card he was so anxious to buy?"

She moved past me as she motioned to the store windows and door—another push of her power, and metal gates suddenly shuttered the glass. Looked like it was closing time. Her back to me, she said, "Actions speak louder than words."

"Speaking of which . . . where were we? Oh yes," I said, coming up behind her to cup her mammoth breasts.

"Actually," she said, "I think we were kissing."

"But I've been thinking about your tits." I fondled them slowly, enjoying their fullness. "How they fill my hands."

I kissed her neck, my tongue flicking over her skin, and she let out a low, sensual moan. Arousal coursed through me, tensing my muscles and tightening my balls, heating my blood until it burned with lust. My heart pounded in my chest, in my ears, echoing through me until all I could hear was its insistent boom *boom*, boom *boom*.

Jezebel.

My erection surged to life, straining against the material of my pants.

Jezebel, here with me; Jezebel, her head thrown back and her eyes closed and giving voice to the pleasure I made her feel.

My Jezebel.

Grazing her neck so very softly with the edge of my teeth, I traced a line from her jaw down to her collar. Her taste lingered on my tongue, splashed over my lips—that suggestion of salty mortality with her demonic scent beneath that, all cinnamon and musk and sex, yes, and sex.

I breathed her in, and she filled me, transformed me.

She was moving now, her hips undulating slowly, rubbing her bottom over my thighs as my hands flowed over her generous bosom. She danced against me, and my body sang.

Oh Gehenna, how I wanted to lose myself inside of her.

Slow, I told myself. Slow. First for her, then for me.

Her tits jiggled in my hands as she arched against me. "How soft their underswells are," I murmured against her neck, stroking her breasts, feeling their weight in my hands. "How sensitive they are."

I splayed my fingers, stretched up until they touched her nipples. Already taut, they pearled even more as I brushed against them.

She moaned again, a soft mewling sound that was utterly intoxicating.

"How hard your nipples get when I touch you," I said, passion roughening my voice. "How you react when I stroke them."

My hands moved over her swells, rolling the sensitive buds of her nipples against my palms. As I caressed her front, I rubbed against her from behind, pressing the bulge of my cock against the small of her back.

Jezebel was panting now, her head leaning on my chest and her body heaving as I teased her. Swirling with her innate aroma of cinnamon and musk, now there was a growing smell of peppermint: the scent of her arousal, of her building pleasure. The smell of her sex.

My thumbs massaged her nipples, then flicked against them. She rewarded me with an urgent groan. Smiling from her reaction, I switched from "massage" to "vibrate," picking up speed and pressure.

"How you like it," I whispered in her ear, "when I pinch them so very lightly."

I captured her nipples between my fingers and gently plucked them.

Jezebel cried out, her hips bucking wildly.

Rrrr.

With a burst of magic, I disintegrated her shirt. Smoke wafted off her skin as I spun her around, and I marveled for a moment over the sheer magnificence of her breasts. The fruit from the Tree of Life could never have looked so ripe. Teardrop-shaped beauty, capped with pink pearls.

"How they feel in my mouth," I growled, and then I bent down to give suck.

Her nipple between my lips now, my tongue lapping as I drank her down. Slowly, so very slowly, I sampled her, drew her deep into my mouth as I suckled. First one breast, then the other, lapping her with broad strokes of my tongue, seducing her with tiny kisses, running over her twin swells until they glistened from where my lips touched her.

She arched against me, her moans the sweetest music. I wrapped my arms around her and crushed her to me, sucking her, sucking until her peaks were swollen and her breathing was ragged with arousal.

Yes, Jezebel. Yes.

I nipped her, a moment of pain lancing her pleasure.

A peppermint splash, heady and overwhelming, and then she shuddered in my arms. I kept sucking as the orgasm took her, kept kissing her breasts as small quakes rippled over her. I kept holding her as she let out a content sigh.

"Yes, I've been thinking about your tits," I said, nuzzling my face into her cleavage.

"Wow." She let out a breathy laugh, fisted her hands in my hair. "I like it when you think about my tits."

Grinning, I looked up at her, soared from the way she was gazing at me right now. "Oh babes," I said. "I've been thinking about much more than your tits."

Jezebel

"Sweetie," I said, my voice heavy from my orgasm, "I love the way you think."

Heat pulsed through me, the aftershocks making my limbs tremble. Bless me, he'd made me come just from touching—and sucking, *ooh* yes, definitely sucking—my boobs.

If this was Daun missing me, I'd have to go away far more often.

"Just you wait." He kissed his way up my breast, his lips tender on my swollen nipple before he peppered his way up to my collarbone, my shoulder, my neck. He said, "You're going to love the way I make you feel."

"I already do."

I felt him smile against the curve of my throat. "Love? How quaint."

Demons don't love. We don't have emotions the way that

humans do. But we do have likes, preferences. And, in my case with Daun, we have attachments that are much deeper than fondness. No, we don't love. But Seducers all know that love belongs to Lust.

And that we had aplenty.

"I'll show you love," I told him, passion roughening my words so that they came forth like a growl. My fingers, still tangled in his hair, pulled him down until his mouth was on mine. I thrust my tongue between his lips, explored his false human teeth, tripping over their edges and then beyond them, touching his tongue with mine. We dueled, rolling and parrying, scoring as we each bled sounds of pleasure. Of desire.

Of a want that stretched across the millennia.

Daunuan. Wicked incubus.

How I want you, deep inside of me . . .

I can do that.

Mmm. Cheater.

I'm a demon, babes. What do you expect?

Bliss. I kissed him harder, crushed his torso against my naked chest. *Rapture.*

In my mind, he laughed. *Not the Rapture, surely?*

No. The better kind. The one with multiple orgasms.

Ah. That kind. You have high expectations.

Are you up for it?

He pressed the bulge of his erection against my belly. *You know I'm always up for it.*

All this, as we continued kissing. His hands slid down my back until they cupped my bottom. Daun broke away from my mouth, kissed his way across my jaw and to my ear, where he sucked on the lobe until my toes curled.

"I've been thinking about your ass," he whispered in my ear. His fingers spread wide, groping my cheeks. "The way it curves. The way it feels in my hands." He squeezed my buttocks, his fingers digging deep.

My hips were rocking now, my body moving of its own accord. Which was very good, because I was having trouble thinking— everything was blurring in a red haze, seductive, consuming.

A smell of burning cotton, and my skirt disintegrated in a wave of his magic. My exposed skin pebbled in the cool air, but then his hands were flowing over my cheeks, and the cold was quickly banished from my body.

"The way you squirm when I rub your hole."

His finger slid into the crevice of my ass, snaking down until he brushed against the folds of my vagina, then back up again, this time pressing against my hole. My cunt throbbed as he teased me from behind, tightening, releasing, tightening again, harder this time, building to something huge and wild and overwhelming.

"Daun," I said, his name a broken rasp as I panted.

Back down came his finger, stroking me harder, spreading my cheeks and nudging my pussy lips, then back up, slow, slow, agonizingly slow, and now dipping into the puckered entrance of my ass.

I spoke his name again, but this time it was nothing more than a groan.

"The way you clench around me when I go inside of you."

He pushed inside of me, his finger digging inside of my ass, reaching deep. Bolts of pleasure, lightning quick, shot through me as I came again, contracting around his finger. I cried out in a long *"Ahhhhhhhhhh!"* as hot liquid slicked my inner thighs.

"Yes, babes," he said. "I've been thinking about your ass."

I was too lost in my orgasm to reply. All I could do was quiver as he slid out of me.

He turned me around, slowly, his strong hands on my waist. Inhaling deeply, he grinned, let out a contented sigh. "You smell so fucking good."

All your fault, I said, waves of lingering pleasure weighing my limbs. I would have swayed on my feet if Daun hadn't been holding me.

"No," he said, "it's all you. Your tits. Your ass. And your cunt. Oh, how I've been thinking about your cunt."

Unholy Hell, his thoughts were slowly turning me into jelly.

He licked a path down my body, from my chin down my throat, pausing to circle the hollow at its base before continuing on, between the valley of my breasts, over the concave plane of my stomach, dipping into my navel. Down more, until I felt his breath at the top of my mound.

"Love the thigh highs," he murmured, running one hand up the inside of my right leg, whispering over the black nylon.

"The client was into it," I managed, but he shushed me.

"They outline your legs so sleekly." His fingers skimmed over my inner thigh, trailing my own wetness over my skin. "And it's such a striking contrast to the cream on your thighs."

He buried his face between my legs.

Eeeee . . .

He started low, slowly working his way up. Tantalizing licks, over the entire length of my inner lips, first one side, then the other, pausing to tease my clit ever so gently with his teeth.

Heat on me, as his tongue probed my folds and his breath tickled that most sensitive spot nestled there. Heat *in* me, as my pussy tingled from his wet strokes, setting fire to my blood.

Oh sweet Sin, what he does to me . . .

His hands on my hips now as I rocked, bucked, thrusting my sex against him almost violently, begging with my body for him to fuck me.

But he tortured me with his tongue and lips and teeth, nibbling and sucking, slurping, gliding over my vulva and back down. And up. And down.

Unholy Hell, Daun . . .

Pressure, deep within, building now, threatening to tear me apart from inside. My head rocked back and forth, and I dug my nails into his shoulders.

He blew softly on my pussy, and I trembled. His fingers danced at the base of my slit, and I cried out.

Please, oh please, fuck me please . . .

"I've been thinking about your cunt," he growled, and then he sucked my clit.

I screamed as another orgasm ripped through me, battering me. Wave after wave of ecstasy broke over me, drowning me in sensation and dragging me under. My knees buckled and I sagged against Daun, boneless with pleasure.

He let out a savage, victorious sound, and then he lapped up my juices.

Quivering with aftershocks, I floated there as he cleaned me, drinking me like fine wine.

"Babes," he said when he was finished, and I was a puddle of ooze in his arms, "I've been thinking about you."

My head on his chest, I smiled as I listened to the steady thumping of his heart. "I can tell." My hand trailed down to his crotch, stroked the bulge of his erection. "Still thinking about me, aren't you?"

Around me, his arms tightened. He shifted, pressing himself ha der against my hand. "Fuck me, yes," he said, his voice ragged. "I never stop thinking about you."

Heh. A pretty lie, that. But one I enjoyed.

"Well then, incubus," I said, unfastening the button on his fly, "it's my turn to show you how much I've been thinking about you."

Daunuan

Her taste still in my mouth, I smiled at Jezebel as she tugged down my zipper. "I can burn away the clothes."

"Don't," she said. "Fucking a man when he's still dressed turns me on." She peeled away my jeans until my dick sprang out, the tip curving up, already glistening with precum.

I inhaled sharply as the cool air hit me, making me half-crazed from the sensation—cool outside, so very hot inside. My balls throbbed, begging for release.

"Babes," I growled, "a change in barometric pressure would turn you on."

She chuckled. "You know me too well." Then she gripped my cock in her hand and squeezed.

Oh fuck me, that feels so good. . . .

Slowly she stroked me, up and down, changing the pressure and the rhythm as her fingers worked. I stood there, my head thrown back, eyes closed, losing myself in the feeling of her hand on my shaft. She rubbed my length, played me like an instrument, and my blood caught fire.

Now her other hand cupped my balls. They tightened painfully as she massaged them, and at that moment, I would have given anything to feel her lips around them.

Ask, and ye shall receive.

I let out a startled laugh. *Now who's cheating?*

What's good for the goose is good for the slander.

"You have a way with words," I said, my voice ragged.

This from the cunning linguist. She laughed softly, even as she stroked me harder. *Now then, I believe this is what you wanted. . . .*

And she dove down.

Her mouth on my balls, sucking me, spiraling me with her tongue, grazing me with her teeth. Getting me wet with her saliva, driving me mad with her lips. Her hand on the tip of my cock, rubbing her palm over the swollen head.

Oh Gehenna, Jezebel . . .

She released my balls from the exquisite torture of her mouth, slowly licked her way up my prick. Her hands planted on my hips, she circled her tongue back down to the base, wetting the pubic hair nestled there. And back up, slower, kissing her way to my ridge, ignoring the crown of my penis as she stroked my shaft with her tongue.

My breathing was coming in hitches now, and my pelvis hummed with sensation, tickling, building.

No. I want to explode inside of her cunt. I want us to climax together.

Shhh, she whispered. *You already got me.*

Jezzie . . . bless it all, Jezzie, do this for me.

Gritting my teeth, I gripped the sides of her head and gently tipped her head up until she freed my cock from her lips. I guided her up, and she let me, and I leaned down to kiss her deeply.

Now, Jezzie. I want you now.

Then take me.

My lips locked on hers, I scooped my hands under her bottom and hefted her up. She wrapped her arms around my neck and her long legs around my waist, tilting her pelvis to rub her sex over the tip of my erection.

Growling with need, I slammed her against the front door. She squealed as I rammed myself home.

Yes.

Jezebel grunted as I pounded her, filled her to the breaking point. She goaded me on, harder, deeper, shouting my name.

Sandwiched inside of her, there was no place I'd rather be.

We fucked there, her back against the door, me supporting her weight. But it was more than giving into the primal force of lust, more than just making the beast with two backs, as we've done time and again across the ages. As passionate, as raw, as our hunger was, there was something soft there, too, something tender that turned carnal desire into something else, something more profound. When my release finally came, I called out the name of the one who'd seduced me from the very start, the one whom I couldn't help but want, couldn't help but think of, no matter where I was, or who else I was with.

Jezebel.

We held each other as our sweat dried—that false human sweat that couldn't mask the deeper aroma of our sexual satisfaction. Her head rested on my shoulder, and I stroked her hair, teased its damp strands away from her brow.

"You know," she said, "no matter how many times we screw, it always reminds me of the first time."

I kissed the top of her head. "You were a wild thing then."

She laughed softly, the sound muffled by my chest. "And you were a tease."

"All you wanted to do was fuck."

"And all you wanted was foreplay."

I smiled, remembering. "No, I wanted to fuck."

"But you were all about the foreplay."

"Hey, I'm an incubus."

She looked up at me, her dark eyes sparkling with mischief and delight, and something else that I couldn't—wouldn't—name. "You're my incubus."

Oh, Jezebel.

We kissed again, softly, as if we were afraid of bruising our swollen lips.

After, Jezebel let out a sigh—full, content. "I really did miss you, you know."

"Babes," I said, hugging her tight, "I missed you, too."

Jezebel

"You know," I said, enjoying the warmth of his arms, "that was a welcome back I could really get behind."

One of his hands slid to my ass. "You mean this?"

Heh. "That, too."

We stayed like that for a little bit, me smiling in his embrace, him stroking my back. And backside. *Yum.*

Finally, reality sank in. As lovely as this was, I had a job to do. With a mournful sigh, I gently untangled myself from Daun's arms.

"Where're you going?"

"Back inside. My client's waiting."

"*Aw,* he'll keep."

"He's kept long enough already. I have to get back to him."

Mischief sparkled in his false hazel eyes. Matt Damon never looked half as wicked. Daun said, "I thought after all this time, I know how to satisfy my little succubus."

Cupping my enormous boobs, I said, "Little? Sweetie, these are big enough to nurse all of Texas."

Daun reached down and grabbed his erection—still huge, even after we fucked. *Ah*, the joys of being an incubus. He said, "And this is big enough to satisfy all the Dallas Cowboy Cheerleaders. At the same time."

"If you do say so yourself." Looking at his cock, my smile turned wistful. "We'll always fit perfectly, won't we?"

When Daun replied, his voice was a small thing, sounding almost human: "Always."

A pause, then, filled with things unsaid. Even our psychic connection was quiet, as if waiting to see what we could do. Silence hummed between us, but not an uncomfortable one: it was laden with nostalgia and whimsy, brimming with memories of times past and anticipation of things yet to come. Daun and I gazed upon each other, him stroking his cock, me standing naked and ready, and we smiled.

"Well then," I said. "Let me get inside and do what I have to do. After it's all said and done, we can . . ."

My voice trailed off. We could what? I'd have to take my client's soul down to Hell and wait in the insufferably long lines for admittance and for processing. And in that time, Daun would move on to another client. It's how it worked: incubi took their clients slowly over the course of a month or two, and succubi took them quickly, in one meeting. By the time I was done filing all the paperwork on my current client, Daun would be involved with another human. And I'd have to start my next assignment.

Who knew when we'd next have time alone?

Steeling myself, I smiled broadly. "We can have a quick good-bye. Maybe you can even accompany me Below."

"Sure," he said gamely, but his voice rang hollow.

There was nothing to be done about it. You didn't complain to the management in Hell; that tended to go poorly. And you certainly couldn't buck Hell's will; that was unheard of. This was how it was with us, and how it would always be. We were what we were: creatures of Lust, bound to seduce and slaughter evil mortals. Any time that we had for ourselves was a small mercy.

Hell isn't big on mercy.

Before I said something I'd regret, I spun on my heel and headed toward the back door.

"Not donning your full costume?" he called after me.

"Why bother? It's all coming off again."

I blew out a frustrated breath as I opened the door at the back of the showroom. I had a job to do. And my client was waiting. I marched down the small hallway to the manager's office. There was a chance that I might go a little rougher than Big Boy would like. But he'd have to deal with it. If he wanted, he could complain about it as I fucked him.

"Well, sweetie," I announced as I opened the door to the office, "I'm back. And I'm ready for you . . ."

Oh . . . crap.

He was on the floor, massive as a beached whale, his face pale and sweaty. I couldn't tell if he'd smacked his head on the way down, or if he'd been dead before he'd hit the floor. Looked like that heart attack I'd been afraid of had made its appearance after all. Possibly when my own heart was pounding from the way Daun was feeling me up. Or maybe it had started when the customers had surged into the store, desperate for last-minute proof of their love.

The when didn't matter. Big Boy was dead as a doornail.

I stood there in a daze, gaping at my client, my mind whirling. He'd died before I could kill him, so his soul had been released on its own. It was brimming with evil, but it was unclaimed by a demon . . . so that meant it was now one of the countless empty spirits floating in the wastelands of Limbo. I could go to Purgatory, try to sniff him out from the thousands upon thousands of lost souls hovering there, unclaimed and shapeless. I had his scent, and I knew his name, so it could be enough. But that would take . . . well, the longer side of forever. Unless I got lucky; then it might only take a couple of centuries.

Shit. Shit, shit, *shit*.

Lying about what happened to my superiors was out of the question. Sure, demons lie all the time, but not to our bosses. That sort of thing was highly frowned upon. In the drawn-and-quartered, pitched-into-the-Lake-of-Fire way. No matter how unpalatable the option was, I'd have to admit that I was too busy screwing an incubus to do my job properly.

Gah.

Shuddering, I sank to my knees. Oh, this was not going to go well for me. I was very, very fucked. (And not in the way that a succubus preferred.)

"Problem, babes?"

I didn't have the energy to turn around to face Daun. "You could say that."

"*Hmm.* Unless you gave 'quickie' a new record, it looks like your client went and died without you."

I bristled. "You're very talented at pointing out the obvious."

"And you're in trouble."

"You think?" Anger surged through me, and I looked over my shoulder to glare up at him. "I was so busy getting reacquainted with you that I let him get away."

Daunuan smiled down at me, and I wanted to claw that condescending smirk off his handsome human face. "There are other fish in the sea."

"But I'm about to get my license revoked." I turned away from him, stared at the cooling form of my client. "Clients come first. And I ignored that. Now I'm going to pay for it."

"I wouldn't say that."

That made me laugh, the sound bitter and so very heavy on my tongue. "No? Then what would you say, Daunuan?"

"I'd say it was time for you to open your Valentine's Day gift."

I blinked, then turned to face him again. He was still smiling, but the condescension had been swept away. That was anticipation tugging at his lips; I'd bet my hooves on it. "But I thought you already did."

"What, fucking you? Babes, I might be the Devil's gift to women, but my Jezebel deserves more than that." He held out his hands, and in a puff of magic, a hatbox appeared, wrapped in a black bow. "This is for you."

I bit my lip before I reached up for the box. "Isn't there a saying about being wary of an incubus bearing gifts?"

"That's Trojans."

"Ah." Letting out a sigh, I tore away the ribbon. Well, maybe whatever was inside would take away the sting of my upcoming torture. *Ooh,* maybe it was a pair of shoes . . .

He laughed in my mind. *I swear to Pit and Paradise, sometimes you're such a girl.*

Hey, it's how I'm built.

I pried off the cover, and then I stared at the chocolate bloody mess inside. And I smiled, delighted.

"A chocolate-covered heart!"

He squatted next to me. "With a soul-filled center."

My jaw dropped. "What?"

"Your client there was just about on his way out when I poked my head inside the office. So I snagged his soul. Popped it into his heart for safekeeping. It's for you." He shrugged modestly, even managed to look bashful. "Thought you'd like the chocolate coating."

"Oh, you wicked incubus! You got me the perfect present! Thank you!" I closed my eyes and let out a relieved breath. No torture for me.

And with my client's soul tucked away for the moment, I had a little free time. Again, I said, "Thank you."

Daun's hand covered mine, so very large. So very warm. "Happy Valentine's Day, babes."

I opened my eyes and smiled at him. Over the millennia, we'd changed our forms thousands of times. We've plied our trade, seducing evil people and taking their souls to Hell. We've fucked countless partners, clients and otherwise, and we'd do so until the Almighty declared endgame and the end of the world was upon us. There were too many times when we'd gone years between seeing each other, and there would be such times to come.

Those times burned, and always would. Even creatures of Hell aren't oblivious to that sort of fire.

But no matter how long those times in between, no matter who else we were with—no matter what else we did—Daun and I would always find each other. Somehow, we'd always find each other.

Oh, the irony of a demon finding the silver lining.

Actually, I thought, it wasn't that difficult. Daunuan, after all, had a silver tongue. Squeezing his hand tight, I said, "Happy Valentine's Day, sweetie."

Demons don't love, not the way that humans do. As much as part of me might have wished it were otherwise, that's just how it was, how it is, how it always will be: demons don't love.

But if we did, I know I'd love Daun.

Preferably, multiple times a day.

Jackie Kessler

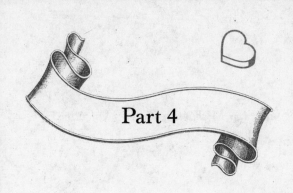

Part 4

By Valentine's Day

by

Jess Michaels

Dedication:
For Michael, my forever Valentine.

♡ Chapter 1

February 1814

It was the worst winter in as long as anyone could recall. Certainly Charlotte Kendrick could remember nothing worse than the bitterly cold weeks that had tormented the entire countryside from Northumberland all the way to Sussex. Even the Thames had frozen solid just before she left London. And now, as she stood at her window, the first fluttering of snow had begun to sweep across the frosty glass.

Charlotte shivered as she turned back to the warm and welcoming glow of the main parlor of her family's country estate. The weather could not bother her here. Besides, when she departed London along the slick roads a few days before, she had claimed she wanted solitude, time to think, peaceful quiet . . . and she would certainly have her wish. This isolation was a godsend really. A *real* chance to ponder her future without the distractions of the city.

Distractions like her friends, who all had their own opinions of what she should do. Of her brother, who talked incessantly. And even of Lawrence Darnell, the man who had put her in this tailspin over her future when he asked her to become his wife a few short days ago.

She had to give him an answer. She had promised it by Saint Valentine's Day. But that was only a week away, and she was no closer to knowing what to do than she had been when he proposed. Only more confused than ever.

"Here I will decide," she murmured to herself. "I *must* decide."

"I beg your pardon, my lady."

Her cheeks hot with embarrassment, Charlotte turned to face the servant who had surely overheard her speaking to herself. Thank heavens that there was only a limited staff on hand while she made this visit home. Only the butler who now stood before her and a few key servants, so the talk of her muttering to herself would be kept to a minimum.

"What is it, Horace?" she asked with a blank smile.

"My lady, you have a guest."

She wrinkled her brow in utter confusion. Her family home, Rosewood Terrace, was at least five miles away from its nearest neighbor. Even if anyone dared to venture out in this terrible weather, no one knew she was in residence, for she had not made her arrival public knowledge.

"A guest?" she repeated, stepping toward the servant. "Is it someone of my acquaintance?"

He nodded gravely. "Indeed, my lady. It is Earl of Atleigh."

Charlotte staggered back, grasping the back of the nearest chair as the room spun around her unexpectedly.

"C-Colin is here?" she whispered when she could finally catch her breath enough to speak. "Now?"

"Yes, my lady," Horace said. "His mount was a bit worse for

wear from the harsh weather, but if you would like to me to tell him that you are not in residence—"

"Gracious, no!" Charlotte said, moving forward again. "If Colin has come all this way through a storm, there must be a very good reason. Please send him in directly and have hot tea and biscuits brought in as soon as Mrs. Horace can prepare them."

"Of course, my lady."

As soon as the butler bowed from the room to collect Colin, Charlotte spun away from the door and clenched a fist to her chest. Her heart was pounding wildly against her fingers and her blood roared in her ears. How she cursed the powerful physical response she had always felt when near the man. The one she had never been quite able to control, to her great detriment.

"Lord Atleigh, my lady."

She turned as her butler stepped aside and Colin Winchester, Earl of Atleigh, moved into her parlor. Charlotte sucked in a breath as she watched him slick long fingers through curling brown locks. Loose snowflakes fluttered to the floor at his feet, and he gave her that crooked, mischievous grin that had made her heart thud painfully for over seventeen years. His dark blue eyes twinkled with wit and playful sensuality as he gave her an audacious wink.

He was an impossibly handsome man, and she had never been able to tame her reactions to him. No matter how hard she tried.

"Colin," she managed to squeak out as she crossed the large room toward him with trembling hands outstretched. "Great God, what are you doing here? Is my brother ill?"

His brow wrinkled as he took her hands in his. He had obviously been wearing gloves during his ride, for his fingers were warm and rough against her inappropriately bare palms. She stifled an involuntary sigh at the touch and fought to keep her expression placid.

"No, of course not. I came here to meet with Damien, in fact." Colin tilted his head. "I didn't expect you to be here, Charlotte, not that I am not pleased to see you."

He leaned back and his gaze flitted up and down her frame with a sweeping possessiveness that weakened her knees. But she knew better than to take it personally. Colin perused every woman he met in such a way.

And Charlotte had never been to his liking.

"You do look wonderful," he said with another playful wink.

Charlotte blushed as she withdrew her hands from his and paced away. The added distance allowed her to remember herself and she turned back with a friendly smile.

"Thank you, my lord," she said softly. "But you must have misunderstood whatever missive you received from my brother. Damien is in London. I am the only one in residence here at Rosemont Terrace. My brother has no intentions to join me, or at least none that he voiced to me before I left just a few days ago."

Colin frowned. Even serious, he didn't look dark or foreboding like so many of his class and rank tried to affect. No, Colin always looked a little like the young man she had met all those years ago when he came home for a holiday with her brother. Far too smart for his own good, a boy with too many pranks and not enough time to execute them all, a boy with a light in his eyes, despite a painful childhood.

When he had laughed back then, it had forced Charlotte to laugh, too.

"How foolish of me," Colin muttered, seemingly more to himself than to Charlotte. "I must have misunderstood his directive, as you say." He shuffled uncomfortably as he looked to her. "If you do not mind, I ask if I may take a respite here and allow my horse to recover from the cold?"

"Of course," Charlotte said, even though inside her stomach was twisting wildly. She had only been totally alone with Colin once. Probably he didn't recall that, but she did. In vivid and humiliating detail. "I could not turn you out into . . ."

She turned to wave toward the window and her sentence trailed off. In the few moments since she had looked outside, the few stray flakes of snow had transformed into a miserable blizzard. Although it was afternoon, it was dusky dark outside and she could no longer see more than a finger's length past the window frame.

She turned back and their eyes met. Colin held up his hands.

"I would not dare invade upon your privacy, Charlotte. I will not stay."

She moved forward, against her will. "Nonsense. I would not send an enemy out into this storm, let alone an old friend. You will stay here until this weather breaks. Until it is safe for you to retake the road."

Colin was still for a moment and Charlotte saw the flicker of humor that was his constant quality fade away. For just a brief flash, he seemed almost . . . *predatory*. But then it was gone and the corner of his mouth lifted into his old grin.

"Thank you, Charlotte. I appreciate that."

She smiled awkwardly and was infinitely grateful when the door behind him opened and Horace returned with a tray brimming with food and tea. Charlotte motioned to the sideboard and thanked the old butler before he left them alone again.

She turned away from Colin and began to pour the tea. Without even asking, she knew that he took three lumps of sugar, no cream.

Suddenly he was at her shoulder.

"Is old Horace studying to be a parlor maid now?" he said with a laugh as he looked at the brimming pile of biscuits.

Charlotte smiled. Mrs. Horace had always adored Colin. Probably because *he* adored her cooking so much.

"No. My return was not entirely expected. Rosemont Terrace has a short staff at present," she explained. "But that is for the best. I came here to think. A quiet house is the best for that."

She expected Colin to move, but instead he remained at her elbow. When she turned, she practically crashed into his very broad chest. The tantalizing, clean scent of his skin wrapped itself around her and she found herself looking up into his eyes as she held out his cup of tea.

For a moment, he didn't take the offering, merely looked down at her with a strangely focused intent in his eyes. Again, Charlotte flashed to the one other time she had been so close to him. They had been in a similar position to this that long ago night, but Colin had had a very different expression on his face.

Today there was a heat in his eyes.

But no, she was imagining that.

"Here," she said, her voice cracking as he finally took the cup from her suddenly shaking hands.

He took a sip and smiled. "You remembered."

"Only you would drink your tea so sweet," she said, trying to laugh off the awareness she felt as she turned back to pour her own cup. It was stupid. Foolish. And she was no longer a girl.

"I have always liked sweet things," he said quietly. Then she felt the whisper of a touch against her neck. Her eyes widened and she spun back toward him, but he had already grabbed two biscuits and was moving away to sit by the fire.

Reflexively, Charlotte moved up to cover the place where she had felt his touch. But she had to have been wrong. Colin hadn't touched her. Now that he had settled into her brother's favorite chair and was wolfing down one of the chocolate biscuits that had always been his favorites, he didn't even seem to recall she was there anymore.

"So," he said with a sigh of pleasure as he swallowed the last bit of his cookie. "What is there to think about?"

Charlotte blinked as she stirred cream into her tea before she joined him. "Think?"

"You said you came here to think. Since I have abominably interrupted your respite, perhaps I can help." He winked. "You and I always came up with the best plans together."

Charlotte dipped her chin with an unbidden smile. As children they had often taken the same side in war games against her brother. Diabolical, the pair of them, they had won almost every time.

But that was very long ago.

"I-I don't need a plan, I'm afraid."

"Then what is it?" he pressed, starting on his second biscuit with gusto.

She shifted uncomfortably before she scolded herself. Why in the world was she hesitating in telling him the truth about why she had come here? He had no reason in the world to care about her plans. He would probably be like her brother and just wave her off with disinterest once he heard the truth.

"I, *er*, I have been offered a proposal of marriage."

He stopped eating and slowly his dark blue gaze slid up to her face. His expression was strangely blank and unreadable, with no emotional reaction to her announcement whatsoever.

"From whom?" he asked, his tone as even and unaffected as his face.

She swallowed, still having the uncomfortable feeling that she was somehow betraying Colin. "I-*er*-Lawrence Darnell. He is the Viscount Darnell's youngest brother."

"I have met him." Colin winced. "He may be the Viscount's youngest brother, but he is not young. He must be twenty years your senior, Charlotte."

She straightened up, defensive at his obvious shock. "His age does not bother me. He has been nothing but kind to me in the few months he has been courting me."

"Nothing but kind?" Colin repeated and his voice was quiet. "What a waste."

"What?" she asked, her brow furrowing.

He shook his head and ignored her question. "So you have come here to consider his offer."

She nodded, confused by his murmured comment and put off by his refusal to explain it. "I told him I would give him an answer by Saint Valentine's Day, a week from today."

Colin set his teacup down on the table between them. "How utterly romantic of you, Lady Kendrick."

Now it was Charlotte who winced. The formality of her married title coming from Colin's lips was like a slap. But his expression wasn't cold as he stared at her. No, it was still heated, and this time she was certain she wasn't imagining things. He was staring at her like . . . like . . .

Well, rather as if she was one of those biscuits that he couldn't get enough of.

And despite all her knowledge that it was foolish, the idea that Colin might feel anything more than friendly concern for her warmed her to her very toes and made her long for things she had long ago convinced herself were out of reach.

Things were going exactly as planned. He was here, he had managed to get an invitation from Charlotte to stay through the duration of the storm. And now she was staring at him with that same combination of sweet innocence and sultry sensuality that had been tying him in knots for years.

Colin settled back. The only problem was Charlotte's impending engagement. Although he didn't tell her so, the news wasn't a surprise to him. He had known all about Darnell's offer before he left London to come here. Her brother had revealed it. But the idea that she was intent on answering the other man's proposal in just a week put even more pressure on Colin than ever.

He only had a few days. He would have to use every single damn moment to perfection.

He stared at Charlotte as she sipped her tea and shuffled uncomfortably in her chair. Great God, but she was a beauty. Her rich hair was the color of chocolate, thick and gorgeous as little tendrils of it curled around her apple cheeks and slender neck. And her eyes, that striking, ever-changing hazel brown that sometimes looked like spun gold and sometimes like nutty depths . . . they had always been where she carried her emotions.

Today they looked confused. And excited.

Yes, Charlotte was still aware of him. Still attracted to him. Still moved by him.

Even though he had once thrown all that away. Now he had one chance to get it back. A last chance, for if she married Darnell, she would never be his.

And Colin knew only one thing, he wanted Charlotte Rosemont Kendrick. He wanted her in his bed, he wanted her in his life, he wanted her in his heart forever.

And he would do anything to make sure it happened.

♡ *Chapter 2*

"There can't be much passion there."

Charlotte choked on her swallow of tea and stared at Colin. He had leaned back in his seat and was staring at her again. She shivered. This time there was no denying that he was appraising her. But not like she saw him look at every woman. This look was different. Sexual, yes, but also something else. Something . . . *deeper.*

She was utterly confused.

"What are you talking about?" she managed to say after she regained her breath.

"In a marriage between you and that old man," Colin explained. His eyebrow arched. "I can't imagine it will be a great passion."

Charlotte shoved to her feet, tea sloshing from her cup to sting her hand. With a frown, she set her drink aside and paced away from Colin.

"This is an entirely inappropriate conversation, Colin."

He chuckled. "Is it? In the proper parlors of London with ladies watching, yes. But we are here in your family home, the door closed, and we are, as you put it earlier, old friends. How can it be inappropriate for me to inquire after your welfare?"

She spun around to face him and found he had gotten to his feet and moved toward her. Instinctively, Charlotte backed up.

"Because you aren't inquiring after my welfare," she said as he came closer and closer. "You are asking after my . . . my . . ."

"Sex life." He smiled as he came to a stop about a pace's length away from her. "Or lack thereof."

Heat flooded Charlotte's cheeks. As devilish as Colin's reputation was, he had never been so forward with her. Now he reached out and caught a loose tendril of her hair. She watched, eyes wide as he wound it around his finger, tighter and tighter, until she felt the gentle tug against her scalp. That little touch forced her to move forward and suddenly they were chest to chest. She craned her neck to look up at him and hated herself for the way her body reacted. Her nipples grew hard and sensitive beneath her silky gown. Her thighs clenched around empty heat and wetness.

"Colin," she whispered, the sound a plea, though she wasn't certain for what.

"It seems a waste for you to marry a man who would be nothing but kind to you, Charlotte." He let her lock of hair spiral away from his finger and slipped the digit beneath her chin, stroking just his fingertip in a silky line there.

"You would prefer me to marry someone cruel, then?" she asked, trying to keep her tone light when she was dizzy and hot beneath his unexpected touch.

He shook his head. "Of course not. But a woman such as you should be worshiped and devoured and seduced. She should be made to beg for more, offered a chance to take more. She should be pleasured and teased. But none of it should be done *kindly*. It should be done passionately. Slowly. Reverently, even."

His mouth came down with every word and Charlotte found her eyes fluttering shut even though she knew she should run away from him, from his words, from his kiss that would mean nothing the moment it was finished.

"Don't you want passion, Charlotte? At least one last time?" he asked softly before his lips claimed hers.

And it *was* a claiming. Despite the fact that it was their first kiss, there was nothing gentle or questing or questioning about it. If she had been a virgin, it would have been the kind of kiss that made her swoon.

But she wasn't. So instead she clung to his shoulders and surrendered herself as his mouth opened over hers. His tongue invaded and claimed. His arms came around her, lifting her up, molding her close. To her utter horror, she arched her hips, rubbing against his very obvious erection as she let out one deep, soulful moan of pleasure.

She shook her head, trying to clear her mind, as she staggered back from him and his confusing touch. He released her immediately, watching her through a hooded gaze as she moved farther and farther from him.

"What are you doing?" she asked, covering her burning lips. "*Why* are you doing this?"

"You were once married to a man of a certain reputation," Colin said softly, his dark eyes never leaving her face. "Undoubtedly you know exactly what I'm doing. I am trying to seduce you."

Charlotte turned away from him as even more blood heated her already flushed skin. Damn him. Damn him for bringing up her marriage that he knew nothing about. For reminding her of exactly why she couldn't involve herself in an affair with a man like him. Even though he was so tempting.

"You don't want me," she murmured, proud she could keep her voice from cracking.

"You are wrong."

She shook her head. "You want a woman, perhaps. But any woman will do. It has nothing to do with me."

He laughed and she looked over her shoulder. He didn't actually look amused, despite his smile. "Darling, if I wanted any woman, there is a chamber maid who passed me in your hall not twenty minutes ago who would have sufficed."

Charlotte's eyes went wide, and she turned her face away with a huffing sound that gave away far too many emotions. He chuckled again, but this time he was right behind her again. Before she could move to face him, his arms came around her, drawing her back against his broad chest even as he moved her forward toward the door, inch by inch.

"When you came to me all those years ago, when you offered yourself to me I turned you down for—" He stopped and Charlotte felt the catch of his breath against her bare neck. She shivered before he continued. "Well, there were many reasons. But I spent the next seven years wondering what would have happened if I had said yes. Haven't you ever wondered?"

Charlotte trembled. Of course she had wondered.

"No," she lied.

"Very well, then, indulge me despite your supposed lack of interest in what might have been. You and I are trapped here, perhaps for many days, all alone. We can play whist and pretend we don't feel the desire that courses through us when we are near each other. *Or* we can have a very passionate affair and purge that desire from our systems."

Slowly, he turned her, pressing her back to the parlor door as he reached around her to lock it. She could hardly breathe now, her dress felt too tight, her *skin* felt too tight as he leaned against her, his body making very clear what he wanted. And what he would give her in return.

"But—"

"You think too much, sweet," he whispered, brushing the tip of his nose against hers. "There don't have to be consequences or regrets; just all that passion that you are so willing to give up by considering Darnell's proposal of marriage."

Charlotte closed her eyes as Colin pressed his lips to her throat. With his mouth on her skin, it was so hard to think. But she had to. For Colin there would be no consequences to an affair. He felt nothing for any of the numerous women he had bedded.

For her, it would be different. She had loved this man for most of her life. Truth be told, that love had never fully died, she had just found a way to ignore it, bury it, forget it. But if she let him make love to her, it would be so easy to feel the emotion again. And the pain when he was finished with her.

His lips slipped lower, as did his hands. He pressed his palms to her breasts, gently lifting them so that the swells were more pronounced over the scooped neck of her silky gown. He pressed his mouth to the valley there, gently licking, languidly lighting her on fire.

She pressed her head to the wooden surface behind her and let out a strangled moan of pleasure and frustration. It was a huge risk to take the sudden offer Colin was making to her. And yet, perhaps without even knowing it, he had given her a good reason to surrender.

Perhaps, if she *did* give in, gave herself to him, she *could* purge those feelings she had for him. And at the very worst, she would have memories, not just fantasies to take into her life after the storm. Whatever she decided about Lawrence's proposal, there was something to be said about *living*, not just wishing to live.

"Say something, Charlotte," Colin whispered, even as his hot hands glided ever lower, bunching her gown up into his fist as he cupped her hip and then skimmed her thigh. "Say yes."

"Yes," she whispered as her hips arched against his hands. "Yes."

He didn't ask again. Immediately, he dropped to his knees before her, shoving her skirt up as he let his mouth move to where his hands had been. Charlotte yelped out surprise as his warm breath breached her stockings, steaming against the skin of her inner thigh.

Her husband had done this a few times in the years they had been married. She had enjoyed it, but the teasing pleasures of this act had ended years before his untimely death. Still, though she had experienced a man's mouth against her before, Charlotte wasn't fully ready when it was *Colin's* mouth that settled against the juncture of her thighs. When it was *his* tongue that burrowed up to tease the wet lips of her slit. When it was *his* fingers that parted her wet folds, revealing her most private areas to his burning gaze, hot fingers, and questing tongue.

"Oh yes," he murmured against her flesh. "I have always loved sweet things."

Charlotte moaned, her head thrashing against the door behind her as he began to lick her in earnest. And he savored every lick, just like she *was* a sweet treat he wanted to relish. His fingers stroked in time with his hot, wicked tongue. First he teased her swollen folds, then he wetted his thick thumb with her flowing juices and stroked her flesh aside until he found the hidden pearl of her clit.

Her legs began to shake as he drove his tongue inside of her with relentless, focused thrusts and swirled his wet thumb around and around the tender bundle of nerves hidden within her folds.

Charlotte's back stiffened against the door. She lifted her hand to cover her mouth as intense, powerful pleasure rushed through her. Every part of her became completely focused on the places where he touched her. She felt every breath between her legs, every strum of her own heartbeat. Her entire life centered in that one pleasure point, and she couldn't help but moan and cry out as he dragged her through one burst of pleasure to the next. Even when her knees buckled, even when her cries turned to pleading words of surrender, he still relentlessly licked and stroked on until her body was on fire and she feared being consumed.

Then and only then did he step between her shaking legs, straightening up to support her trembling backside as he unfastened his trousers and freed his cock. Charlotte did not protest as he fitted the hard, hot head of his erection to her trembling entrance. She simply held her breath and waited for the tremors of pleasure to move to their next level.

He didn't disappoint. As he leaned his hips in and slipped inch by inch into her body, Charlotte sighed with pleasure. Oh yes. This was what she had dreamed about. He was bigger than her husband had been, and when he fitted himself to the hilt and ground his hips in a slow circle against hers, Charlotte realized Colin was also far more talented. Immediately another orgasm overtook her.

She clung to his shoulders, which were still cloaked in his heavy coat. She slammed her hips to his, no longer caring that her fine gown was caught between them and likely to stain. She even stopped trying to muffle her cries of release as he took her in one hard, long thrust after another. Until finally, as she climaxed a final time, he withdrew from her body and cursed loudly as he spilled his seed against his palm.

Charlotte slowly lowered her legs, letting her feet touch the ground as her heart rate began to slowly ease its way back to normal. She waited for doubts to enter her mind, for her thoughts to race with all the reasons why she shouldn't have allowed the animal coupling that had just transpired.

As if reading her mind, Colin met her gaze as he fastened his trousers. "Do you regret what just happened?"

She stared at him a long moment. It was impossible to lie to him. It always had been. So she slowly shook her head.

"No. I regret nothing."

He smiled, an expression of relief as much as pleasure. Then he leaned forward and kissed her so gently it brought tears to her eyes that she blinked away.

"Then I would like to go up to your bedroom and do that again," he whispered as their lips parted. "Only this time I would like to savor every moment."

Charlotte's breath caught. This was her last chance to withdraw from the agreement she had made for an affair that lasted the duration of the storm. She could refuse him.

But she didn't. She simply smoothed her skirts, unlocked the door behind her and took his hand.

♡ *Chapter 3*

There was no night and no day. At least no discernable difference that Charlotte could see out her dark window. All she saw was swirling snow. The lack of markers of time made the powerful experiences she was having seem all the more strange and out of context.

Snuggling deeper into the covers, she rolled onto her side to face Colin. The roaring fire that warmed her chamber also cast a flickering glow over his naked skin. Since they reached her room hours ago, they had made love two more times. Once slow, sprawled across her bed as he explored her body for over two hours. And once quick and fast and hot against the wall after he got up to stir the fire. She shivered at the memory of both.

He slept now. His handsome face was relaxed and calm.

How many times had she imagined a moment just like this with Colin? An intimacy that had little to do with the passionate sexual encounters they shared. It felt so right that it was easy to imagine that it would be permanent. That she might wake up every morning to Colin's warmth beside her.

She shook her head, even as she reached a trembling hand out to trace the hard line of his jaw with a featherlight touch. Those kinds of thoughts would only lead to heartbreak. This was an affair, not a lifetime commitment. And that was how she intended to keep things.

Colin's eyelashes fluttered and then lifted. Charlotte caught her breath at the deep blue heaven revealed. Despite her very strong thoughts, she was still moved by this man. And when he smiled at her, his gaze still bleary as he cupped the back of her neck and drew her close for a searing kiss, she couldn't deny that she felt a connection to him that went beyond a mere affair.

"You are as beautiful in the morning as I imagined you would be," he murmured as he released her.

She smiled at the compliment. "It may still be night. I have no idea. The storm is so bad that I don't have a good sense of time."

"That is perfection," Colin said with a yawn. "I don't want there to be time or space. Just us."

He tugged her closer and she settled her head against his shoulder. His arms came around her and they lay that way for a long while. Almost until Charlotte thought he'd fallen back asleep, but then he broke the comfortable silence.

"Was there a reason you picked Saint Valentine's Day to give Lawrence Darnell your answer to his proposal?"

She winced. The last thing she wanted to think about was the man she might marry. She certainly hadn't let a thought of him cross her mind since the moment Colin's lips touched hers. A little guilt poked at her at the realization.

"It is the day of love," she said with a light laugh that she hoped would serve as a dismissal. "I thought it was as good a day as any to become engaged."

"Or to refuse him," Colin said with a chuckle. "The day is based upon a pagan tradition, you know. Long before there was a 'Saint Valentine,' the Romans worshiped their goddess Juno. They held love lotteries where a young man and woman would be paired by drawing their names from slips of paper floating in water."

Charlotte glanced up at him. "A fine thing, to have your fate determined by a slip of paper."

He shrugged. "Fates have been determined by far worse, my dear. I rather like the idea. I think we should play that little Valentine game together."

Charlotte pushed up on her elbow and stared down at him with a light laugh. "In case you haven't noticed, we are the only two in the room. It will be fairly easy to match us. Unless, of course, you intend to bring in my servants as potential suitors. You already admitted to having an eye on one of my chamber maids."

She said the words lightly, with a teasing smile, but she was glad when Colin sat up and cupped her chin. Drawing her close, he kissed her with such possessiveness and sweetness that it was entirely clear who he wanted.

And if the kiss wasn't enough, he whispered, "The only one I have an eye for is you. And I don't mean that we play the traditional Roman game. I want to play our very own version."

Charlotte shook her head. "And what are your rules?"

"Instead of writing the names of potential suitors on our papers, I want us to write our fantasies. And whichever fantasy we draw is the one we must fulfill."

Even though Charlotte was naked in this man's arms, she still blushed. The idea of sharing her fantasies was not a particularly comfortable one. She was a lady. Frank sexual talk had never been something she was schooled in. And sharing those deepest, darkest thoughts with Colin was almost worse. It made her so vulnerable.

"Do not turn your face away," he said, lifting her chin to force her to look at him. "If this affair between us is to truly be your last chance at passion, I want to fulfill every fantasy you have feared to share." He moved closer and just barely brushed his lips back and forth against hers.

"And I certainly have more than enough fantasies you can fulfill in kind," he continued, his voice gruff with the renewed desire she felt in the hot erection that pressed against her thigh.

"Very well," she conceded with a shiver as his fingers glided up and down her bare spine. "I agree to your game."

"Excellent." Colin pushed the covers away and motioned to her washbasin on the dressing table. "We can use that as our fountain. Do you have paper and writing instruments?"

Charlotte nodded as she got out of the bed. Wrapping a robe around herself, she collected the items he required.

"Now we shall part company until our fantasies are written," Colin said.

"We aren't going to write them together?" Charlotte asked, annoyed by how her heart leaped at the idea of even this brief parting.

He shook his head, solemnly engrossed in the "game." "No. The fantasies must be secret until they are chosen. You write five and I will write five. When you are finished, fold them up and we'll put them in the bowl. I'll empty it for our purposes. We wouldn't want disintegrated fantasies."

Charlotte shook her head with a laugh as she crossed the room so he wouldn't be able to see what she wrote. She stared at the blank paper for a long time. It was funny, despite being married, even to a man of known lusts, no one had ever asked her about her fantasies before.

Her husband had slaked his own needs, he had tried to be

mindful of her pleasure, but her *wants* hadn't ever entered the equation. Now she had five chances to have exactly what she wanted. And from the man she really, truly wanted those pleasures from.

She bit her lip. This exercise might be a little embarrassing at the outset, but in the end, Colin was correct. If this was to be her only chance with him, and perhaps her last chance at true passion, she couldn't waste it. With renewed purpose, she began to write.

Colin tilted his head to the side, watching as Charlotte dropped all five of her folded sheets of expensive paper into the empty washbowl. He had a powerful urge to run over and open every note up, soaking in the sensual words of her deepest fantasies.

But he didn't.

His little "game" had a purpose and he had to stay on plan if he was going to reach his goal. And the goal was Charlotte. All of her. Forever. That was worth sacrificing everything for.

He could only hope she would come to see that.

But for now, he was her temporary lover. And if the last few times they had made love were any indication, her body was a gateway to the rest of her. It wasn't that far of a step from the surrender of her body to the ultimate surrender of everything else.

He smiled as he moved beside her and dropped his own collection of papers into the bowl. She smiled up at him, part playful, part wary.

"And now what, Colin?" she said with a light laugh. "How does your game proceed?"

He turned her toward the bowl gently and stepped behind her. She sucked in her breath as he placed one hand over her eyes and wrapped the other arm around her waist. Beneath her silky robe, he felt the magical shift of her naked body and his erection flared to full hardness instantly. As he pressed against her backside through the fabric, he leaned down to let his breath brush her ear.

"You choose a fantasy. Whose ever is chosen, the other one will fulfill it," he explained. "No arguments, no denials. Just as in the old love matches of Roman times."

She let out a low, almost imperceptible groan, but then she reached forward. Her fingers found the edge of the bowl and she glided her hand inside. She swirled the papers around, mixing their fantasies together before she found the folded edge of one of the sheets and withdrew it. Wordless, she handed it over her shoulder to him.

Colin released her as he opened the page, though he kept her back pressed to his front, enjoying how she gently moved against him, rubbing herself against the cock that was aching to fulfill *any* fantasy, as long as it ended buried deep within her quivering flesh.

He unfolded the paper and smiled. It was one of his own fantasies, which was probably best. Charlotte was still resistant, uncertain, wary. Reading one of his fantasies, letting her have all the control on how she fulfilled it, those things could only give her more certainty in their blossoming relationship.

And he rather liked the idea of what she was about to do.

"What is it?" she asked, peeking over her shoulder at him and nearly unmanning him with the combination of innocence and pure carnal heat in her dark eyes.

"It is mine," he explained and then read from the paper. " 'In honor of ancient Roman tradition, I would like to be bathed by my lover.' "

Charlotte laughed. "Would you like to be adorned with oils and fed fruits, as well?"

He leaned forward to nip lightly at the perfect shell of her ear. "Surprise me."

She spun around, leaning her breasts against his chest with her full weight.

"I wonder if I *could* surprise you, Colin?" she whispered and there was something earnest behind all the teasing.

She leaned up to snatch the paper from his fingers and pressed a quick kiss to his lips.

"Your fantasy is my command," she said. "Now run along to my dressing room. It will take me a short while to prepare for your bath, my lord."

Colin shook his head as he gave her a courtly bow and backed from her warm arms. At the door that separated the two rooms, he looked back. Charlotte was already flitting about the room, gathering up clothing, straightening the sheets so it wouldn't be even more obvious to the already-aware servants that she was carrying on with Colin.

Her dark hair tumbled around her shoulders and as she turned so that she was in profile, Colin saw a little smile turning up her lips. That smile made his chest swell with emotions and pride. He loved seeing Charlotte playful and happy.

And if he had his way, he would be able to keep her in that state for the rest of her life.

Chapter 4

Charlotte adjusted her outfit carefully and took one last look around her bedroom before she smiled. Everything was perfect. She only hoped Colin would agree.

She opened the door between her two chambers and found him sitting at her writing desk, staring out at the swirling snow, his back to her. For a moment, she smiled at the image. He was such a large presence at her very delicate and feminine escritoire.

"I'm ready for you," she said.

He got up and turned toward her. "And it's about time . . ." he began with a teasing tone that trailed off as he saw her outfit.

Charlotte grinned. She had carefully modified one of her prettiest, silkiest chemises so that it looked quite like an ancient roman shift. She had piled her hair high on the crown of her head and wrapped her upper arms with golden bracelets.

"This is better than a fantasy," Colin breathed as he crossed toward her slowly. "I asked to be bathed by my lover, and instead I am greeted by the goddess Juno, herself."

Charlotte turned her face with pleasure and embarrassment at the compliment. She would never grow accustomed to such words coming from Colin's mouth. At least, she never intended to. She intended to drink them in and revel in them.

"Come inside," she said, stepping aside to motion him into her bedroom.

He sucked in a breath as he looked around him. She had transformed her bedroom as well. Her large bathtub sat in the middle of the room, steaming from the hot water awaiting him. Candles had been lit all over the room, adding to the glow of the firelight. Rose and orchid petals spread on the floor and floating in the bathwater gave the heady scent of flowers to the air.

Colin bent and picked up a petal from the floor. Holding it up in wonder, he said, "Flowers? In the midst of a storm?"

She smiled. "In the orangery I keep a few plants to have fresh flowers in winter. I had the servants pick the prettiest ones."

"This *is* a fantasy," he said as he let the petal fall from his fingers to the ground. His gaze grew heavier, more taut with desire as he stared at her. "Better than a fantasy."

"Divest, my lord," she ordered softly. "If I am to bathe you, I do not want your bathwater to get cold."

"Yes, goddess," he said with a deferent nod as he released the knot that closed his robe and let the fabric fall away.

The air left Charlotte's lungs in a whoosh of heavy breath. Dear God, but he was a specimen of a man. Lean muscle tapered down his chest, his arms, and his legs. Years of fencing and riding had kept him in perfect condition.

And then there was his cock.

Charlotte had not seen a great many, of course. Her husband had been her one and only lover. But she had heard a great deal of discussion of such things from her married and widowed friends. Enough talk that she had a sense of what to expect from the average man.

Colin was in no way average.

She shivered just thinking of how good it felt when he pressed that long, heavy length of muscle deep into her body. Already her thighs clenched, wet heat trickling from inside of her as she anticipated the moment when these little games of fantasy ended and they joined together once more.

Colin seemed immune to her perusal. He turned away, revealing buttocks as muscular as the rest of his lovely form, and lifted one foot into the steaming bath. He sighed as he slowly eased himself under the surface of the water.

"Great God, I needed that."

She moved forward and knelt on the pillows she had stacked beside the tub in preparation for this moment.

"I imagine you would after your long, cold ride," she said as she took up a sponge and soap.

He arched a mischievous brow at her. "If you recall, my last ride was quite hot and wet, my dear."

Rolling her eyes, Charlotte wetted the items in her hands, lathering the sponge until the foamy soap soaked every pore. Then she leaned forward and began to swirl delicate circles across Colin's broad, wet chest. He made a hissing sound of pleasure and shut his eyes.

"I am at your mercy, great goddess of . . ." He hesitated and one eye came open. "What was Juno goddess of?"

Charlotte faltered in her strokes before she said, "Marriage, I believe."

"*Ah.*" He settled back again. "How appropriate."

She was quiet for a while. The only sounds in the room were the soft sloshing of water, the swish of the sponge across Colin's skin, and his occasional groan of pleasure when she teased her fingers below the surface of the water and stroked his belly.

"You know, I do not think I was specific enough in my fantasy," he finally said as he sat up a little and looked at her.

Charlotte couldn't help but smile, even as she let her fingers under the water one more time. But this time she did a little more than tease. She cupped his cock and found him fully erect beneath the cloudy water.

"Weren't you?" she asked innocently, while she took him in hand and stroked him base to head. "Where do you require more detail, my lord?"

"I should have said that I wanted to wash my lover, as well," he groaned as he caught her beneath her arms and pulled her closer.

The soap in her hand fell away as Charlotte kissed him. Water sloshed between them, wetting her chemise until it was transparent and dripping between her breasts, but she didn't care. She didn't even care when Colin pulled a little more and she was forced to rise up until she was half in the tub with him.

"Wouldn't you want your lover to have a few less layers?" she finally asked when he let his mouth leave hers and instead trailed it to her neck, where he sucked ever so gently on the tender flesh he found there.

"Oh yes," he purred in her ear. "Most definitely."

She shoved away from him to rise. She knew what he saw. Her chemise clung to her breasts, revealing her taut nipples, her flat stomach. The heated humidity of the bath was causing her hair to fall from its updo. But he still looked at her like he would like to rip her clothes away and devour her whole.

She decided it was best not to make him wait. Shrugging out of the wet chemise, she let it fall to the ground around her ankles. She reached up to remove her bracelets, but he shook his head.

"Leave those on, my beautiful, delectable goddess," he said as he reached for her.

She stepped over the edge of the tub. Although it was large, there wasn't much room for the two of them together, and Colin didn't make it much easier, forcing her to straddle his lap.

"You are a cad, sir," she whispered as she settled over him. His cock rubbed between them, pressing to her belly as she rocked her hips back and forth against his.

"I think I'll lick you clean," he murmured back as he lifted her a little higher until her breasts were at the level of his mouth.

She let her head dip back as he captured one aching nipple. He sucked, tugging the swollen flesh between his teeth and swirling his hot, talented tongue around and around the bud until she was groaning with utter pleasure. Then he switched to the opposite nipple and repeated the action.

And all the while his wet fingers moved. He stroked along her sides, massaging her naked flesh until he cupped her gyrating hips. When he found the curve of her backside, he smiled against her flesh.

"I have always admired your beautiful body, Charlotte," he whispered as he continued to lick and caress her breasts.

His fingers slipped down, parting the globes of flesh, granting him access to the little rosebud there. Charlotte gasped as he circled his wet finger around the opening.

"What are you doing?" she gasped, but she didn't resist him. His mouth felt too good, his body felt too right, even that finger, which was pressing with greater intent and pressure, awoke nerves in her she never knew she had.

"I won't hurt you," he said softly.

She groaned as his finger slipped inside a fraction. A strange combination of pleasure-pain rocked her. Part of her wanted to pull away, but another part, a greater part wanted to feel more. To give something to him that she had never shared, or even thought to share, with another man.

As he eased deeper with that questing finger, he positioned her wet and ready slit over him. She moaned softly as he thrust upward, gliding into her sheath with no resistance.

It was as deliciously full feeling. His hard, heavy cock invading her in a way that was pure pleasure and comfort. And his thick finger in a way that was foreign and wicked. Meanwhile his mouth was so hot on her breasts, licking her nipples, stroking the valley between in a way that reminded her of the intimate kiss they had shared in the parlor.

Her senses were overloaded, overwhelmed and without warning a powerful orgasm rocked her. She arched against him, driving both cock and finger deeper as she clenched and tremored against both. He let out a low curse and thrust up into her release, pounding into her from below and swirling his finger in and out from behind.

She clenched and relaxed against the pressure as her first orgasm faded away. Now that the intense driving need for pleasure had been sated, she settled down against him, rolling her hips in time to his thrusts, really feeling the strange invasion of his body in hers.

"It's so good," she panted, amazed by how something that was surely wicked could make her feel so alive.

"I want everything to be good for you, Charlotte," he panted from below her. "I want to make you tremble and scream and beg for more. I never want you to forget this."

She rocked back, forward, always being filled on every stroke. Shutting her eyes, she drowned in sensation, and once again the intensity of pleasure, the impending anticipation of release, mounted deep within her loins, pounding in time with her heart.

"Come for me, Charlotte," he whispered against her breast.

His permission set off the second explosion. This time she did scream, writhing and thrusting against the hardness of his body, milking his cock, almost desperate to draw out his pleasure with her own.

She opened her eyes and looked down at him. Colin's wet hair was slicked away from his eyes, his neck strained with pleasure and the attempt to hold back the flood of his own release. He held her stare steady, watching every flicker on her face, drinking in each shudder and thrust of her body.

"Come for me, Colin," she cried, mimicking his words.

His eyes widened and he bit back a groan before he pulled away from her body, leaving her bereft as he spent himself away from her. She frowned as he moaned and collapsed against the back of the tub. Although she knew exactly why he was so careful, she couldn't help but feel cheated by not sharing that moment of his ultimate pleasure with him.

"That was magnificent," he said after they had been quiet long enough that their panting breaths had calmed. He straightened up and shifted so that she had a little more room in the cooling bathwater. "Better than every fantasy."

Charlotte smiled, strangely triumphant that she could give this man his fantasies when he had so much more experience than she had.

"And now it is your turn," he said, giving her a wicked wink.

Charlotte felt a thrill low in her belly, but she ignored it as she pushed to her feet and climbed from the tub. Wrapping a large towel around herself, she shook her head.

"My only fantasy at this moment is food," she said, and laughed.

His eyes lit up with desire and Charlotte cocked her head in wonder. He truly did only have one thing on his mind. Not that she wasn't grateful that one thing involved her, but the fact that anything and everything she said could arouse him also served as a reminder that for him this was just a physical affair. Just sex.

For her own sake, she couldn't want anything more. She already knew the consequences of such a thing.

"Food to *eat*, Colin," she said with a laugh. "I think it is morning."

He pushed to his feet and suddenly her appetite for breakfast faded. Water sluiced from his muscular frame, trickles trailing along his stomach, his legs. Even his cock, still semierect after their encounter, had rivulets dripping from it.

Turning her face away with a gasp, Charlotte grabbed for her robe. "I-I believe your things were placed in your usual room down the hall."

Colin nodded and didn't ask for further direction. He had always had a room of his own in the house. Her parents had accepted him as family almost from the moment he first appeared with Damien at thirteen. Whereas other guests were ensconced in the guest wing, Colin's room was next to her brother's, just across the hall from her own; and this nearness had caused so many long and sleepless nights for her as an infatuated girl.

Thank goodness she wouldn't have to sleep alone now that she was an overheated woman.

"I will meet you in the breakfast room in an hour," he said, interrupting her thought as he wrapped himself in his own robe.

"Colin," Charlotte said, facing him again.

He crossed to her in a few long steps and wrapped his arms around her waist. Their bodies molded. Charlotte felt the heat of his touch, but there was something more. Something *comforting* about his embrace.

It made her want to push him away, but with great effort she remained steady.

"Do try not to make it utterly obvious what is happening," Charlotte said, and blushed. "The servants will already guess and whisper about it, but if you are seen walking half naked from my chamber . . ."

He smiled before he placed a kiss on the tip of her nose. "I will be cautious. The breakfast room. One hour."

She nodded as he slipped away from her and headed out the door. When he was gone, Charlotte let out the breath it felt like she had been holding since he first walked into the parlor the afternoon before.

She looked around. Her bed was a tangle of sheets, petals and clothing had been strewn along the floor, and bathwater dripped from the edge of the tub and pooled along the hardwood beneath.

No one who came into this room would have any doubt as to what had occurred here. Charlotte sighed as she attempted to ignore her embarrassment.

She did trust the servants. Word of her transgressions would never 'eave this house, and they would tidy up while she and Colin breakfasted. Upon her return, no doubt all evidence of the night she had shared with Colin would be gone.

Nonetheless, she would never again view this room in the same way. For the rest of her life, when she stepped into this chamber, she would think about how Colin had looked in her bed. She would recall their bodies tangling in the sheets, in the tub, on the floor, against the wall.

The servants could erase the evidence, but no one could take the memory. And as she rang for her maid to help her clean up and dress, she wasn't certain if that was a blessing or a curse.

Chapter 5

"That was delicious," Colin said as he set his napkin beside his plate.

Charlotte couldn't help but smile. "I had a feeling you were enjoying it when you took the third serving."

He arched an eyebrow and gave her the most wicked smile. "A little excess never hurt anyone. If one enjoys something, why not relish it? Over and over."

She shrugged delicately, although she was painfully aware that they were no longer discussing food. Her nipples began to tingle as he stared at her with such heat.

"No particular reason, except that overindulgence sometimes leads to boredom."

"Not if one does it right," he said as he pushed back his chair and moved down the small table to offer Charlotte an arm.

She slowly got to her feet and took his elbow. A flash of powerful desire greeted her when she wrapped her fingers around his arm. He must have felt it, too, for his smile broadened.

"You see. Overindulgence hasn't changed a thing between us yet."

"But isn't *yet* the sticking point to that argument?" she asked as they exited the dining room and walked through the halls slowly. To her surprise, Colin didn't steer her immediately back to her chamber, but guided her toward the music room instead.

"Explain," he pressed.

She cast a quick glance at him out of the corner of her eye. This was dangerous territory.

"Even the ladies of Society have heard of your reputation," she explained. "They cluck their tongues, but secretly I think it thrills them to talk about men like you. Men who take what they want. Men who leave a string of well-pleasured women in their wake."

Colin remained silent as he released her arm and motioned toward the beautiful grand piano that was the centerpiece of the brightly painted room. Even with the storm darkening the windows, the chamber gave a sense of summer and sunshine. It had always been one of her favorite places in this house.

"You wish for me to play right now?" Charlotte asked, blinking in surprise.

He nodded. "We can continue our conversation, but I would dearly love to hear you play. It was always a highlight of any visit to this estate as a boy."

Charlotte hid a surprised smile as she settled herself onto the piano bench, adjusting her skirts carefully before she pressed her fingers to the keys and began to play.

"Pray continue," Colin said as he sank into a nearby settee and closed his eyes.

"I suppose I mean that you indulged yourself, *overindulged* yourself, with many women before. And ultimately you bored of them and discarded them."

He opened one eye, but only to wink at her. "A few did discard me."

Charlotte found that difficult to believe, even in jest. What woman in her right mind would dispose of Colin if he still wanted to be in her bed? A foolish, silly woman, indeed.

"It still proves the point, whether it was you who ended the liaison or the woman. You indulged in sex until one of you bored of the other. Therefore, it is just like the meal we ate. If you eat ten or twenty servings of Mrs. Horace's biscuits, one after the other, you will soon tire of them and not desire them any more."

"Impossible."

She ignored his impish response. "And if you make love to me a hundred times in the next three or four days, by the time the storm lessens, you will be dreadfully sick of me."

"Even more impossible," Colin said, and this time both eyes came open.

He continued to slouch negligently on the couch, but there was something different about his stare. More focused. Like this conversation was somehow very important to him.

Charlotte broke her stare from his and bit back a curse as her fingers faltered on the piano keys. Concentrating, she corrected herself and continued to play.

Slowly, Colin rose from the settee. She tried not to look but could hardly help herself. It was such a slow, sensual unfolding of long, lean limbs that it was impossible not to stare.

She hesitated at the keys, but he waved her off. "Continue playing. Please. It gives me great pleasure."

Charlotte's heart was pounding hard now, driving against her ribcage as she watched him come around the large piano. He dragged his long fingers along the length of the shiny wood as he drew nearer and nearer.

"Variety is always the way to fight boredom," he said softly as he slipped behind her. "I may eat ten of Mrs. Horace's biscuits, just not ten of the same flavor."

"Then you will never settle with one woman . . ." Charlotte choked as she felt his warm fingers caress the sensitive skin at the back of her neck.

"I never said that. One can have intensely pleasurable variety with one woman," he whispered, and suddenly his fingers glided lower. He found the little pearl buttons that fastened the back of her gown and slipped one free with delicious slowness.

Her fingers fell from the piano keys with a discordant tone when he dropped his lips to the small opening he had created in her gown.

"Play," he whispered against her skin while he unfastened a second button.

Charlotte could scarcely breathe, let alone think about chords and notes, but somehow she placed her fingers onto the keys and began to move them. And as she moved her hands to play chords, he did the same, only his instrument was her body. With each note, he unfastened another button. With every beautiful turn of musical phrase, he touched her spine as he brought her closer and closer to nudity. To him.

She fought for concentration as he freed the final button and slowly eased her gown forward. The fabric was tangled around her elbows, which made it hard to play, but he soon remedied that by lifting first one hand, then the other, and tugging her sleeves away so that her dress bunched around her hips and her fingers were free to dance along the piano keys.

"I never knew you enjoyed my playing so much." Charlotte panted as he began to nibble his way along her neck, following the slope of her shoulder until he found the thin chemise strap and caught it with his teeth.

"You have always looked so passionate when you played," he murmured against her skin as he dragged the strap lower and slower, lapping at her flesh with each movement. His wet, hot tongue lit her body on fire. "I have long wondered if I could combine your passion for music with a much more wicked endeavor."

Charlotte stopped playing and surged to her feet to face him. "Do you mean that you wish to make love to me *while* I play?"

He nodded, never taking his eyes from her even when he reached out and flicked aside the other strap of her chemise. The filmy fabric fell forward, revealing her breasts.

Charlotte considered her options. She could refuse his request, and part of her wanted to do just that. Music had always been a refuge for her, a true passion that had nothing to do with anyone but herself. Once she associated with Colin, it would be marked by him.

And yet, that was an equally tempting reason for her to say yes. How delicious would it be to recall Colin making love to her the next time she played a musicale for her prudish friends?

"That is two fantasies for you, Colin," she finally whispered.

He smiled as he stepped forward and gently lifted her breasts together. As he bent to drag his lips from one hard nipple to the next, he whispered, "I will make it up to you later."

She nodded, her chin jerking up and down. He released her sensitive breasts and slowly dragged the piano bench away. He stepped back to her and tilted her chin up, pressing his mouth to hers with possessive heat before he turned her back to the instrument.

"Play for me."

"S-standing?" she stammered as he caught the bundles of fabric around her waist and began to shimmy them over her hips.

"Yes," he whispered, his voice ragged when her gown and chemise fell around her ankles, leaving her utterly exposed except for her pretty slippers and finely stitched silk stockings.

Charlotte drew a long breath of calm and then leaned forward. Without the bench to sit upon, she had to bend over quite far. But, of course, that was part of Colin's fantasy. To see her utterly naked and on display as she gave him a private concert.

And she intended to give him that fantasy in every way. She began to play a new song, this time not one she chose without thought. She picked a composition filled with building crescendos and intense passion.

He chuckled as she lifted her backside just a little, enough to give him better access visually and physically.

"You could kill a man, you know," he groaned before he dropped to his knees behind her and began to gently lick her thighs.

Charlotte shut her eyes, overtaken by the music, overwhelmed by the heated touch of the man who was spreading her folds and tasting her as if she were the best food and wine. As the music built to its first crashing crescendo, she tensed. Colin was licking her in time to the rhythm, sucking her clit, stroking his fingers along her wet slit and finally driving inside of her.

Pleasure wound its way through her body, but this time it wasn't urgent or overpowering. It swirled through her, as pleasing as the music she played. It touched every part of her from the roots of her hair to her toes as they curled in her slippers. Her body felt weightless, floating in time to the music, moving in time to Colin's touch.

She felt him pull away from her, but didn't despair. She was too wrapped up in the pure passion of the moment. She continued to play, pouring all the desire she felt for him into the notes, continuing to writhe in pure ecstasy as she awaited his return.

He wasn't gone for long. She felt his heat wrap around her from behind and realized he had stripped his own clothing away. He reached around, deftly avoiding her arms so as not to disturb her music, and cupped her breasts. Charlotte moaned, but to her overstimulated mind it almost sounded like a note in the piece. She arched back against him, surrendering fully as he spread her legs a bit wider, tilted her hips.

And then he was inside of her. Her fingers clanged against the keys as she cried out, but she forced herself to keep her eyes closed. She didn't want to lose the magic of the moment by separating the music from the power of their lovemaking.

"God," he groaned as he filled her completely. His hand smoothed along her spine and fingers tangled in her hair before he started to move.

Like he had with his tongue, he drove his hips in time to the music. The second powerful crescendo was coming, and Charlotte found herself pounding her hips back to greet his thrusts in time to the composition's beat. The pleasure that had been twisting through her like a lazy snake suddenly took on a more purposeful drive. She rolled her hips against him, panting and moaning as it grew ever higher, ever more pronounced and finally, just as she crashed out powerful notes, her eyes flew open, her hands fell from the keys, and an orgasm that nearly took her breath roared through her.

Colin held her close through her crisis and then drove against her a few more times before he withdrew and she felt the heat of his release against her back.

Together, they leaned against the piano, their breath sucking in and out in perfect time.

"You see, Charlotte," he said as he kissed her sweaty neck gently. "Infinite variety."

"I will give you that, my lord," she said with a laugh as she peeled away from his embrace to grasp her dress. Pulling it back up around her, she held still as he began to fasten her buttons.

He pressed a final kiss to her neck from behind. "And besides, all those other women did not have the one thing that you most definitely do."

"And what is that?" Charlotte asked with a smile, ready to have him tease her in reply.

Instead, he grasped her shoulders and turned her around to face him. Suddenly his face was serious, despite that fact that he was standing naked in the middle of her music room.

"My heart, Charlotte," he whispered. "No one but you has ever had my heart."

Charlotte stared at him as her world came to a complete halt. Was he toying with her? No, his face was utterly earnest. Honest. This was not part of some game.

Her blood whooshed in her ears as she continued to stare at him. What could she say to that declaration? Hell, how should she *feel*?

"Say something," he murmured, searching her face for her reaction.

The reaction she couldn't seem to have, she was so utterly confused. Finally, she merely shook her head and ran away.

♡ *Chapter 6*

Charlotte paced the length of her chamber, her head spinning. For so many years, she had longed for Colin to make the admission he had made in the music room. She had gone so far as to utterly humiliate herself in that hope.

But now that he had said it, all she felt was fear. Pure, unadulterated terror. There was no way he could mean those beautiful words. A man like Colin would never love, never settle down with just one woman, no matter what he said about infinite variety.

She shook her head. He had said the words in the heat of passion. That was all.

As she paced, she passed by the dressing table where she and Colin had left their washbasin full of fantasies. Charlotte stopped moving and stared at them. Colin had written sexual things here. And they could serve as reminders that all he wanted was her body. No matter what he said in the afterglow, the things he wrote were more truthful than his words.

She reached into the bowl and drew out a sheet of paper. She opened it. Colin's hand greeted her.

I wish to eat a meal from your lush body. And you are my dessert.

Well, no wonder he'd been so excited when she mentioned food. She shivered as she set the fantasy aside and drew another paper. This was hers and she discarded it for a third. Colin again.

I want to make love to you outside. But since it is cold enough to kill us, I would settle for your orangery, surrounded by flowers and plants.

She smiled. Again, he had tapped into one of her passions to mix with his fantasy.

She pulled another paper and unfolded it.

Let me love you, Charlotte. Give me another chance to make you mine, not just in body, but in spirit, in soul. Forever. Let me love you.

Her heart lodged in her throat as she read the words again and again. She dropped the paper, letting it flutter to the floor like one of the puffy snowflakes outside her window.

Unlike his statement downstairs, she could not dismiss this as meaningless words spoken in passion. They had both been quite calm when they wrote down their fantasies.

Colin had wanted her love even then. And from the wording of that "fantasy," it wasn't just for a fling. He said *forever*.

Forever with Colin.

No, that was impossible. And it was about time she explained to him why.

Colin surged to his feet with a start when the door to the parlor flew open and Charlotte barged inside. She held a piece of paper in her hand, which trembled wildly as she marched inside and closed the door behind her.

"What is the meaning of this, Colin?" she asked, holding out the paper.

He didn't have to look at it to know what it was, but he did regardless. It was one of the fantasies he had scribbled down that morning. His ultimate fantasy. The only one that really mattered to him.

"It means exactly what it says," he said softly, even though her response meant everything. And this was not the one he had hoped for when he came here.

"What kind of game is this?" she snapped.

He moved on her as desperation unlike anything he had ever known swelled in his chest. He supposed he deserved it. He'd fallen in love, and now he was going to have to deal with everything that came along with that. Including a need to prove himself to the utterly tempting woman who stood, trembling, before him.

"There is no game, Charlotte." He shook his head in frustration. "I meant every word I wrote on that paper. And every word I said to you in the music room earlier today. I am in love with you."

She bit back a cry, but from her expression, it was not one of pleasure. It was a sound of pain. Anguish.

"I came to you, I stood before you seven years ago, and I offered my heart to you," she whispered, her tone harsh. "And you refused me. You *do not* love me."

Colin squeezed his eyes shut and thought of the night to which she referred. She had been twenty and he twenty-three. He was just coming into himself in Society, just realizing how much power he could wield with a smile, a wink.

One night Charlotte had appeared in his chambers, unescorted and uninvited. She had confessed that she wanted to be more than his friend. She had laid her heart out to him, much like he was doing now.

But youth and fear and a longing to experience more of life before he settled down had won out over the curious draw he felt toward her. Colin had refused her, as kindly as he could. Even as a callow youth, he had known he hurt her deeply. Their friendship had barely survived it.

"Do you not believe a person can change in seven long years?" he asked. "I was hardly more than a boy when you came to me. And a very stupid one at that."

"And why have you never said anything to me before now?" she asked, her hands still shaking, her voice quavering just as hard.

He shook his head. "You married someone else. I didn't want to ruin your marriage or our remaining friendship by telling you my feelings had changed. And then your husband died."

Charlotte sucked in her breath. "You could have told me then."

He barked out a humorless laugh. "God knows I wanted to. I could have screamed it from the rooftops on the day of his funeral, but that would have been wrong. I realized it was better to bide my time, allow you to complete your mourning. Only I waited too long. When I found out Darnell asked you to marry him, I panicked because I knew I might lose you again."

"So you followed me here," she whispered, her voice barely carrying in the quiet room.

He nodded once. "I did."

Charlotte swallowed hard and her eyes were wide as saucers as she stared at him. "But you-you said you came here to meet with my brother. You lied."

He held up his hands in acknowledgment of what he'd done. "I had no choice. I didn't want to burst into your home and simply blurt out my heart. I feared you would be too shocked to accept it.

My hope was that if I won your body, I could win your heart. But make no mistake, Charlotte. I came here for you. For all of you."

Colin took a few long breaths before he moved forward and took both her hands. Charlotte flinched when he touched her, but she didn't pull away. She only stared at him, still filled with disbelief and confusion.

"I came here because I love you. You owe me no quarter and I deserve none, but I hope that there is something in you that still wants me. Wants me for more than just your bed." He released one of her hands and brushed his fingertips along her satin cheek. "Please, Charlotte."

There was a long moment of silence in the room, and finally Charlotte spoke. Her voice cracked.

"You are right, Colin. So much can change in seven years. When I came to you that night, when I offered my heart to you, I was young and naïve. I didn't know what kind of damage a man like you could do. When you refused me, it broke my heart. I thought I would never want anyone else."

She pulled away from him, pacing across the room restlessly. "And then I met Griffin Kendrick. I can admit now that I married him because he was . . ." One glance over her shoulder was all she afforded him. ". . . *you*. He was a wit. A rake. He even looked like you in some light."

Colin flinched, but let her continue uninterrupted, as difficult as it was.

She shook her head. "He tried to be a good husband, God knows he tried. But he couldn't fight his nature. Ultimately, he only wanted me until he had me. Then the desire faded. He found other women to fill his time and his bed. By the time he died, we sometimes only spoke when we said a passing hello in the hallway."

"I would never—"

She spun on him, anger in her gaze. "Do not say you would never, for you have no idea. And it was one thing to experience that kind of pain and humiliation from him. It would be far worse from someone I love."

Now it was Colin's turn to let his mouth drop open in shock. "You love me still?"

"Of course I do," Charlotte said, though there was no pleasure in her voice or her face. "I always have. And being here with you, feeling your arms around me, having this time alone when we could be friends and lovers . . . it only made it stronger, no matter how much I hoped it would make the feeling lessen."

"Then we should be together," he insisted.

She lifted a hand to ward him off when he moved toward her. "No."

It was one word, but it was spoken with such finality and conviction that it stopped Colin cold.

"No?" he repeated.

"I may love you, but I wish I didn't. And I certainly don't want a life with you. There is nothing you can say to convince me that you could stay faithful. That your heart would stay true to me." She frowned, an expression so sad that it broke his heart as much as her words. "I won't go through that a second time. Not with you, Colin. With you it would break me."

Colin stared at her. As a child, he had always admired the stubborn set of her jaw. How she could make up her mind to do something and see it through no matter how difficult a task it was.

Now he hated those things he'd once admired. They meant his doom. His loss. His heartbreak.

"The storm is easing," Charlotte said softly as she turned away to stare out the window. "I think you should go and leave me to consider the offer I was made."

Colin flinched at her coldness. It made him angry.

"You are a coward," he snapped. "You run from love because it is frightening, you deny yourself happiness because of the *chance* of heartache."

"You are correct, Colin," she said without turning. "So you would be better off not to waste your time here any longer."

He stared at her stony back. Then he executed a quick bow. "Very well, my lady. I shall depart at first light tomorrow and leave you to your peace as you require."

Then he turned on his heel and left the room. He did not look back, so he did not see Charlotte slip to her knees and sob silently into her hands.

Chapter 7

February 13, 1814

Charlotte braced herself against the cold and stepped from her carriage. After two long days in the cramped and uncomfortable quarters of her carriage, traveling along snowy and sometimes dangerous roads, she was finally back home in London.

Back to her real life. No longer the fantasy Colin had tried to create for her. After he had gone, she had tried to forget what had happened, but it was impossible. In the end, she had moved into a new set of quarters just to sleep at night.

But her dry, tired eyes mocked her. There had been no rest, no dreams that didn't involve Colin. Nothing had erased what had happened between them, no matter how far away she pushed him or how hard she ran.

She trudged toward her London home as if she were returning to a firing squad. One comprised of one man who wanted to marry her. She was not looking forward to refusing her second proposal in less than a week, but it was what had to be done. Lawrence Darnell was a good man and at least deserved a bride who wasn't desperately in love with a man she refused to have.

The door opened, and her London butler met her with a wide smile.

"Welcome home, my lady," he said as he ushered her in and took her wrap. "We have missed you."

"Thank you, Weasley." Charlotte touched the elderly man's hand briefly before she removed her damp gloves. "I trust all was well in my absence?"

"Of course, madam. There are several messages for you from Mr. Darnell, as well as Ladies Chatsford and Meyerscrosse. Oh, and your brother is in the parlor."

Charlotte had hardly been attending, but now she let out a groan. "Damien is here?"

"Yes, my lady. He seemed to know of your impending arrival and refused to leave until he had an audience with you." Her butler smiled, accustomed to her brother's demands and theatrics.

"Thank you, Weasley. Please do send in tea directly," she said as she strode down the hall to the parlor.

The last person she wanted to see at present was her brother. Damien would only bring up more memories of Colin. The two had been inseparable as boys and remained best friends even now.

Besides, her brother was almost always in some fix, and she didn't have the energy to deal with his latest disaster.

But she had little choice, so she pushed the door open and affixed a false smile on her face.

"Damien," she said as she crossed the room to him.

He turned at the sound of her voice and a bright smile lit up his face. She suppressed a sigh as she kissed both his cheeks. No one could resist her brother's charms.

"It's about time you made your way home," Damien said as he leaned back against the mantel with a playful scowl. "I was worried sick."

She shook her head and gave his arm a little slap before she sat down in the nearest comfortable chair. "You have never been worried sick about anyone in your life, Damien."

His brow furrowed. "What a perfectly awful thing to say."

Now Charlotte laughed, and it actually felt good. "And true, admit it."

"Sometimes true. But not today." Her brother shook his head. "I'll tell you who I am worried sick about. Colin. What in God's name did you do to my friend?"

All the good-natured fun Charlotte had been allowing herself to have bled away as she stared up at her brother. She felt the blood draining from her face, rushing to her racing heart and filling her ears with a horrible whooshing that she could not shake away.

"I'm sure I don't know what you mean," she said slowly. No matter how close Damien and Colin were, she doubted—or at least hoped—that Colin wouldn't go so far as to share his plans of seduction with her own brother.

"Perhaps not, but he returned to London in a wretched mood. I've only ever seen him like that once before, after *you* got married. So forgive me if I suspect your involvement in his current spiral into melancholy."

Charlotte blinked, sudden tears stinging her eyes. She was the one responsible for Colin's mood. He thought himself in love with her and she had refused him—not to hurt him, though, never to hurt him. Just to protect herself from the empty and painful future she was certain surrender would lead to.

"I'm sure any melancholy Colin feels will fade quickly enough," she said softly. "Whatever it was caused by. A few women in his bed and he'll—"

"That's exactly what I said," Damien interrupted as he pushed away from the fireplace and began to pace around the room. "I told him he ought to break this ridiculous celibacy and come round with me to Arabella Nichols's place at Wills Cross. It's all the rage and a friend of mine has membership and will take us in. But he refused me. *Again*."

Charlotte swallowed. She could only imagine what kind of place a woman named Arabella would run. She was about to remind her brother that this was an utterly inappropriate conversation to be having with her when his words really sank in.

She stared as Damien went on and on, but she didn't hear anything else he was saying. Finally, she raised a hand to silence him.

"Did you say something about Colin's celibacy?"

He stopped, midsentence, and his cheeks brightened with color. "Blast, I did. I'm sorry, Char, this isn't right for me to talk about with you. You're a lady and my sister and I—"

Charlotte jumped to her feet and hurried toward him. "No, please! That isn't why I asked. I'm not offended. I just want to know what you mean. Even the ladies speak about Colin's reputation."

Her brother sneered. "Well, it was once true, but not for over a year. Right around the time your bastard of a husband tucked up his toes, Colin stopped bothering with women entirely. He said something about being 'ready.' Being 'worthy,' whatever the hell that means. He's been positively no fun ever since. No woman can tempt him! And trust me, many have tried."

Charlotte tried to catch her breath, but her lungs felt tight and restricted. She had rejected Colin because she presumed he would not be able to remain faithful. And yet, without any reason to do so, he had apparently *been* faithful to her—to the *idea* of her—for well over a year.

"What is wrong, Charlotte?" her brother asked, catching her elbows for support. "You are very pale. Here, sit back down."

He took her to the nearest chair and helped her take her place. She continued to pant for breath, overwhelmed by the facts that Damien had laid at her feet.

"The travel in this weather was too much for you," her brother said, motioning for the servant who had just arrived at the door with tea. "You never should have gone to the country estate."

After the girl had gone, he poured Charlotte a cup, added cream and a bit of sugar, and handed it over.

"Here, drink this slowly."

Instead, Charlotte held the cup in trembling hands, staring at the steaming liquid with unseeing eyes. She cast a sidelong glance at her brother, who had settled into a chair near hers, his expression deeply worried.

"D-Damien," she choked, setting her tea aside. "Did you know that Colin loved me?"

Her brother straightened up with a sharp intake of breath that gave her the answer she sought even before he nodded slowly.

"I did. He confessed it to me one night when he was very drunk not long after you married. It seems he had many regrets."

She let out a low sob. "Why didn't you tell me?"

Her brother took her hand. "You were married. What was I to do? Offer you what you always wanted and now could not have? You were already miserable enough with that ass Griffin Kendrick. I didn't want to make it worse."

One solitary tear made its way down Charlotte's cheek as she smiled weakly at her brother. He could be utterly selfish, but in the end, she knew full well that he loved her.

"But Colin is just like Griffin," she choked, clinging to the biggest argument she had against surrendering to Colin's claim of love.

Her brother was on his feet so fast that Charlotte jumped at the sudden movement.

Damien scowled at her. "I may not be much, but I am loyal. And you ought not to malign my friend that way. Colin has loved you, despite knowing it was desperate and foolish to do so, for a long time. *Never* put him in the same category as Kendrick, who was selfish and stupid and even cruel if it meant getting what he desired. You have known Colin for nearly twenty years. Have you ever known him to be any of those things?"

Charlotte dipped her chin in embarrassment and shame. Damien was right. In more ways than he knew. Colin's love had been true, even when it was hidden, yet she had thrown it back in his face.

She staggered to her feet. "I have to find him, Damien. I must go to him."

"Now?" he asked in shock.

Her heart pounded. "This moment! Please, do you know where he is?"

Her bother hesitated for a fraction of a moment, but then he nodded.

"You will find him at his home here in London." Damien stepped back and motioned to the door. "Go change and ready yourself, I will make the arrangements for you to be taken there."

Charlotte wrapped her arms around her brother and hugged

him close. As they broke apart, she was surprised when he whispered, "You deserve to be happy, Char. Be happy."

And then he was gone, departing the parlor in a few long strides. Her heart throbbed as she raced up the stairs, calling for her maid with every step. Tonight, on Valentine's Eve, she would take the biggest risk of her life.

And she hoped by Valentine's Day that she would have everything she had ever hoped for and more.

Colin sat alone in his shadowy parlor, watching as the firelight played along the walls. He swirled the sherry in his glass as he recalled the last time he had watched firelight. It had been in Charlotte's bedroom as it played over her satiny skin.

Only it was highly likely he would never have that chance again. She was too afraid. She blamed him for another man's sins. Colin could fight almost anything, but there was no weapon against that.

So for the second time in less than a decade, he had lost her. Probably she would marry Lawrence Darnell because he was safe and that would be the end of it.

Only Colin couldn't make the love he felt for her end. It had been made all the more sharp and painful by the two days they had spent together in the country. He wished he could regret that time, but he couldn't.

The door to the parlor opened and Colin's grip on his glass tightened. "I think I told you I didn't want to be disturbed," he said without looking over his shoulder to the door.

The door shut again and he let out a sigh. Damn the servants for trying to coax him from this rare mood. He wanted to revel in it. Bask in it. He had bloody well earned darkness after being refused.

A shuffle of feet behind him made him lunge from the chair and turn to face whoever had disturbed him.

"I said—" he began, but then he stopped, for it was not a servant who stood in his parlor, but Charlotte.

She was wearing a red cloak that covered her body from head to toe. As he stared at her, she pushed the hood back to reveal her pale face in the firelight.

"I heard you, my lord," she murmured. "But I'm afraid I have no time to indulge your desire to be alone."

He opened his mouth, but no words would come. He was too overwhelmed by surprise and wonderment. And deep down inside something far more insidious and dangerous.

Hope.

For why would she come here after practically kicking him out of her life forever?

"You see, you owe me, Lord Atleigh. And I want to collect my debt." She moved forward, the red velvet swinging around her without opening.

"What debt?" he managed to growl out, fighting to remain still. He had made a cake of himself once already this week, he had no intention of repeating that until he was certain of her intentions.

She reached up and untied the slender velvet tie that held her cloak to her throat. With a shrug, it fell away and the glass in Colin's hand hit the floor less than a second later.

Charlotte was naked. Utterly, delectably, beautifully naked.

"We never fulfilled any of my fantasies," she whispered as she moved forward with a sinful twitch of her bare hips.

Colin arched a brow. "I suppose we didn't. I'm afraid I no longer have those slips of paper we wrote our Valentine wishes upon, Charlotte. You will have to say your fantasy out loud."

She nodded. "I'm perfectly willing to do so. You see, Colin, *you* are my fantasy. You always have been, and even though I tried to deny it, you always will be."

Colin shut his eyes as relief and joy washed over him. She was here because she loved him. That truth shone in her eyes, though she had not yet voiced it to him. She loved him and she had chosen him, after all.

"But you said I had not given you the fantasy," he said as he let his eyes open and drank her in. "I recall giving myself to you quite freely while we were at your estate."

She nodded as she finally stopped a hairsbreadth away from him. Her hands came up to flatten on his chest, and he felt as if she had lit him on fire. She gently shoved, and he let himself fall back on the settee as she straddled his lap.

"You did," she said softly and stopped moving, stopped teasing. She looked down at him with tears in her eyes. "But I didn't. You were right when you called me a coward. I was too afraid to give myself completely. I came here tonight to finally do that."

Before he could answer, she reached between them and cupped his cock. It was already fully erect, and had been since even before she revealed her naked form to him.

She smiled at the discovery before she snaked away from his lap to her knees before him. Colin settled back against the pillows as he watched her unfasten his trousers and free his cock. He sucked in a harsh breath of pleasure as she stroked him from base to tip in one firm motion.

She dipped her head, little tendrils of hair tickling his balls before she drew him between her lips. His hips arched up off the couch. Her hot mouth ignited an already out-of-control fire in his loins that slowly spread throughout his entire being. Never before had he felt so alive. Never had a woman's touch moved him in every way.

Her head bobbed, her tongue rolled around him and he found himself moving toward release with rapid and terrifying speed. But he didn't want that release this way. Not when she had come to him and laid out her heart.

He caught her arms and lifted her away, settling her back onto his lap as he caught her mouth for a hot, wet kiss. She straightened up, holding his cheeks as their tongues met and tangled wildly. He felt her positioning over him and he cried out as her wet sheath enveloped the first few inches of his cock. She eased down slowly, holding her breath, shivering and shaking as she took him farther and farther into her willing body.

When he was finally fully seated, she rested her forehead against his with a sigh of utter contentment. The moment stretched out, washing over him, making him complete. And then she began to roll her hips.

Almost instantly, the coupling became out of control. He dug his fingers into her hips, she mewled and cried as she thrust over him with a wild abandon that spoke of her high emotion and the passion it had caused. The hot swirl and thrust, clench and release of her tight body was almost immediately gratifying. He felt her clench and shiver with release first, her keening cries lost against his lips as she clung to him and begged him to join her.

Knowing she had experienced her pleasure, Colin didn't hold back. He thrust upward a few final times and then a white, blinding explosion of pleasure overtook him and he let loose, filling her body with his seed for the first time.

Charlotte clutched at him, holding him close as she whispered, "I have wanted you to lose control with me like that from the very beginning. I felt like I was missing something when you spent away from me."

He kissed her sweaty neck, reveling in how warm and soft her body was, still draped around him. How right it was to hold her, to be with her.

"You said you were afraid before," he said when their breathing had returned to normal.

She glanced down at him and gave a little nod.

"Are you still?" he whispered, reaching up to trace the angle of her cheekbone with a fingertip.

She thought about that before she nodded a second time. "I am. But I am more afraid about living my life without you. Of wondering what would have happened if I wasn't the coward you accused me of being. I love you, Colin. Parting myself from you will not make that better, it will only make it worse. I know. I lived it the last seven years of my life."

"I love you," he said, drawing her mouth down to his. "I will always love you. Marry me and I will grant your fantasies every day for the rest of my life."

Tears filled her eyes as Charlotte held him even tighter. "Yes, Colin. Yes!"

Jess Michaels

Although **JESS MICHAELS** came to romance novels later in life than most, she always knew what she liked: ultra-sexy, emotional reads. Now she writes them from her purple office in central Illinois. She lives with her high school sweetheart husband and two supportive cats. Readers can contact her at http://www.jessmichaels.com.